# THE PHANTOMS

To Mary
I hope you enjoy!
Elizabeth A Wilson

# THE PHANTOMS

***Mission: Justice***

---

**Elizabeth A. Wilson**

The Phantoms



ISBN-13: 978-1-7332401-2-3 (Paperback)
ISBN-13: 978-1-7332401-3-0 (eBook)



Photo Credits:
Cover: ID 139065639 © Assoonas | Dreamstime.com
Back: ID 96519259 © Ultramarine5 | Dreamstime.com

Cover Design: Elizabeth A. Wilson

First Edition, 2019

# Dedication

In a world where nearly everything is geared to the under thirty crowd, this story is dedicated to those over fifty who are living proof that vitality, productivity, love, romance and life in general, don't end with graying hair.

# About the Author

**Elizabeth A. Wilson** delivers action-packed crime novels, filled with suspense, unexpected twists and engaging characters. Her ***Mission: Justice*** series has been well-received by readers across the globe. Published in both non-fiction and fiction, she is happily retired from the world of business and now devotes her days to weaving danger and intrigue into the lives of her fictional characters. A lifelong resident of Lancaster County, Pennsylvania who shares her home with one very spoiled German Shepherd Dog, Elizabeth loves to hear from readers. Visit her author page at amazon.com/author/eawilson for updates on her other books.

**Books by Elizabeth A. Wilson**

***Mission: Justice Series***

Double Deception (Book I)
The Phantoms (Book II)
Ghosts from the Past (Book III)
Christmas Hostages (Book IV)
Trail of Death (Book V)

# Acknowledgements

The late Edgar J. Hartung, FBI Supervisory Special Agent, Retired. His patience and willingness to answer my many questions concerning the Federal Bureau of Investigation and to share some of his experiences as an agent were invaluable in helping me weave fact with fiction. And his input gave me a whole new level of respect for agents in the field. While I have taken literary license with my lead characters, I've hopefully presented them in an honorable light that reflects the integrity of the Bureau and its agents. Any errors are solely my responsibility.

Shirley Quevedo. Without your boundless help, advice and encouragement during every phase, this entire series would most likely still be tucked away in my computer. A *thank you* hardly seems adequate, but it is sincere.

My editors: Shirley Quevedo, Tamera Gehris, Susan Weaver and Dorothy Yohn. Thank you for encouraging me to keep the stories coming; your willingness to proofread and offer suggestions; and your ability to catch my typos. Any remaining goofs are my fault alone.

My creative design consultants: Beverly and Judith Beats, Tamera Gehris, Shirley Quevedo and my entire family. Thank you all for your help with the cover designs.

And lastly, but certainly not least, my family. You are the best. Thanks for being there through thick and thin.

# Table of Contents

# Chapter One

Lifting back the starched cuff of his shirt sleeve, Gary Thornton glanced at his watch and blew out a breath of impatience. Eight fifteen. If he didn't know better he'd swear time was going backward. The twenty minutes he'd been trying unsuccessfully to get someone to let him inside the bank seemed like an hour.

It didn't help that he could see people moving around and knew they heard him rattle the door. A blonde-haired woman had even looked his way several times, but she'd continued to ignore him. He couldn't even get anyone to come close enough to the door so he could show them his identification. And apparently they ignored their phones until eight-thirty sharp too, because they hadn't answered his calls either.

Under normal circumstances he'd take the delay with a grain of salt. His line of work could be tedious at times. But the day was going to be far from ordinary and the reason for his meeting was anything but routine.

Resigning himself to the fact he had fifteen more minutes to kill, he turned around to study rush hour traffic flowing along the National Pike.

"Good morning!"

Lost in thought, the cheerful greeting coming from somewhere close behind gave him a start. Spinning around, Gary found an elderly woman pushing her walker up the sidewalk toward him. She stopped a few feet away and gave him a friendly smile.

"Thank you. Same to you," he replied, smiling down at the pretty white-haired woman who looked like she was dressed for a fashion show with shoes and a pocketbook he'd swear had been dyed to match her baby blue dress. Even her eyes matched her outfit.

He had countless wonderful memories of his maternal grandmother, but besides her infectious laugh, probably the most striking memory was of the perfectly coordinated outfits she had always worn. This woman reminded him of her.

"Isn't it beautiful out here?" the woman mused.

Gary shifted his gaze upward. She was right. Mid-seventies, slight breeze, bright sunlight and a blue sky dotted by puffy white clouds. June didn't get much better.

"Yes, ma'am. It sure is."

She eyed him up and down. "You're a tall one," she said with the bluntness of many older people.

Her frank assessment pulled a chuckle from him. At six-six and weighing in at two hundred thirty pounds, he'd been told more than once that he presented an imposing figure.

He wasn't sure how imposing he was, but he'd long ago gotten used to his height and rarely thought about it unless he was approaching a low overhang. Considering his diminutive companion stood about five feet tall, the height difference was definitely significant, so her comment wasn't surprising.

"So I've been told," he replied.

"You look awfully familiar, but I can't place how I know you."

A sinking feeling developed in the pit of Gary's stomach, but before he could divert her attention, she uttered something totally unexpected.

"I must be getting old. You'd think I'd remember a handsome devil like you. What's your name, young man? And are you single?"

That brought a grin to his face. At fifty-four, it wasn't often someone called him young man, nor was he used to octogenarians flirting with him. But he liked the woman's friendly demeanor, even if he was a little wary of continuing the conversation.

"My name is Gary Thornton and I'm flattered, ma'am, but I'm married."

The woman nearly doubled over laughing and it was several moments before she could reply. "Dear heavens! I wasn't asking for myself, though Lord knows you're easy on the eyes even for someone as ancient as me."

Gary couldn't help chuckling at another dose of her blunt honesty. "Sorry."

"No…don't apologize. I was asking for my daughter. She keeps telling me to stop meddling, but I figured there was no harm in asking." Her eyes narrowed on him again. "Gary Thornton, you say….hmmm!"

When surprise suddenly widened her eyes, he realized the cat was out of the bag. She'd connected the dots and figured out who he was. When she snapped her fingers for emphasis, he knew he was right.

"Yes. I knew I recognized you. I've seen you on the news recently. I didn't know you were from Hagerstown."

"I'm just in the area on business," he replied, being intentionally vague.

But Gary could tell by the way she was studying him, she was trying to piece together what the news reports had been about. Since his business was confidential, it was time for a diversion. The last thing he needed was for her to figure out exactly who he was and realize why he was here.

"And to whom do I have the pleasure of speaking?" he asked, hoping the change of subject would distract her.

She grinned up at him, "Rose Eshleman."

"Well it's nice to meet you, Rose. Have you lived in Hagerstown long?"

His strategy worked. For several moments as he continued to feed questions to her, she chattered away and by the time Gary heard the snick of the lock indicating the bank was finally open for business, he'd learned Rose, a widow for two decades who'd lived in Hagerstown her entire life, was a retired school teacher who had just celebrated her eighty-fifth birthday and still enjoyed playing pinochle twice a week.

"Well, it's about time they let us in," she quipped sarcastically, turning her walker toward the bank entrance.

His sentiment, exactly. "Here…let me get that for you," Gary said reaching for the door.

She graced him with a smile. "Thank you. And thank you for letting an old lady bend your ear."

"I enjoyed talking with you, Rose." And he had. She'd help pass the time and for a few minutes had taken his mind off the reason for his visit. "You take care," he added as she preceded him through the door.

A heartbeat later, he realized his chivalry had back-fired when she made a beeline directly into the manager's office. Gary wouldn't have thought it possible for her to move so quickly with her walker, but she motored along better than many people half her age.

Heaving a frustrated sigh, he headed over to the receptionist.

**EMMA CARPENTER CONSIDERED** the day she'd landed her job to be the luckiest day of her life. A year ago when her husband dumped her for a woman twenty years younger, her self-esteem had taken such a beating she'd felt as if a part of her had died. After all, what were the odds a graying, slightly pudgy, forty-five year old would have a second chance at happiness?

But once she'd gotten over feeling sorry for herself, she'd decided to make the most of her newfound freedom. A gym membership had helped her shed the excess pounds, a make-over and a younger-looking wardrobe had opened up a world of possibilities and then landing the job had given her a new lease on life.

One of the things she loved most about being a receptionist was the opportunity it provided her to meet men. She'd learned quickly that by adding a little well-timed flirtation to her greeting, she could usually attract their interest. And what a difference a year could make. She was having the time of her life.

The sound of the front door bolts being unlocked by the security guard signaled the start of another day, one Emma was sure would be busy. Friday was payday for most companies and an event beginning tomorrow at the convention center across the street had brought nearly a thousand tourists to town.

Emma figured her opportunities for some action would be endless with a steady stream of customers.

Sure enough the moment the doors swung open an elderly woman pushing a walker raced inside like they were giving away free currency. But it wasn't the old woman who caught Emma's eye. It was the good-looking man who followed her inside.

Incredibly tall and athletically built, with a square jawed face capped by a head of snowy white hair, the man was completely masculine and quite simply, gorgeous. And his intelligent blue eyes seemed to miss nothing of his surroundings.

He was the kind of man any woman with a pulse would remember and she was positive he'd never been in the bank before. But he looked familiar; she just couldn't place why.

Watching the confident long-legged stride of his approach, she gave his solid body a lustful appraisal.

His hair was neatly trimmed with just enough length to tempt a woman's fingers. And from his well-tailored black business suit, crisp white dress shirt and dignified maroon tie to the small round pin on his jacket lapel, his appearance was immaculate. Nicely packaged and definitely yummy.

She sat up straighter to emphasize her bust line and when his gaze met hers, she gave her head the slight toss she knew would give a sexy jiggle to her bleached blonde hair.

"Good morning. May I help you?" she asked, tossing in a smile designed to telegraph that she liked what she saw and was interested.

Instead of the receptive response she'd come to expect from her practiced greeting, he barely seemed to notice her as his left hand flipped open a leather case he'd drawn from the inside breast pocket of his jacket.

"I'm Supervisory Special Agent Gary Thornton, Federal Bureau of Investigation. I need to speak with your manager as soon as he is free," he stated in the sexiest bass voice she'd ever heard.

But she suddenly realized why he looked familiar and a gasp of horror erupted from her mouth. "Oh my God! You called yesterday. I'm so sorry. I didn't…I mean…oh, no…I forgot to give him your message."

She knew she was babbling, but she couldn't help it.

She'd seen a man pacing back and forth outside the bank door for the past half hour and had even heard him knock several times, but she'd ignored him, figuring he was just a customer impatient to get his banking business over with early. It happened all the time.

But the FBI Agent had been all over the news in recent months and now that she saw him up close she knew he was the man she'd seen outside the door. Even worse, she clearly remembered her phone conversation with him.

He'd told her he'd be here at eight and that it was imperative he speak with her boss immediately. She hadn't recognized his name when he'd identified himself on the phone, but now that she saw him, she connected the name to his face.

And of all people, she'd forgotten to give her boss a message from him! She couldn't believe it. But worst of all, she knew why.

She'd no sooner hung up from his call when her ex-husband had come into the bank with the latest in his long string of gorgeous young playthings and he'd taken great relish in announcing he and the voluptuous brunette were getting married. She'd been so upset she'd completely forgotten the message she was supposed to give Ron Chandler.

Emma rarely cursed, but a few well-chosen words silently bounced around her head. She was in trouble. Big trouble. And if she didn't manage some damage control quickly, she might find herself out of a job.

# Chapter Two

Gary could feel a slow boil rising in his blood, but he held his tongue. No point in giving the woman a piece of his mind. He was fairly certain her boss would do it for him once the reason for his visit was learned. And he knew from experience that well-placed silence could be more effective than any words, so he merely stared at her, letting her feel his wrath.

It worked too. She nearly knocked over her coffee mug when she reached for her phone while glancing into the manager's office.

"I'll get him for you now," she stammered.

As urgent as his business was, Rose had beaten him fair and square to the man's office and Gary wasn't about to pull rank on her. At this point a few more minutes wouldn't matter.

"Let him finish with Mrs. Eshleman," he answered tersely. "There's no point in inconveniencing her, too." He let the censure stand without bothering to point out it was Ms. Carpenter's fault he wasn't already in the manager's office.

Turning his back on the ditzy receptionist, he surveyed the bank lobby, familiarizing himself with the layout while assessing the security.

A line of six teller windows currently manned by four tellers backed up against a wall housing the bank's vault. Hi-tech cameras. Alarms. Narrow teller windows with a high façade to impede someone attempting to jump over the counter. A locked gate to prevent unauthorized entry into the open vault. And a few other standard deterrents.

No glaring deficiencies, but then again none of the other banks had been lacking in their security either.

The elongated colonial style bank, situated in the middle of a plot of ground just off the National Pike, had entrances on both ends of the building. Those dual entrances presented a problem, but it was the uniformed armed guard posted in the lobby that concerned him most. They'd have to do something about him.

"I am sorry about the message, Agent Thornton. Can I get you some coffee while you wait?"

"No thanks. I've already had my limit," he answered absently, while continuing to assess the bank. Surrounded by a parking lot and sitting adjacent to a shopping center, traffic could pose…

"Limit! Your doctor must be a tyrant," the receptionist retorted.

His thoughts interrupted again, Gary turned slowly to gaze incredulously at the woman, astounded she'd jump to the conclusion his doctor had imposed the limit and that she'd offer such a blunt and unflattering assessment about someone she didn't know. And he doubted his wife would appreciate the opinion since she was his doctor.

Beautiful, sexy, intelligent, athletic, funny…the love of his life. That was Katie. Tyrant never crossed his mind. And the whole issue of coffee had begun when a joke of his had backfired.

As health conscious as Katie was, she had one weakness. The woman was a chocoholic. And one evening about ten years ago, after watching her search the cupboards for something to satisfy her sweet tooth, he'd teasingly challenged her to give up chocolate for a week, saying if she succeeded, he'd do whatever she wanted for the same time frame.

When the idea had first come to him, he'd figured it was a sure win for him because he'd never known her to pass up a piece of chocolate. But the moment he'd spoken, he'd seen a glint twinkling in her eyes and realized immediately the dare had been a colossal mistake on his part. And by the time she'd successfully breezed through the week, he'd reconciled himself to the fact he was going to have to uphold his end of the deal.

He'd fully expected a long honey-do list or possibly having to cook dinner for a week. But Katie had caught him completely off-guard with a challenge of her own, daring him to give up coffee for a week.

Gary supposed his male ego had suckered him into agreeing because it sure hadn't been his head, which after only two days without caffeine had been pounding so hard he thought his skull was going to explode and he'd been so irritable other special agents in his field office had avoided him like the plague.

Apparently the body didn't appreciate going cold turkey from eight or more cups of coffee per day to zero. And the only sympathy he'd gotten from his loving doctor wife, who'd seemed amused by his suffering, had been to offer him some ibuprofen.

In the end, the traded challenges had been a blessing in disguise for both of them though, because Katie had conquered her insatiable craving for chocolate and now only occasionally indulged her sweet tooth. For his part, he'd self-imposed a limit of two cups of coffee per day and he had to admit he was sleeping better at night and felt significantly healthier without all the caffeine in his system.

Since none of that was any of Ms. Carpenter's business, he didn't dignify her comment with a reply.

Undaunted by his silence, she gave him a suggestive smile. "Well, I'll give you anything you want and it'll be just between the two of us. In fact, why don't I cook dinner for you tonight at my apartment," she said, running her tongue along her lips invitingly. "And afterwards, I'm sure we can find a way for me to make it up to you for forgetting your phone message."

Gary stared at her in disbelief. Early in his career when he'd been working for Houston P.D., he'd met hookers who had more finesse and tact than this woman.

"Did you really just proposition a federal agent?"

Her eyes went wide as if she realized her error, but if he'd been expecting an apology, he would have been sorely disappointed. Good thing he wasn't because a guilty grin curved her lips and she eyed him as if sizing up a decadent dessert.

"Can't blame a girl for trying, can you?"

"She's pretty. But you'd better watch out, Romeo. She's got the hots for you."

The voice in his ear came so suddenly and loudly, it startled Gary, but he caught himself before visibly reacting. The miniscule receiver that fit inconspicuously in his ear had been quiet all morning, he'd actually forgotten someone was monitoring the audio and video feed from the Bureau's wireless communication link.

But that someone was Special Agent Zachary Taylor.

His son.

Zach's parents had been his and Katie's best friends and when they'd died in a plane crash, as his legal guardians, Kate and he had taken Zach to live with them. They'd legally adopted him two years later on Zach's twelfth birthday and loved him as if he was their own flesh and blood.

Gary had been honored and flattered by Zach's decision to follow in his footsteps and join the Bureau. And with Zach's graduation from the FBI Academy eight years ago they'd joined an elite group within the Bureau.

Between its minimum age requirement of twenty-three and the mandatory retirement age of fifty-seven, there were very few instances of fathers and sons working as special agents at the same time.

"This might require some hush money to keep you know who from learning she's got some competition."

Recovering from recent hernia surgery, Zach was officially on limited duty. So instead of being in the field, he was working from home monitoring and coordinating communication for Gary's task force.

And apparently plotting some friendly blackmail. Maybe it was time to reconsider that *honored and flattered* thought.

Zach was right though. Gary had seen the way Emma Carpenter had studied him when he'd entered the bank and just now had felt her eyes undressing him.

While he wasn't vain, he also wasn't blind. He saw his face every morning when he shaved. Personally Gary didn't see what the fuss was about, but he was used to women coming on to him, especially in his line of work. Usually those women were trying to distract him from their criminal activity, but it never worked.

Unlike some men who'd be more than willing to take the receptionist up on her offer; Gary was too professional to be sidetracked by anything so frivolous. And he was also very happily married. He took his vows and the gold band on his hand seriously and the only woman he wanted to share a bed or anything else with was Katie.

Letting the Carpenter woman's innuendo slide without comment, he walked further away from the reception desk to deal with Zach.

"Very funny," he growled softly into the miniscule microphone pin he was wearing. So sensitive it could detect a whisper, he had no doubt Zach heard him. "But if a photo or anything else from that conversation gets back to your mother, you're going to find yourself reassigned to a field office in the middle of nowhere."

Based on the laughter that came through his earpiece, Zach viewed the threat as an empty one. And it was.

Zach was a well-respected agent; the Bureau wasn't about to transfer him anywhere, let alone to some remote "punishment" locale. But more importantly, Katie would never forgive him if Gary had anything to do with their son being transferred. And in truth, Gary enjoyed working with Zach; he'd never do anything to change that.

Glancing into the manager's office again, Gary saw movement.

"Looks like the manager's conversation is winding down, Zach," he said relieved on so many levels he couldn't begin to count them all. "So cut the comic relief. It's time to go back to work."

"Killjoy!"

The smile twitching on Gary's lips over his son's irreverent reply, blossomed when Rose toddled out of the office and tossed a wink at him, as she headed over to the teller line.

Still smiling, he gave her a wink of his own before turning back to Emma Carpenter, ready to remind her he was waiting. To his surprise, she'd already picked up her phone.

"There's a man here to see you," Emma told her boss while tapping her pen rhythmically on her desk.

*A man here to see you?* Was that the best she could do? Hell, for all the manager knew from that pathetic comment, Gary could be selling a set of encyclopedias. What a ditz. Apparently it hadn't crossed her mind to mention he was a federal agent or that his business was urgent.

Before Gary could make the obvious suggestion, Zach's voice suddenly resounded in his ear again and this time there was no trace of humor in his son's voice.

"Head's up, Gary. Someone recognized you and notified the press; a TV crew is on its way to the bank."

In addition to coordinating communication for the team, Zach was monitoring numerous sources for information that pertained to Gary's task force.

Cursing silently, Gary glanced toward the door. The last thing he needed was for reporters to plaster his picture all over the news today. It would ruin everything his team had arranged.

"Mike is with the police chief," Zach continued. "And they've contacted the television station to ask them to recall the crew, but he's sending some officers down to the bank to help you avoid any reporters who are still there when you leave."

Special Agent Mike Devlin was Gary's second in command on the task force. If anyone could get the press to back off, it was Dev.

And Gary hoped he was successful because a media circus could have catastrophic results.

Relief pushed aside Gary's frustration but since he was too close to the receptionist desk to reply aloud, he tapped his transmitter twice in acknowledgement.

"He'll be with you in just a moment," Emma Carpenter said letting her smile turn suggestive again. "But be sure to let me know if you change your mind about my offer, handsome."

Fully expecting another smart comment from Zach, Gary was just as glad when his comm link remained silent because the blatant innuendo left him speechless. And after more than thirty years in law enforcement that was no easy task.

From the background check they'd pulled on bank employees, Gary knew Emma Carpenter was a divorcee in her mid-forties. But he had a hunch someone had done a real number on her self-esteem. Nothing else explained why an attractive woman would be dressing in skin tight clothing that bore no resemblance to professional attire and propositioning a complete stranger…on company time, no less.

He actually felt sorry for her. But ignoring her again, Gary turned, using his vantage point to watch the branch manager as the balding bespectacled man finished a phone conversation with someone and then rose from his desk.

After straightening his striped tie, adjusting his khaki sport coat and sucking in the ample gut that hung over the belt on his dark brown pants, the man waddled out to the lobby in no particular hurry to greet the *man here to see him.*

Background information on Ron Chandler had been interesting. Born and raised in Hagerstown…fifty years old…began his banking career a quarter century ago at a Richmond, Virginia office of Hamilton National Bank, a nationwide financial institution. Chandler had bounced from one branch to another, rising through the ranks to be a regional manager for the bank's Maryland branches. But at the beginning of the year, he'd been named branch manager for the National Pike office.

Looking for an explanation for what appeared to be a demotion, Gary had examined Chandler's background report carefully, but the information hadn't provided any clue. The incongruity had tweaked Gary's curiosity, but since he couldn't find any tie between Chandler's career and the Bureau's investigation he'd gone on to the next employee file.

But as he watched the man approach, he was looking forward to meeting Chandler and hopefully getting a better sense of why the man's career appeared to be going backward.

"I'm Ron Chandler, the branch manager," the corpulent man said, peering at him through bifocals. "What can I do for you?"

"Supervisory Special Agent Gary Thornton, Federal Bureau of Investigation," Gary replied, flipping open his credentials again. "We need to speak privately in your office."

Chandler's brow knit with concern, but he nodded. "Certainly. Follow me." He turned to lead the way, but as an afterthought tossed instructions to the receptionist over his shoulder.

"Hold my calls. I don't want to be disturbed."

Gary followed Chandler into a large, front corner office brightly illuminated by sunlight flowing through two enormous colonial style windows. His eyes swept the prime piece of real estate admiringly. Custom drapery, upholstered furniture, plush carpet…and several signed, numbered art prints depicting the Battle of Sharpsburg, expensively matted and framed, hanging on the walls.

The tastefully decorated office was dominated by an enormous cherry desk devoid of any kind of paper. Fellow agents teased Gary all the time about the orderly state of his own office, a habit he'd adopted due to his forensic accounting background. Finding financial information was a hell of a lot easier in a neat space than having to dig through papers scattered haphazardly around an office or desk.

So, yeah, he was guilty of being neat…but this place made his office look like a pig sty. Nice, very nice. But, the entire room was so immaculate it looked more like a show room than a working office, which made him wonder what Chandler did all day.

The click of the door closing redirected Gary's thoughts to the reason for his visit and settling into one of the exquisite wing-backed visitor chairs, he got right to the point.

"We have credible evidence the Phantoms will hit your bank branch this afternoon."

Chandler's double chin wobbled with a shake of his head. "Oh, no! The Phantoms! Are you certain?"

"Certain? No," Gary replied. "But all indications point to it."

"Why am I just now learning about it?" Chandler shot back sharply.

Gary glanced out to the lobby considering how to answer, but any thoughts he had of cutting Emma Carpenter a break disintegrated when in spite of being engrossed in a phone conversation, she gave him a provocative wave.

"I spoke with your receptionist by phone yesterday afternoon, telling her I'd be here at eight this morning and that it was imperative I speak with you immediately. Apparently she forgot to give you the message, so we've lost an hour that could have been used productively to plan for their arrival."

Chandler muttered a curse under his breath.

From the manager's reaction, explaining the seriousness of the situation obviously wasn't necessary. While most bank robberies drew local news coverage, only someone with their head in the sand would be unaware of the Phantoms.

The notorious group of bank robbers, named for the grotesque masks they wore, had been running rampant through Maryland for months and their national headlines grew each time they pulled off another brazen heist.

In February, when the Phantoms hit their first bank, a suburban branch in Catonsville, the case landed squarely in Gary's lap as head of the Bureau's Criminal Investigation Division in Maryland. When three subsequent heists by the same group occurred around the state, the Bureau named him to head a task force charged with bringing the bank robbers to justice.

After frustrating weeks of investigating six ensuing hold-ups and studying every aspect of all ten robberies, they'd finally found a common theme.

Each hold-up had occurred in a community hosting some unique event that drew large crowds and generated significant cash flow. The pattern hadn't immediately been obvious because the size of the events had varied drastically from one town to another.

But trying to identify their next target on such a scant lead had been an overwhelming process considering Maryland had countless communities, hundreds of which held events that could potentially fit the profile.

As they'd developed their list, though, one upcoming event caught their attention. And it was that event that had led Gary and his team to the Hagerstown branch of Hamilton National Bank.

A large national labor union was holding its annual meeting at a convention center in Hagerstown, bringing an influx of conventioneers to town. And with the flood of visitors, larger than normal amounts of money would be changing hands at hotels, restaurants and stores located near the convention center. All that translated into banks needing more cash on hand than normal.

Its convenient location across the National Pike from the convention center, made Hamilton National Bank the logical choice for the center to use for its daily financial transactions. The task force had easily confirmed that to be the case. They'd also learned many of the stores and restaurants in an adjacent shopping area used the branch as well. So it was no surprise to have Federal Reserve verify the bank was expecting a much larger than usual cash shipment.

The easy access and quick escape routes around the bank, similar to those in previous robberies, were additional factors pinpointing it as a prime target.

Every instinct Gary had developed during his years in law enforcement told him the bank was ripe for an attack by the Phantoms. And after an exhaustive effort failed to poke holes in his theory, the entire task force agreed the bank would be too tempting for the brazen robbers to resist. Chatter on the streets from criminal informants supported their suspicion.

To date, the Phantoms had hit so swiftly and with such precision that they'd been long gone before law enforcement could react. Gary was hoping to throw a wrench into the gang's well-oiled machine this time.

And while he'd been cooling his heels waiting for the bank to open, Mike and other agents had been coordinating with local and state police to enlist their aid in plugging potential escape routes the bandits might attempt.

"Why this bank?"

Gary wasn't about to show all his cards, so he only told the manager the obvious. "You've got an unusually large currency shipment arriving this afternoon and their M.O. to date has been to strike right after a shipment is delivered. So that's when we're expecting the robbery to occur."

"How are you going to stop them?" Chandler asked with a blend of curiosity and alarm.

"We aren't," Gary answered bluntly. The task force had weighed every scenario imaginable and in all but one the outcome put innocent civilians at risk. So they'd opted for caution and decided to allow the robbery to occur and concentrate on cutting off escape routes.

His team and a small army of plainclothes state and local police planned to be in strategic locations outside waiting to take the robbers into custody once they exited the bank.

No one on the task force had any delusions about the potential outcome; things could get ugly very quickly. But the hope was to convince the bandits they were outnumbered and have them surrender peacefully. If that didn't work, the team was prepared to use whatever force was necessary to end the Phantoms' reign of terror.

When he explained the plan to Chandler, the manager begrudgingly agreed. A good thing since Gary had no intention of altering his plans because of a diffident bank manager.

"With any luck we'll be able to take them into custody without bloodshed."

At least that was the plan.

"For you and your employees, it's business as usual," Gary continued. "But your armed guard in the lobby is a problem. The Phantoms have routinely killed guards they've encountered during other bank robberies. I don't want to see that happen here. So I suggest you either send the guard home or have him change into plain clothes and lose his weapon."

Chandler stared out into the lobby at the guard before nodding mutely.

Gary shot a glance at the teller line over his shoulder. "Is Rachel Washington reliable?"

The Bureau's background check of the forty-three year old head teller identified her as a married, mother of three teenagers. She'd worked for the bank for twenty years and all indications pointed to her being a good steady employee with no red flags in her past.

Chandler's response was immediate. "Oh, yes. Rachel has been with us for years and is an excellent supervisor."

"Then I suggest you call her in here and let me explain things to her so she can help keep her staff calm when the robbery goes down."

Clearly unhappy with the entire situation, Chandler picked up his phone.

A few moments passed before the woman knocked on the door. When Chandler waved her inside, Gary stood to greet her.

He recognized Rachel Washington from the photo in her file, but the picture hadn't done her justice. Tall and with a dignified carriage, the woman could easily have been a fashion model. And her professional appearance in both dress and make-up was such a contrast to the ditzy receptionist's barroom skin tight, pick-up attire that the two women didn't seem to belong in the same building. It was a no brainer which one of them projected the image of a career banker.

Rachel stared at him curiously for a moment before turning to her boss. "You wanted to see me, Ron?" she asked, shooting another questioning glance at Gary.

"Yes, Rachel, come in and shut the door."

Once the door closed, Gary didn't wait for an introduction. "Mrs. Washington, I'm Supervisory Special Agent Gary Thornton with the Federal Bureau of Investigation."

"FBI?" she echoed, clearly concerned and turning to her boss. "Is something wrong?"

"Agent Thornton has some disturbing news for us."

When Chandler's reply caused her gaze to swing back to Gary, he motioned to a chair, waiting until Rachel sat down before doing the same. And then because they were in a time crunch, he bypassed any idle chatter and went right to the reason for his visit. But as soon as he began to explain when the robbery would go down, he noticed her eyes widen in alarm and she began to shake her head.

"No…what?" he asked wondering if she was merely trying to deny the inevitable.

"We just got a call that the delivery was changed," she uttered breathlessly, glancing down at her watch. When her eyes met his again, they were filled with panic. "The truck will be here in less than fifteen minutes."

"Dammit!" The curse flew from Gary's mouth unchecked and it took a moment for his brain to reorganize for the new development. The fact Zach hadn't reacted audibly to the news was odd, but Gary didn't have time to figure out if he'd lost the communication link or if Zach was just busy scrambling to get the rest of the team notified as to the change of plans.

But Gary couldn't afford to take any chances. The last thing he needed was a group of uniformed officers descending on the bank and being massacred in the process.

Snatching his cell phone from the clip at his waist, he quickly typed a text message to his entire team.

*Plan is OFF!!! Do NOT…Repeat NOT approach bank; Phantoms arriving any minute. Get into position to cut off escape. Do it NOW!*

As soon as he hit Send, his gaze snapped up to the two bank employees.

With upstairs space currently empty while being renovated to accommodate corporate offices, his task force had discreetly halted work crews from accessing the site today. But he had to secure the first floor quickly.

"Okay…here's what we're going to do. We've got to make things look like business as usual, but I want as few people as possible caught up in this mess. I'm going to clear the bank, but I want the two of you to remain behind the teller line. Keep the receptionist at her desk and one other teller behind the line with you. Everyone else goes."

"You're staying?" Chandler asked incredulously.

If they hadn't been discussing a potentially deadly situation, Gary would have found his reaction comical. Chandler's tone made no secret that he thought the idea of Gary intentionally subjecting himself to a bank robbery was insane.

And maybe it was. But with his original plan flushed down the toilet, Gary was creating a new one on the fly.

To date the task force had a lot of silent security footage and conflicting statements from scores of terrified witnesses. His team could use a set of eyes and ears inside during a robbery to get first-hand knowledge of how the gang operated and some good solid intel on the members of the group.

By virtue of the fact he was already inside, Gary was the most logical person to handle the assignment. And the communication equipment he was wearing would allow Zach to capture sound and video of everything that happened.

"Hopefully I'll be able to help you defuse any incident before it gets out of hand," he explained. "But I don't have a death wish, so I won't be attempting to stop the heist."

Chandler merely nodded. "How are you going to clear the bank?"

Gary shot a quick glance at the lobby, counting a dozen customers. "Trust me…I'll clear it." He just needed to figure out how and with the clock ticking down, he'd better come up with an idea pretty damn fast.

"Can't we just lock the doors and stop the robbery from occurring?" Rachel asked.

Gary gave her an understanding smile. "I wish we could, Mrs. Washington, but the Bureau wants to stop this group once and for all. To do that we need to catch them in the act. If we lock the doors, they will just hit another bank and we don't make any headway in catching them. If we let them carry out the robbery here, we still have a chance to capture them afterwards and put an end to their crimes."

When she nodded understanding, he paused for a moment to let them digest everything. "Any questions?"

Looking less than enthusiastic, they both shook their head.

They might not have questions, but Gary had a ton of them rolling around his brain and all of them centered on who had changed the cash delivery schedule at the last minute and why. And when he found the answer to that one, the person damn well better have a good reason for it or the task force would be all over them.

"Okay, let's go," he said standing up.

When neither of them reacted, he rapped his knuckles on Chandler's desk, loudly. "Move!"

That snapped them out of their trance and as soon as they cleared the office door, Gary quickly headed to the lobby where he pulled the security guard aside.

The Bureau's background check had identified the guard as Robert Kendall, a sixty year old retired police lieutenant. Gary flipped open his identification.

"I don't have time to explain," he said while Kendall studied the credentials. "But we believe the Phantoms are going to hit this bank any minute now."

That caught Kendall's attention and Gary kept going.

"I need you to help me get these customers out of here and with that guard uniform of yours…I want you to go with them. And if there are any uniformed cops in view out there, get them away from the building."

Kendall evidently knew the Phantoms' reputation because his response was immediate. "Will do. How do we clear the lobby?"

Fortunately Gary had come up with a plan he prayed would work.

"This way," he replied, turning his attention to the customers. "Folks, I need your attention," he called calmly. One advantage to his deep bass voice was it projected well and everyone turned his way. "We've got a gas leak in the building and need to evacuate immediately. I'm sorry for the inconvenience, but we'll reopen as soon as we receive an all clear. Until then, you should either head home or over to the shopping center, but you need to leave and get far away from the building now."

To Gary's immense relief customers began funneling to the door before he even finished his explanation. He saw Chandler motion one teller and the receptionist to remain behind while Rachel Washington shooed the rest of the tellers out, with loan officers, financial advisors and a customer service rep on their heels.

In short order Kendall rounded up the lingerers and ushered them out the door as well. With a nod to Gary, the guard followed the last person out.

Gary spun around to the skeleton crew remaining and from the petrified expressions on all their faces, he realized Chandler had already informed them what was about to happen. Standing between the reception desk and the teller line, so he could see everyone, he tried to ease their concern.

"I know it's difficult, but try not to worry. When the Phantoms arrive…don't argue, don't hesitate and don't resist. Your life is worth more than any money; just give them what they want, do whatever they say and try not to draw attention to yourself. You'll be fine."

"What about the armored car delivery?" Rachel asked. "How do we handle that?"

Impressed by her ability to think under extreme pressure, Gary gave her an admiring smile and nodded. "Good question. Previously, the Phantoms have appeared within a few minutes of the armored car leaving the bank. We don't want to tip off the robbers that we're on to them, so handle the delivery the way you normally handle it. But just be aware that if the Phantoms are planning to hit here today, it will happen shortly after that delivery. So just stay calm and cooperate."

He made eye contact with each of them and satisfied they were as ready as they'd ever be, he quickly stepped back into the bank manager's office where he'd noticed security monitors showing wide angle camera footage of the approaches to each of the bank's doors. Another monitor displayed images from the parking lot, showing only five cars, one of which was his. He figured the others belonged to the four employees inside the bank with him.

To Gary's relief, no people were lingering anywhere in the vicinity outside. Kendall had done a good job of clearing the area.

Orienting himself to the different views, Gary made sure his identification and badge were safely tucked out of sight in his inside breast pocket where he always carried them.

"Zach, do you read me?" he asked. "The robbery is going down any minute. Is everyone in place?"

Nothing. No feedback, no static, no nothing. Just deafening silence.

Frowning, he took the receiver from his ear and tapped it, then repositioned it and tapped his pin transmitter. "Zach!"

Again, nothing.

Cursing the untimely break in their communications, motion on a monitor drew Gary's attention. He watched as the armored vehicle pulled to a stop at the side door. A few short minutes later, the money had been unloaded from the truck and brought into the bank.

Through it all Gary could feel tension knotting his shoulders. Those knots only twisted tighter as he watched the armored truck pull away from the bank. He imagined the employees were holding their collective breath, wondering what would happen next because that's exactly what he was doing.

Any hope he had that the change in schedule would foil the Phantoms' plans dissolved as five masked men swarmed out of a black SUV that suddenly appeared on the camera. And with the impending danger for everyone involved, he took no satisfaction in the fact the task force hunch about the robbers' target had been correct.

Giving up on the communication device, he grabbed his cell phone again and texted an update to his team.

*Phantoms are here; black SUV at front door; I'm inside bank.*

Shoving aside his anger over the breakdown in their communication and what was about to happen, he hit Send and turned the phone off so it wouldn't distract him or attract unwanted attention. And slipping it back into its clip, Gary watched intently as the Phantoms, carrying an impressive array of weapons, surged into the bank.

A heartbeat later, amid blasts of gunfire from their weapons, the robbers fanned out.

# Chapter Three

Doctor Kate Thornton knotted her surgical thread and stood back to study the neat row of stitches closing a gash on her sixteen year old patient's forehead.

"You're good as new, Chase." Peeling off her surgical gloves and tossing them in with the other medical waste, she gave him a smile. "And if I must say so myself, I did such a beautiful job with that sewing you won't even have a scar."

Considering his car had been one of many caught in an I-83 pile up when a semi jackknifed during rush hour, he'd been fortunate to sustain nothing more than the laceration. But he didn't look as pleased as she would have thought.

"That's good, right?" she asked, seeing a frown crease his numbed brow.

"How can I impress the girls if I don't at least have a scar to show them?"

Kate let her gaze travel over her patient.

With a solid set of biceps and athletic body rounded out by dark brown wavy hair, hazel eyes with Bambi-like lashes and killer dimples, he personified the kind of boy teenage girls were drawn to like flies to fly paper. She knew this because her now grown son, Zach had the exact same assets and she wasn't so old she didn't remember all the girls who'd fawned over him at that age.

She couldn't help chuckling. "Somehow I doubt you have any trouble in that area." When he grinned guiltily, she let the smile slide off her face and fired off some instructions. "Keep them clean and dry and when they start to itch, don't scratch."

The kid gave her an unconcerned shrug. "No sweat. I know the drill, Doc."

She smiled at his nonchalance and turned to his distraught mother.

As a wife and mother, Kate could relate to the terror Carol Hampton must have felt when she'd been notified Chase had been injured. Kate had been there and done that more times than she cared to remember.

"Mrs. Hampton, he's going to be fine," Kate said reassuringly before giving her final instructions and a prescription for pain medication in case the boy needed it. "Unless you have questions, you're free to go."

"Thank you for everything," Carol said, draping a protective arm around her son's shoulder as he got down from the exam table. And as she led him out of the room, Kate smiled after them wearily.

The highway pile up had occurred during the first twenty minutes of her shift and almost immediately, casualties had begun pouring into the emergency room. As head of the trauma unit, one of her responsibilities was to prioritize treatment, but she wasn't one to sit back and watch others work. When her trauma team was busy, all hands chipped in to help and she'd been up to her elbows in patients since the first gurney had arrived.

Thankfully the excitement had subsided and since there was a lull in activity, she had time to run to the cafeteria for a cup of tea.

She was just coming out of her office with her wallet in hand when she spotted her son and daughter-in-law, Cassie walking toward her, hand-in-hand. They were the last people Kate expected to see in her emergency room.

"What brings the two of you here? You're not hurt or sick are you?"

"No…we're fine," Zach said dropping a kiss on her cheek. "We were just in the area and decided to stop to see you."

If anyone other than Zach had given her that line she might have bought it. But like any other mother who'd raised a teenager, she'd finely honed her truth meter. And at age thirty-five he still wasn't able to pull one over on her.

But whatever it was he was trying not to tell her, she intended to find out because her mind was already traveling in dangerous directions imagining all sorts of things she didn't want to think about.

Leading them into her office, she shut the door and then turned back to face them, planting her hands on her hips.

"Now…tell me why you're really here."

The minute she saw them exchange a glance, she knew she'd been right. Something was up and something about their expressions sent a trace of alarm creeping along her spine.

Zach gazed at her thoughtfully for a moment and then heaved a deep breath. "The Phantom's are hitting another bank right now and Dad is inside the building."

For a moment, Kate couldn't breathe.

Although Gary never went into details, she usually knew the general nature of one of his investigations. And this one was no different. She'd known his trip had something to do with the string of bank robberies by the Phantoms. But the idea of him being caught inside a bank with violent bandits who'd left a string of bodies in the wake of their previous robberies absolutely terrified her.

It was as if she could see Gary teetering on the edge of a cliff and Kate was afraid to blink for fear when she opened her eyes again, he'd be gone.

Grabbing her cell phone from her purse, Kate pressed the speed dial for Gary's phone. When Zach reached toward her, she spun away to prevent him from taking the phone away and glared at him.

"Mom…he's not going to answer," Zach insisted quietly. "He can't. If the robbery is still in progress, he'd only draw attention to himself and if the Phantoms are gone…well…he'll be too busy to answer."

Realistically Kate knew what her son said was true, but the last thing she was feeling was rational. She needed to hear Gary's voice, to know he was alive and okay. But the call went to his voice mail.

On the edge of panic, she slid the phone back in her pocket and tried to make sense of what was happening. It was impossible.

Kate knew better than most the inherent dangers FBI agents faced. The rational side of her brain had long ago reconciled to the fact that one day her husband might not come home from work. But faced with that stark reality now, it was impossible to accept. Just the thought of life without Gary caused a wave of nausea to swirl in her stomach.

Feeling her legs give out from under her, Kate sat down on one of her visitor chairs.

"Are you sure?" Even she heard the tremor of fear in her voice.

Zach knelt down in front of her and took her hands in his. "Yes, Mom. But try not to worry. Dad's been studying this group for months; he understands exactly how they operate. And there's no way he'll do anything to jeopardize his safety. He'll be fine; I know he will."

Kate wished she had her son's optimism. It wasn't that she lacked confidence in her husband's ability. Gary was one of the smartest men she'd ever met and having survived four years working the streets as part of the Houston police department and twenty-seven more years with the FBI, he knew how to handle himself in a crisis situation.

Kate was certain he would never intentionally do anything to endanger himself, but it wasn't him that worried her; it was the entire situation. Criminals were unpredictable and things could get out of hand quickly; things Gary would have no way of controlling.

"The bank is in Hagerstown, isn't it?" she asked. The question was really rhetorical. When Gary had slipped out of bed at five o'clock that morning Kate had known he was leaving for a meeting, but she hadn't known where. But then a little after eight she'd gotten a text from him telling her he'd thought of her when he'd driven past a restaurant they'd discovered a year ago during a romantic weekend getaway at a bed and breakfast in that town. And since his meeting had been set to start at eight, she figured he had to be somewhere near Hagerstown if he'd seen the restaurant.

Zach nodded confirmation. "We suspected they'd hit the National Pike branch, but we were expecting it to happen in the afternoon when their cash shipment arrived. Dad met with the branch manager this morning to get everything set up for when the robbery went down. I don't know what happened, but a little after nine…just about ten minutes ago in fact, Dad sent the team a text saying the robbery was going to happen any minute. And he just sent another text a few minutes ago telling us the Phantoms had arrived and that he was inside."

A faint hint of amusement lit in Zach's eyes. "I think he added that last part because he didn't want anyone getting trigger happy."

His humor fell flat on Kate. She was too worried to find anything funny about her husband's life being in danger. "Oh dear Lord, no. If they do that…" her voice trailed off when her brain refused to let her finish the terrifying thought.

Apparently Zach realized where her mind was traveling because he patted her hand again. "Mom…I'm sorry; I was just kidding. Dad will be fine. Mike's on his way to the bank; he's probably there by now and he'll be assuming command until Dad is free. Jimmy and Lucas are there too. They won't allow anyone to do anything that would put him in more peril. And as soon as we hear from him or know anything, I'll let you know."

Kate closed her eyes praying Zach was right.

She knew it was killing him to be left behind while the rest of the task force was on the scene, but Kate had mixed feelings about it. Part of her wished Zach was there too. He adored his father and she knew in her heart he'd never let anything happen to Gary. But as a mother and doctor she was relieved Zach was safely away from the danger.

Since he couldn't be with Gary, she was glad Mike Devlin, Jim Barrett and Lucas Shaw were. Those men were like members of her family and Kate knew they'd do whatever they could to ensure Gary's safety. She tried to take comfort in that knowledge, but it wasn't easy.

"If he just sent these texts, how did you get here so quickly?" she asked.

"I don't know if a reporter was following Dad this morning or if someone else recognized him, but I picked up chatter from the press on our communication links. They knew he was at the bank and were lining up to talk to him when he came out. That worried me because I knew it would only be a matter of minutes before one of them figured out why he was there and plastered his picture all over the news and I figured I'd better give you a head's up before that happened. Cassie and I were on our way here when Dad sent his first text and his second one arrived as we were pulling into a parking space outside."

The fact Gary had been recognized scared Kate even more than she had been, because whoever had notified the press that he was at the bank had potentially signed his death warrant. If the Phantoms learned who he was…well…she didn't even want to think about that outcome.

She supposed the one positive thing in this nightmare was that Zach and Cassie only lived a short distance from the hospital and had gotten here so quickly to break the news before she'd learned about it accidentally. She dreaded to think how she would have reacted if she'd heard about it on television or if one of her co-workers had drop the news on her in the middle of the ER.

A heavy sigh lifted Kate's chest. "The wait for information is going to be unbearable."

As soon as she said it, her mind latched onto an idea that quickly became the sole focus of her thoughts. She stood up suddenly. "I'm going to Hagerstown."

"That's not a good idea Mom," Zach countered. "Besides the fact it's an hour away, even if you could get close enough to the bank to see Dad, he's going to be tied up with the investigation and won't have time to talk to you."

Every day Gary left for work she thought about the dangers of his job and it made their every moment together more precious to her. And during his twenty-seven years with the Bureau, he'd been injured a handful of times, but she'd always learned about those injuries after the fact, the danger to him had been over. This time was different. The robbery was ongoing and Gary's peril was not over; it was happening now.

As a wife and doctor, there was no way she could know that and do nothing. And no one was going to talk her out of going to him. "I don't care. I'm going."

Cassie stopped Zach before he could protest again. "Zach, I understand what Mom is feeling and this is something she needs to do. Trying to talk her out of it is only wasting precious time." Her focus shifted to Kate immediately. "But Mom…you're not in any shape to drive. I'm taking you. And I'm staying with you until we know Dad is okay. And then if you want to stay and ride home with him, I can come back alone."

Zach heaved a resigned sigh. "I wish I could go with you, but I can't. I shouldn't have left the communication link unattended as it was, but I wanted to be the one to tell you what was happening. I've got to get back."

"Go!" Cassie said, giving him a quick kiss. "We'll be fine and I'll call you when we get there."

Zach gazed at his wife for a moment and after giving her another kiss, he hugged Kate. "Dad will be fine. I know he will."

Kate wasn't sure if he was trying to convince her or himself. But as soon as he left, she turned to Cassie. "Give me five minutes."

Heading the ER had its advantages and perks, but she'd never been one to abuse her position. Today she made an exception. And after quickly rearranging the schedule to cover for her absence, Kate dashed back to her office where Cassie was waiting and grabbed her pocketbook and the medical kit she took with her everywhere.

"Okay…let's go."

# Chapter Four

"Everyone get down!"
"On the floor…now!"
"Face down! Do it!"

Screamed orders accompanied by automatic gunfire intended to terrify their captives into cooperation came from the bandits.

Five of them…all men and probably in their thirties.

Gary doubted that last observation would stand up in court, but over the years, he'd gotten pretty good at guesstimating ages by the maturity tone of a voice. The bandits hadn't sounded youthful or middle aged, so he pegged them in their thirties.

First chance he got, he intended to have Zach run a voice analysis on sounds being captured by his communication equipment. He'd only heard them speak a few brief words, but they all sounded as if they had southern accents. If they could pinpoint the dialects it might help them identify the bandits.

Right now, though, he had more immediate problems than their accents. Namely, making sure he and everyone else survived this robbery. Stepping into the lobby to a scene where terror definitely reigned supreme, the first thing he saw did nothing to alleviate his concern.

A pretty young brunette with two children in tow had apparently slipped inside the back door of the bank just before the Phantoms descended on the lobby and they were now caught up in the robbery. Terrified by the gunfire and masked bandits, the woman stood frozen in shock while the toddler she was carrying screamed hysterically. The boy, who looked to be about five, clung to her with a look of quiet bravado, obviously shaken, but trying not to cry.

Drawing attention to himself was the last thing Gary intended, but when one of the gunmen swung a weapon toward the family, he knew he had no choice. No way in hell could he stand by and allow the woman and her children to be hurt without at least trying to stop it.

Moving faster than was wise with bullets flying around, Gary raced out of the office and in a few long strides captured the woman around the shoulders. Her startled scream echoed in his ears as he dragged her and her children to the floor.

He'd managed to get her out of the line of fire just in time, too because the gunman had unleashed a hail of bullets aimed where she'd just been standing. He knew this because one of those bullets had seared through his suit jacket, grazing the top of his shoulder. It stung like hell, but Gary figured the injury was minor considering the woman would be dead if he hadn't acted when he did.

"Stay down," he whispered at her ear, while sheltering the boy beneath him.

"Th…thank you," the young mother stammered, staring at him as if he was an angel of mercy.

"Don't mention it. Just stay down and you'll be fine."

"Get down old woman. Move it."

The angry demand and the sound of metal crashing to the floor drew Gary's attention. His heart dropped to his stomach when he saw one of the Phantoms manhandling Rose. He hadn't realized the elderly woman was still in the bank, but considering the noise he'd heard had been her safe deposit box hitting the floor, she must have been inside one of the privacy booths and not heard his order to leave.

Disregarding her age and physical condition, the bandit was attempting to force her to the floor. Already unsteady on her feet, she teetered on the verge of falling, which at her age Gary feared would result in a broken hip.

A powerful wave of anger surged inside him. He patted the boy's shoulders. "Stay down, son. I'll be right back," he said scrambling to his knees.

"Rose," he called, holding his hands up to show the gunman he was no threat. "Cooperate with them. Do what they say."

The bandit, a man appearing to be of average height and weight, watched him warily.

"Please…let me help her get on the floor," Gary said with a calm he didn't feel.

"Who the hell are you?"

Before Gary could answer, Rachel Washington piped up from behind the teller line.

"He's our loan officer."

Her voice quivered nervously, but the lie had been spoken so convincingly no one questioned it. No surprise there. These men weren't here to apply for a loan.

Grateful she hadn't revealed his true identity, Gary played along with the ruse. "I'm just trying to help so no one gets hurt."

To his surprise the bandit released Rose and with his urge to deck the man temporarily assuaged, Gary stood up and reached out to the elderly woman.

"Let me help you," he said, taking her hand.

"He was trying to knock me over," she protested furiously.

"I know, but Rose you've got to cooperate with these men or they'll hurt you. I don't want that to happen and I'm sure you don't either."

Rose patted his hand and let him guide her to the floor.

He straightened to find a different bandit, a human refrigerator, standing in front of him with an AK-47 aimed at his chest.

Gary considered himself to be in good shape, but this man, although a couple inches shorter, was a wall of solid muscle and easily outweighed him by more than a hundred pounds. The guy belonged on the forward defensive line of a pro-football team; he was huge. Definitely not someone Gary wanted to tangle with under these circumstances…or any other, for that matter.

He lifted his hands again. "I was just trying to help her," Gary explained calmly, glancing down at Rose again to make sure she was okay.

Pain suddenly exploded in Gary's side, spiraling through his body and sucking the air from his lungs as a groan shot from his mouth. It took a lot to double him over, but the behemoth's blow, ramming the butt of the assault rifle into his ribs, managed to do just that. And it felt like his liver had flown across his innards and slammed into his stomach.

Before he could correct his vulnerable position, the bandit brought the gun down hard on the back of his head, dropping him to the floor like a ton of bricks.

Coherent thought fled Gary's brain for a heartbeat, only to return with a resounding…Not again!

Just last October while he was part of Zach's drug task force, a dirty FBI agent helping the cartel, tried to kill him by cutting the brake line of his car. In the resulting crash he'd sustained, among other injuries, several cracked ribs…the same ribs that now screamed with pain again.

"No…no…no! He was just trying to help me," Rose protested, her voice quivering with emotion.

"Shut up," the gunman screamed at her.

Ignoring his pain, Gary looked over at Rose, seeing the shock and anger in her eyes. "Don't antagonize him," he whispered, catching her gaze. "Let it go. I'm okay."

He wasn't sure where he found the breath to utter the words and doubted she believed him. He didn't even believe it. His ribs hurt like hell and if his head wasn't bleeding from that last blow it would be a miracle. The force of the hit had momentarily made the room spin. He figured he was lucky that he hadn't blacked out.

But he glanced over in time to see the gunman swinging a heavily booted foot in his direction.

Gary had gone into this situation with the goal of not attracting attention, of doing just what he'd warned others to do. Comply. He'd gone against his own advice by helping Rose and the young family. But no way was he going to let the jackass kick him in the side because if the first blow hadn't broken any ribs, a second one definitely would.

Self-preservation kicked in and he flinched away. The dodge worked, too.

Almost.

Gary avoided the blow, but instead of connecting with his ribs, the gunman's foot catapulted his cell phone from its carrying case, flipping up the flap of his suit jacket. The phone skittering out of his reach was of minor concern considering the gun clipped at his hip was now in full view for anyone to see.

"Well, what have we here?" the refrigerator taunted.

A creative string of expletives raced through Gary's mind. So much for his cover as a loan officer. He doubted many of them carried concealed weapons on the job.

Law enforcement was inherently dangerous and a measure of fear was always present. A healthy fact of life that never completely went away. But it was something Gary had gotten used to, something he was able to work through and overcome. If he hadn't, he wouldn't have lasted in his job.

Now though, staring into the icy blue eyes of the gunman standing over him, there was no working through anything. From months of investigation Gary knew all too well how these bandits dealt with anyone they perceived as law enforcement. Casualties during previous robberies had already claimed the lives of three bank guards who'd merely been doing their job and four police officers who'd had the misfortune of accidentally interrupting robberies in progress.

With as much dignity as a man could muster while awkwardly sprawled on the floor, Gary met the gunman's gaze and forcing his voice to remain calm, he splayed his hands again in a non-threatening gesture.

"I'm not here to cause trouble."

But the moment the gunman's lips curved into a cold smile, Gary knew he was as good as dead and there was nothing he could do about it.

Reaching for his gun would amount to suicide and would be a futile effort at best. Considering his position on the floor, the gunman would kill him before he even had the weapon in his hand. And on the off chance, slim as it was, that he could grab his gun and get off a shot, Gary knew damn well the rest of the Phantoms would respond by opening fire and a lot of innocent people, including children, would die in the mass carnage.

It was a no win situation all around.

Sounds of chaos that had filled the air moments before vaporized and the entire world shrank down to just one deadly gunman and him. Gary's jaw clenched, but he stared directly at the SOB, refusing to show even a hint of defeat or fear.

"Say goodbye," the bandit taunted.

Feeling the remaining seconds of his life ticking away, Gary continued to stare unblinkingly at the man and blanked his mind of everything except thoughts of Kate and how much he loved her.

But the sound of a metallic click robbed him of the moment and he held his breath, awaiting the instant the fatal bullet slammed into him. A second later he realized nothing had happened.

It made no sense. He knew the man had pulled the trigger; he'd seen and heard it.

Suddenly, coherent thought fired to life again and his years of experience handling weapons gave him the answer. The trigger had been pulled, but the sound had been that of an empty magazine. The weapon was out of ammunition.

Gary kicked himself mentally for not recognizing the sound immediately, but apparently with all the gunfire and confusion in the lobby, the bandit hadn't realized it either.

Suddenly, a different man, a tall, thin Phantom whom he hadn't seen before appeared, shoving the would-be executioner away from Gary while he was in the middle of loading a new magazine.

"Go help 'em load up," the new man demanded.

"But he's a fe…"

The new man held up a hand, cutting off the protest and poked *Refrigerator Man* in his stomach with his weapon. "Shut up and follow orders. Cowboy again and you're out."

For a tense moment, it looked like *Refrigerator Man* wasn't going to obey, but then he turned abruptly and disappeared behind the teller line, leaving Gary facing the business end of the new bandit's M-16.

Pain fueled Gary's anger and he met the bandit's light hazel eyes, refusing to blink or look away. If this man was going to kill him, he too was going to have to do it eye to eye. For several agonizing seconds they stared at each other, tension building to an almost unbearable level until the bandit finally blinked.

"This is your lucky day, Fed. Don't do nothin' stupid."

For an instant Gary didn't process the hissed whisper, spoken so softly it had barely been audible. A second later, though, a tidal wave of relief flooded through him.

He imagined it was the same feeling a condemned prisoner had, learning he'd just received a last minute reprieve from the Governor. But what he couldn't reconcile in his mind, was that the man had recognized him as a federal agent and yet, for some inexplicable reason had allowed him to live, when *Refrigerator Man* was going to kill him for the same reason. It made no sense at all.

What did make sense…what was crystal clear was that the gunman didn't want the rest of his comrades to know he was being charitable to a lawman.

Not about to argue over his good fortune, Gary gave a subtle nod in reply.

The bandit stared at him for another brief moment, then turned and disappeared behind the teller line. And just that quickly, the action and noise in the room roared to life in Gary's ears again.

And there was plenty. Most of the noise though seemed to be coming from one source. A young woman whose chestnut hair was pulled into a prim bun at the back of her head. Gary had noticed her in the split second before he'd been doubled over, but wasn't sure when or where she'd entered the bank.

Regardless, screaming hysterically, she was causing enough noise for a chorus of people and that meant trouble where this group was concerned.

His eyes made a quick scan of the lobby to check on the other captives. Other than the toddler who was crying quietly in her mother's arms, everyone else was quiet. But from the look of horror on Rose's face, Gary knew she had witnessed every terrifying second of his near execution.

What worried him more than Rose's reaction was the wide-eyed terror contorting the young boy's face, indicating he'd seen the violent encounter, too.

Gary wasn't sure when or why the child had moved closer to him, but preoccupied soothing her terrified daughter, his mother probably hadn't even realized her son was watching. Even if she had, the boy was too far away from her to do much of anything about it.

But with the bandits randomly shooting their weapons, Gary knew damn well it wasn't safe for the kid to be moving around. Reaching his long arm out toward the boy, he snagged him around the shoulders and slid him into the shelter of his side again.

"How you doing, buddy?" Gary whispered, gritting his teeth against the pain his movement sent cascading through his body. "You okay?"

"I'm scared," the child murmured softly as if instinctively knowing he needed to be quiet. "Dat bad man tried to kill you."

Gary cursed silently. No child should have to witness something like that or be subjected to the terror of a group of ruthless robbers.

"What's your name, son?"

"Tyler." The voice quivered with fear.

"Well, Tyler…I'll tell you something. I'm scared too, buddy."

"You are?"

The quizzical expression on the boy's face indicated some idiot had apparently convinced him real men never admitted being afraid of anything. Hell, only an idiot wouldn't be scared when confronted by a group of masked bandits wildly spraying deadly bullets all around them.

Gary met the boy's questioning gaze and nodded. "You bet I am. But if we're real quiet and do what they say, we'll all be fine. Do you think you can do that?"

"Uh huh. But I'm still scared."

The child's honesty tugged at Gary's heart and he snugged the boy closer, reassuringly. "Stay here with me, son; I won't let anyone hurt you."

A grateful smile tugged at the boy's lips. "Fank you."

With Tyler safe and silent, it was time to go to work.

Quickly realizing that lying on a hard floor in the middle of an armed robbery probably wasn't the best place to conduct a criminal investigation, Gary kicked his brain into analytical gear anyway. No easy task with the woman still screaming right at his ear.

Not for the first time in his life, his photographic memory came in handy, though, as he recapped the mental notes he'd been capturing on each of the bandits…voice, appearance, anything he'd thought might help identify them later.

Granted, gunfire being sprayed over his head didn't provide optimal conditions for testing his memory. But in spite of the chaos surrounding him, Gary knew the information he was gathering was more than they had to date. None .of their witnesses had been able to give detailed descriptions of the robbers and images from previous security film footage hadn't provided any useful identification leads.

But Gary was certain *Refrigerator Man* hadn't been in any of the camera footage from previous robberies. No way would they have missed noticing someone that large. That meant either the gang had lost a member and acquired someone new or not all their members participated in every robbery. And if it was the latter, then the task force was looking for more than five people.

Gary couldn't do much with the information now, but it would come in handy when the task force began to piece together details of this latest robbery.

"Hey, boss man!" a different southern accent called.

Figuring the man was addressing him, Gary looked up to find a fourth bandit, this one about six two and two hundred pounds, staring down at him. Yeah, the task force was definitely pursuing the southern connection.

"You wanna help? Shut the bitch up or I'll do it…permanently," he taunted. Firing his weapon over the woman's head, elicited another scream from her.

Gary cursed beneath his breath when the spray of bullets flew too close for comfort to where Tyler and he were lying and lodged in the nearby reception desk, drawing a terrified shriek from Emma Carpenter.

As angry as he'd been with the receptionist earlier he didn't want to see her hurt. "Stay calm…and stay down," he mouthed in her direction, motioning the second order with his hand. In spite of the terror etched on her face, she nodded understanding and laid her head on the floor.

If only the screamer would be as easy to convince, but Gary doubted she would be. The way he saw it, he had two choices. He could do nothing and the Phantoms would kill her or he could try to calm her down and be caught in the crossfire if the gunmen got impatient.

Ignoring the tiny voice in his head pushing for self-preservation, he kept Tyler tucked protectively sheltered and turned his head toward her. "Ma'am, you've got to calm down. Trust me you don't want to make these men any angrier."

Caught up in her hysteria, she didn't seem to hear him. So he covered her hand with his, hoping the physical contact would capture her attention. A hiss of pain passed through his lips, stealing his breath.

"Ma'am, calm down, please," he said when he found his voice. "Just do what they say; you will be fine."

He hoped to hell he was right.

**A DEEP BASS** voice filtered through her terror and Patti Henderson turned toward it, her bespectacled gaze colliding with a pair of incredibly blue eyes. But never in her life had she been more terrified. If he'd spoken she hadn't heard him. How could she?

Crazed masked men shouting orders were spraying gunfire wildly inside the bank.

She was a gardener, for God's sake. She led a calm and peaceful, if somewhat boring, existence amongst her plants in the nursery greenhouse.

But this! It was insanity, like a horrific nightmare come to life and she was so scared she could barely breathe.

Patti saw his lips move again and this time his voice, his plea and the warmth of his hand filtered through her panic. And when she clamped her lips shut to listen, she surprised herself with how much quieter it suddenly became.

Yes, the men were still hollering orders and she heard a young child's quiet crying, but an eerie silence had settled over everyone else. It was as if they'd resigned themselves they were going to die.

That thought sent a new wave of panic racing through her and threatened to ignite another wave of hysteria. And it took every ounce of her courage not to start screaming again.

"That's good," the deep voice murmured in such a calming tone she looked at him again. Really looked at him.

Patti's eyes widened in disbelief.

It was him. He was alive. She'd thought for sure the bandit had murdered him. She was so relieved, for several moments she could only stare at him.

His large hand suddenly gave hers a gentle squeeze. "You're doing fine. Just stay calm."

Patti couldn't believe he'd come to her rescue, that he was trying to help her after what had happened to him when he'd helped the elderly woman. And now he had a small child sheltered under his other arm as well. The man had to be in incredible pain from the beating he'd taken, but all he seemed to care about was protecting everyone else from these monsters.

"What's your name?" he whispered.

The soft rumbling tones of his deep voice eased the tension in her body, miraculously lifting the tightness in her chest and somehow she managed to find her voice.

"Patti."

"Hi Patti. I'm Gary."

His calm, friendly tone and those incredible cobalt eyes soothed her tattered nerves. Turning her hand, she twined her fingers with his. What possessed her to do something so bold, she didn't know. But the slight smile that curved his mouth hitched her breath.

The man might be old enough to be her father, but he was gorgeous. How he managed to muster a smile, though, in the midst of all this madness, she'd never understand.

"That's right. Hang on to me and we'll get through this together."

Well there was an idea that was certainly no hardship and the warmth of his hand gave her something to focus on other than the danger surrounding her. Laying her cheek on the cold floor, she gazed at him, letting her thoughts wander.

# Chapter Five

Gary breathed a sigh of relief. The danger was by no means over, but thankfully Patti had settled down and now that she'd stopped rattling his brain, he could refocus his attention. After whispering a few words of encouragement to Tyler, he went back to studying their captors, trying to commit to memory as many details about them as possible without attracting any further attention his way.

He didn't have much time to do it, though, because suddenly all five Phantoms were back in view and a new order was given by a short squat guy built like a fire hydrant. No surprise…he was another southerner.

"Y'all get up. And keep your hands where we can see them."

While it seemed as if they'd been on the floor much longer, Gary knew it had only been a matter of minutes. Definitely less than ten from the time the gang had burst through the back door until the bandits had everything they wanted.

Getting to his feet set off a whole new world of pain, but Gary bent down again to retrieve his cell phone. He cursed under his breath noticing the screen was shattered. Guess he wouldn't be calling anyone anytime soon.

With a sigh, he snapped the useless phone back into its holder anyway and turning, he noticed Tyler trembling uncontrollably. The sight quickly put his problem into perspective. A broken phone was nothing compared to the trauma the child had just endured.

Disgusted with himself, he hoisted the boy up into his arms protectively, gave him a hug and a couple words of encouragement and then led the way as bandits herded them all into the vault.

Gary had known ahead of time what was going to happen, but in spite of that, the heavy door thudding closed and the locking mechanism bolting them inside the pitch black space set off a myriad of memories…physically and mentally painful ones. All of them at the hands of his old man, a sadistic bastard he refused to call father.

Every bit as tall as Gary was now, with hands the size of a side of beef and muscles toned by years of farming, Chester Thornton preferred intimidation and brutality over nurturing. And considering the severe beatings his old man had inflicted on him for indiscretions like outgrowing a pair of shoes, getting his jeans dirty…or usually just because the bastard felt like it, Gary figured he was lucky to have survived his early childhood.

But to this day he had flashbacks to the punishment and especially to the root cellar where, due to its sound-proof sodden walls, most of those beatings had occurred. He'd been left, locked inside that cold, damp, pitch dark prison until he was so hungry and grateful to be free, he'd promised not to tell anyone how he'd gotten the bruises that covered his body.

Thankfully, the abuse had ended when Kate's father, a veteran investigator with the Texas Rangers had made a surprise visit to the farm to check on Gary's unexplained absence from Kate's thirteenth birthday party, a party Gary had helped plan and been looking forward to attending, much to his old man's displeasure.

Already suspicious of Gary's endless supply of bruises, Thomas Callahan had noticed the root cellar door ajar and heard Chet hollering. And when he'd looked inside, he'd seen Gary half conscious and bleeding on the ground while Chet continued to pummel and kick him.

While Gary was in the hospital recovering from his injuries, police detectives gathering evidence in the root cellar found human remains buried there. Remains quickly identified as those of his mother, a mother who had vanished five years earlier. His old man had delighted in tormenting him with claims that she'd abandoned Gary; that she hadn't loved him enough to stay or take him with her.

The coroner's examination of her remains had uncovered the truth.

Cold as it may sound, Gary hadn't shed one tear when his old man had been arrested and sentenced to life imprisonment for her murder or when the bastard had been killed in his prison cell several years later.

Gary had spent the rest of his youth living with his maternal grandparents, a couple he'd grown to adore. And Kate and her parents had also been a support system, like a second family to him; so had Zach's father and grandparents. Between the Callahan's, Taylors and his grandparents, Gary had found the first sense of security he'd ever known and more importantly at age thirteen, he'd finally learned the true meaning of the words love and family.

But the wounds of his childhood still reared their ugly head at times and one of those times was now.

Embarrassing as it was for someone his size and age to admit, small enclosed spaces, especially if they were dark, still unnerved him.

Gary had thought he had his phobia under control until a couple years ago when he and Kate had taken a tour of Alcatraz while vacationing in San Francisco. He could only attribute it to a moment of temporary insanity, but he'd agreed to go with her when Kate, along with several other brave tourists, had volunteered to spend a few minutes in one of the old prison's soundproof solitary confinement cells which had been used to punish incorrigible inmates.

With walls painted black, no windows, no light and furnishings consisting of only a bare toilet and a sink, those isolated seconds of pitch black absolute silence in "the hole", as the cold, damp cells were called by inmates, had seemed endless. And Gary's heart had been racing so fast by the time the door had opened that Kate had initially thought he was having a heart attack.

Strangely, while planning this assignment, knowing full well how the Phantoms secured their prisoners afterward, he'd never experienced so much as a ripple of unease. But he figured it was because he was focused on the idea his team would be capturing the bandits outside the bank. And when the plan had gone haywire so quickly and he'd decided to remain inside during the robbery, he hadn't had time to think about the ramifications of the vault.

But the thud of that heavy door had sent his heart into such an arrhythmia, it felt like a stampede of stallions was thundering through his chest. Just like when he'd been inside the Alcatraz cell.

This was worse, though. There was no tour guide on the other side of the door who intended to let them out.

And if that wasn't bad enough, a chorus of blood curdling screams erupting around him did nothing to help the situation. To keep from completely embarrassing himself by joining the chorus, he clamped his jaw shut and comforted the frightened child in his arms by running a soothing hand along Tyler's back.

Several deep breaths focused Gary on the pain in his ribs rather than the tiny confined space he was trapped inside. So, he hauled in a couple more breaths just to make sure he had himself under control before he opened his mouth.

"Calm down, everyone," Gary called, feeling like a hypocrite since it had taken every ounce of his self-control to keep from losing it. "Chandler…get the light," he added, hoping the branch manager had had the presence of mind to stay near the switch.

He heard some fumbling around in front of him and then to his immense relief, and he assumed everyone else's, light illuminated the room. It had a magical effect on everyone as even the toddler's wailing stopped.

And just as amazingly, the wild pounding in his chest ceased and Gary could feel his body relax. So did Tyler's. But glancing around their small prison Gary got his first look at the teller he hadn't yet met, a woman who appeared ready to deliver a baby at any moment.

Gary bit back a curse. What the hell had Chandler been thinking keeping a pregnant woman behind the teller line during a bank robbery? The man needed his head examined.

He shook away the thought. It was too late to rectify that situation now, and thankfully the woman appeared to be unharmed. But with the way his day was going, the trauma of the robbery would probably send her into labor right here in the vault.

God, there was a thought he didn't even want to entertain. Gary shook it away with even more determination and glanced around again.

Ten people packing the vault was entirely too many for the cramped space. It wouldn't be long before the air became stale and heat became a problem. Setting Tyler down so the boy could go to his mother, Gary glanced up looking for an air-conditioning vent which he knew he wouldn't find. And he didn't.

Duct work would be a potential way to breach security and gain access to the vault. Still, if they were all going to come out of this alive, they were going to need some fresh air soon.

He kept the thought to himself. No point in panicking anyone. There was no doubt they were all shaken. Hell, so was he. But he pulled in another calming breath and took charge.

"Is anyone hurt? Does anyone need medical attention?" he asked hoping the answer would be negative since he saw no sign of a first aid kit in the vault. To his relief, no one did. So he reached into his jacket and pulling out his identification, flipped it open.

"Some of you have already met me, but for those who haven't, I'm Supervisory Special Agent Gary Thornton with the FBI," he said, stifling a smile when Rose's expression revealed she finally understood why he looked familiar.

"The bandits we just encountered were the Phantoms and as you may know they've got a reputation for violence."

Continuing, his gaze swept over the group. "Every one of you deserves a pat on the back for keeping your cool and letting them get in and out without hurting anyone."

"You're the reason we all survived," Rose asserted before explaining to her companions. "Gary kept them from killing her," she said pointing to Patti. "And he stopped one of them from knocking me over. They paid him back for that by clubbing him in the ribs and over the head with their machine gun."

Gary didn't bother correcting her misconception about the weapon. The important thing was no one had been seriously injured or killed. Before he could say anything, though, her sympathetic gaze met his.

"I hope you weren't hurt too badly, dear."

His ribs hurt like hell, his shoulder was on fire and his head was pounding, but he saw no reason to worry Rose or anyone else over something no one could do anything about at the moment. It wasn't like medical attention was available inside the vault.

"I'm okay," he assured her. "And if they were going to hit someone, I'm glad it was me and not you…or any of you for that matter."

Turning to the two women he had not yet met, he introduced himself to the pregnant teller and Tyler's mother, but before he could learn anything more than Jessica Myers' and Brittany Franks' names, he noticed Ron Chandler conferring with Rachel Washington. And given the small space, he realized Chandler was trying to determine the amount of cash taken during the robbery.

Normally during a bank heist, there was a time delay between the event and the arrival of law enforcement and in the interim there was no way to control what discussion took place between witnesses to the crime. Ideally, though, law enforcement wanted untainted statements from each witness. Since he had the opportunity to make that happen, he intended to take it.

"Folks," he interrupted. "I'm going to have to ask you not to discuss the robbery with each other until you've been interviewed by my team. That goes for everyone in here."

Chandler puffed up his chest and glared at Gary, indignantly. "That's ridiculous! I'm in charge of this branch. If I want to discuss the robbery with my employees, I'll do it."

Gary had known his order wouldn't be popular. And Chandler was upset. Gary got that. Hell, if the robbery hadn't been enough to throw a person off his game, being locked inside a stuffy old bank vault would have tipped the scales.

But while a hostile environment was the last thing Gary wanted to create, considering they were going to be stuck with each other until the door could be opened, he had no intention of allowing Chandler or anyone else to undermine his authority.

Keeping his expression neutral and his voice calm, he pressed his point. "Mr. Chandler, the moment the Phantoms fired their first shot, this entire bank became a crime scene. And as I'm sure you know, bank robbery is a federal offense. I'm the head of the Federal Bureau of Investigation's task force investigating the Phantoms and it is my responsibility to maintain the integrity of our investigation…"

Face contorted with anger, Chandler interrupted. "Fine, then get to work; take our statements," he fired back.

Gary studied the man silently for a heartbeat, wondering if Chandler's combative attitude was the reason for his demotion. It certainly seemed a good possibility. But the bold challenge surprised Gary. Usually his badge was enough to bring people into line and when that didn't work his size usually did.

After the upbringing he'd had, he preferred using his wits and intelligence over violence, but he wasn't averse to intimidating someone with his stature when necessary. In this instance, he didn't think that would be required. More than likely the threat of being arrested for interfering with a federal investigation would make the bank manager see reason.

But with two small children present, especially two who'd already been traumatized, Gary didn't want to create a scene of any kind and kept the arrest threat as a last resort. Still, a mutiny was unacceptable, which meant he had to get the man to back off.

Taking as much of a calming breath as his ribs permitted, Gary forced his voice to remain even and his stance relaxed.

"Look…I understand that this incident was terrifying for everyone. We are all stressed and I know talking helps. Under other circumstances I would take your statements, but there are two reasons I can't. First and foremost, I was caught up in the robbery like the rest of you. My team is going to want my statement too. But even if I hadn't been involved, in this small enclosure it would be impossible for me to speak privately with each of you."

"May I text my husband? He's a reporter for the…"

"This is between Mr. FBI and me, Jessie," Chandler growled at the pregnant teller. "Stay out of it."

The television station and newspapers both would know about the robbery by now since they monitored emergency dispatch scanners. And if Jessica's husband worked as a reporter for either of them he had to be frantic with worry about his pregnant wife. Chandler was an ass to not recognize that and show some compassion.

Gary shot a glare at the manager before turning to the young woman and softening his expression. "Certainly. He's got to be worried about you." Gary's gaze shifted to include everyone. "All of you are free to call or text your family and let them know you are okay."

But his eye contact immediately locked on Chandler again and he adopted the stern tone he used with difficult witnesses. "But I have to insist, robbery details are off-limits for discussion until you've been interviewed. That's an order and it is not negotiable."

Apparently, Chandler wanted to leave the vault in handcuffs because he cursed aloud and opened his mouth to continue arguing. But he was cut off by an unexpected ally.

"Oh for pity sake, Ron, hush up. You're acting like the headstrong, disagreeable teenager you were when I had you in my ninth grade algebra class," Rose Eshleman admonished.

Gary nearly burst out laughing at Chandler's mortified expression, but with Rose on a roll, he had no intention of interrupting her and managed to contain himself.

"Anyone who has ever watched a crime show on television knows the police separate witnesses," she scolded. "And if you stop being bull-headed for a minute you'll realize Gary is just doing his job and he's doing it under very difficult conditions."

She heaved a sigh before issuing an order perfected by years in front of a classroom. "Get over yourself and stop arguing."

Gary wanted to kiss the elderly woman for her vote of support, especially after the disagreeable bank manager gave him a concessionary nod. Instead he settled for mouthing a silent *thank you* and gave Rose a discreet wink.

But when dead silence descended on the vault, Gary realized something needed to be done to lighten the mood. After all, they had to put up with each other until the vault could be opened. Might as well try to make it as pleasant as possible.

# Chapter Six

"At the risk of sounding like a camp counselor," Gary said. "Why don't we all sit down, get comfortable and maybe get to know each other a little, while they work to get us out of here."

The suggestion had the desired effect, as people began shifting around to find a place to sit, some leaning against the door and front wall and others along the bank of safe deposit boxes that lined the back wall. Gary helped Rose ease down to the floor again. Then to give everyone a little more space to get comfortable, he folded her walker and put it on top of a floor safe that, until it had been emptied by the robbers, had housed the bank currency.

Out of habit, Gary chose a spot in the far corner where he could keep an eye on everyone and easily see the door. Tugging his necktie loose, he shrugged out of his jacket, transferring his live-feed camera pen to his shirt pocket before sitting down.

He'd no sooner settled when he felt someone staring at him. Glancing up, his gaze met the inquiring sapphire eyes of the young boy.

"Hi Tyler. How are you doing?"

"Okay," his little voice replied. But he studied Gary curiously. "Are you really a FBI agent, Mr. For…"

The boy's face screwed up quizzically as he tried several times to pronounce the name and then gave up. "How do you say your name?"

Recognizing that like many young children, Tyler was having trouble with the 'th" combination, Gary helped him out and repeated his last name slowly. "But how about if you just call me, Gary…and yes I am an FBI agent."

Confusion fled the boy's expression on a wave of relief. "Den I call you Agent Gary, okay?" Tyler countered.

Gary had meant the boy could call him by his first name, but apparently the child liked the title. "That works."

To his surprise the little boy extended a small hand his way and Gary gave him a gentle handshake.

"How old are you, Tyler?"

"Five and a half," he declared, emphasizing the half as if that made him so much older. Gary supposed to someone that young, it probably did.

"Well, you've got an impressive grip there, young man. A nice firm handshake. I like that."

Tyler grinned at the compliment, but then his eyes locked on Gary's and he took a step closer and peered toward the back of Gary's head.

"Dat man was bad, Agent Gary. He hit you real hard for tryin' to help da lady and he hurt you. He made you bleeded."

Gary hadn't been able to hide the fact his ribs were killing him. Every time he moved it sucked the air from his lungs and with his coat off, the line of blood staining the shoulder of his shirt was clearly visible. But while his head was pounding, he was fairly certain the wound there was superficial and had already begun to clot. And he'd hoped, since he was so much taller than everyone else, that none of them would notice that wound.

But by sitting down he lost that height advantage and apparently not much got past Tyler.

"I'm okay, son…just a little sore," Gary answered, hoping that reassurance would satisfy Tyler. One look at the kid's face, though and he knew it hadn't worked.

"When I hurt myself, Mommy kisses it to make it feel better. Maybe she could kiss your booboos too."

"Tyler!" Brittany exclaimed, her face turning beet red with embarrassment.

Gary chuckled softly, amused by the innocence behind the boy's suggestion. But his amusement came to an abrupt end a second later when Emma Carpenter piped up from across the vault.

"I'll be happy to kiss or massage you, handsome, and my offer from before still stands."

While Rachel Washington and Jessica Myers gave the receptionist looks of disapproval and Ron Chandler whispered something to her that turned her face red, Gary chose to ignore Emma and instead focused his attention on the boy.

"That's a real nice offer, Tyler," he said shooting a smile at Brittany. "And I appreciate it. But my wife has magic kisses…"

"Magic kisses," Tyler parroted, staring at him wide-eyed.

If the kid was lucky someday he'd meet a woman like Katie and learn all about the magic powers of love. But he was too young for that explanation, so Gary stuck with a simplified version of the truth. "Yup! Magic kisses. So, how about if we let your mommy save her kisses for you."

Tyler gave a childish giggle and nodded. "'Kay." But the smile vanished quickly and cupping his hands around his mouth he leaned close to Gary's ear.

"Were you tellin' da troof when you said you were scared?" he asked in nearly a whisper as if he was embarrassed for anyone to know he'd been afraid.

Gary figured some jackass had probably reprimanded Tyler or made fun of him for crying or showing signs of fear. He wasn't sure anything he said would rectify the damage done, but at least he could try. Respecting the boy's wish to keep the conversation confidential, he kept his voice to a whisper too.

"You bet I was scared, Tyler. The bandits were shooting guns all around us and one of them tried to kill me. That would scare anyone."

Tyler nodded, but didn't look convinced, so Gary tried again.

"There's nothing wrong with being afraid, son, especially when something scary happens. But what's important is that you don't let that fear stop you from thinking..." — he tapped his temple for emphasis — "from using your head to figuring a way out of the scary situation or trying to find some way to make it less frightening."

The boy's brow knit as he processed the explanation. "You mean like if it's a scary show I could turn it off?" he asked softly.

Smart kid.

"Exactly," Gary agreed with a smile. "You can turn it off or leave the room…or just think about something else besides the scary show. Of course, during the robbery we couldn't leave, but even though we were both scared, we didn't panic. We just kept quiet and did what we were told…and everything worked out okay. Right?"

A grin spread across the boy's face again. "Right."

For several moments the boy didn't say anything and Gary imagined he was thinking about ways he could conquer his fear the next time something scared him. But with the typical attention span of most five year olds, his train of thought quickly moved on to something else.

"Are you gonna arrest da bad men when you find 'em?" the boy asked aloud with a look that said the answer better be affirmative.

As much as the boy's challenge amused him, Gary kept a straight face. Clearly Tyler considered this a man to man conversation and while Gary didn't know anything about the boy's background he had a gut feeling it was important to Tyler to be taken seriously. And while the boy might only be five, his question was a fair one that deserved an honest answer.

"Yes, sir, I am," Gary replied sincerely. "And hopefully I'll be able to do it real soon."

With a look of satisfaction, Tyler shoved his hands into the pockets of his neatly creased khaki pants and straightened proudly. "I'm gonna be a FBI agent like you when I grow up, Agent Gary."

Gary recognized a case of starry-eyed, hero-worship when he saw it and was flattered, but he couldn't help wondering how such a young child even knew about the FBI.

He let his questioning gaze travel to Brittany.

She rolled her eyes and gave a frustrated sigh. "My 'ex' wants him to be a macho man and has him watching shows that give him nightmares, but something he saw recently had FBI agents in it and that's all he's talked about since."

Macho man? Really? What kind of idiot does that to a five year old child?

Swallowing the choice words that came to mind for her ex-husband's lack of judgment, Gary nodded his understanding and turned his attention back to the boy, as Tyler plopped down next to him.

"FBI men were good guys," the boy explained proudly. "And I wanna be just like 'em…like you, Agent Gary."

Gary figured the boy was just going through a phase and within a month or two would probably set his sights on some other profession. Hell, in elementary school he'd wanted to be a doctor like the ones who'd been so gentle and compassionate caring for injuries his old man had inflicted on him. But by seventh grade he'd forgotten all about a career in medicine and aspired to be a pro football player. It wasn't until his sophomore year, after some long talks with Kate's father that he'd set his sights on law enforcement and ultimately the FBI.

Tyler had plenty of time to change his mind. But on the off chance he didn't, Gary saw no harm in encouraging an honorable profession.

"Well, Tyler, the FBI will be lucky to have you working for them and I know you'll make an excellent agent when you're a little older."

Looking like he'd just been paid the highest compliment possible, the boy grinned at him. But his grin turned to a frown when his mother called to him.

"Tyler, come back over here and stop bothering Agent Thornton," she admonished.

Considering she had her hands full trying to entertain her toddler, Gary figured she could use some help distracting the boy and since none of the others stepped up to help her, he decided to do it himself. After all, it wasn't like he could do much of anything else stuck in a vault. And besides, he liked the kid.

"He's fine Ms. Franks. He's not bothering me."

From the appreciative smile that lit the little boy's face, Gary figured he had a new best friend. And apparently a curious one at that. He could almost see the wheels turning in the child's head.

A tiny index finger pointed at the gun clipped at Gary's waist.

"Is dat gun real?" Tyler asked continuing to whisper as if it was classified information he shouldn't divulge.

"Yes it is."

"May I hold it?"

Gary had dealt with enough children over the years that he'd seen that question coming. He began shaking his head before Tyler even finished asking.

"No, son."

The boy recoiled at the refusal, looking confused. "Why not? Daddy lets me play wit his gun."

Gary heard Brittany suck in a startled breath and the expression on her face was murderous. He had a feeling she'd be giving her "ex" a piece of her mind and if Gary ever met the man so would he. But he wouldn't criticize the father in front of Tyler.

"Well, son, I won't let you handle mine. Guns are not toys; they're dangerous…very dangerous. You could hurt or kill someone with it." In all sincerity he met the child's gaze. "You wouldn't want to do that, would you?"

The boy shook his head solemnly. "Uh uh."

Gary saw the disappointment in the boy's eyes, though and didn't want to discourage him completely. A moment of thought produced an idea, one he had a feeling would be an instant hit.

"I can't let you handle my gun, Tyler, but I sure could use your help," he said watching the boy's discouragement turn to eager curiosity.

"How?"

"Well...since it hurts for me to move too much, I'm hoping maybe you would like to be a junior FBI agent and help me out with some official work while we're in here. Will you do that?"

The boy's mouth gaped open and he nodded mutely.

"Great," Gary said suppressing a smile. With Tyler staring at him curiously, he removed the small Bureau pin from the lapel of his suit jacket and handed it to the boy. "This is something agents wear so people know they work for the FBI."

Gary let him examine the pin for several moments, taking time to point out and explain the various features of the Bureau's seal, including its motto, Fidelity, Bravery, and Integrity.

"Dat's a F, a B and a I...FBI!" Tyler exclaimed.

Gary stared at the boy for a moment, unable to hide his amazement. A five year old. Hell, some adults Gary had met didn't even notice the correlation between the motto and FBI, but Tyler had nailed it immediately.

"Very good! I'm impressed," he replied in all honesty. "You are one smart young man, Tyler."

Tyler smiled broadly at the praise.

Plucking the pin from Tyler's small hand, Gary fastened it to the collar of the boy's navy blue shirt.

"There you go," Gary said. "Now you're official, Junior Agent Franks."

Mouth agape, Tyler stared at him for a moment before he let out an excited squeal and hopped to his feet, nearly falling over when he spun around to show the pin to his mother.

"Mommy look! Agent Gary made me a junior FBI agent," he exclaimed excitedly.

Shifting her now sleeping daughter in her arms, the mother shot a grateful smile at Gary and he gave her a little nod, smiling at the big fuss she made over her son's pin.

Gary waited several moments to let the boy bask in the attention he was getting and then called to him. "Come on back over here, partner. We've got work to do."

Tyler raced the few steps back and crouched down on his haunches. "What do we gotta do?"

Maintaining a poker face when he really wanted to chuckle at the adorable boy's enthusiasm, Gary pulled some business cards along with a small notepad and pen from his jacket and handed them to the boy. "We need to get information on everyone in here and give each of them one of these cards," he explained to the boy. "Do you think you could do that for me, partner?"

"Uh huh," Tyler agreed excitedly.

To ease the way for the boy, Gary raised his voice for everyone to hear. "Folks, Junior Agent Franks is going to come around with a pad and pen. We need you to print your name, address and phone number for us. And I would really appreciate it if you'd please do it neatly so I can read your handwriting."

Amid the responding chuckles, he continued. "Junior Agent Franks is also going to give you one of my business cards. Feel free to contact me anytime if you have questions or concerns related to the robbery."

Beaming broadly Tyler began a circle around the vault proudly showing off his FBI pin as he went about his assignment with youthful professionalism. Gary couldn't help smiling watching him.

**SOMETHING STIRRED DEEP** inside Brittany Franks as she watched the FBI agent, something she hadn't felt in a long time. He was a giant of a man in both height and heart. His stature was obvious, but a lot of men were tall…including her ex-husband.

Brittany heaved a sigh.

Just thinking about Adam Franks was enough to ruin a good day.

Marrying him had been the worst mistake of her life. The only thing she didn't regret about the marriage was that it had given her two wonderful children. But Adam had been a poor excuse for a man and an even worse husband and father.

Seriously, what kind of man let a five year old play with a gun?

Adam wanted nothing to do with his daughter and since the divorce, if Tyler had a dollar for every scheduled visitation Adam missed, he'd have a hefty balance in his college fund.

Selfishly, Brittany was glad when Adam didn't show up for those visits, though, because after every one of them, Tyler had nightmares about some inappropriately violent show or activity Adam had subjected him to. It took her days to undo the negative effects of the visit.

It had gotten so bad, in fact, that her attorney was petitioning the court for another custody hearing. She was hoping to suspend Adam's visitation rights completely, but even if the court made the visits supervised, it would be an improvement. She was tired of Adam's negative influence on her son.

From what little she could tell about Agent Thornton, he was the polar opposite of her 'ex'. What touched her about the man was his heart…the kindness and sincere interest he was showing her son and his protective nature.

When gunfire erupted around her in the lobby, she'd been so terrified she'd stood there like a statue, unable to move or think. She still couldn't believe she'd reacted the way she had. Her inaction had endangered her children.

What kind of mother did that make her?

But Agent Thornton, a complete stranger, had risked his own life to protect her and her children. God only knew what would have happened to them if he hadn't tackled them to the floor when he did. But even that he'd done gently, taking the brunt of the fall himself to ensure they weren't hurt or crushed in the process.

Her glance swept over the handsome man again, zeroing in on a streak of red along a ragged tear on the shoulder of his starched white dress shirt. Was that blood?

Studying it more closely when he wasn't paying attention, she realized it was. Guilt trickled through her.

Had that happened when he rushed in to help them? The thought it may have, did nothing to assuage her guilt. Clearly he'd saved their lives, but there'd been so much happening all at once it had been impossible to process it all.

She'd heard Agent Thornton tell them all to stay down and had seen him scramble over to help the elderly woman. After that she'd been so preoccupied trying to console Nikki, she'd lost track of everything else…including Tyler.

When she'd first realized he wasn't at her side, she'd nearly panicked thinking the robbers had taken him. Then she'd spotted him lying tucked practically beneath the big man. Of course, she hadn't known then that he was a federal agent; all she'd known was that he was the man who'd helped them. But he was still a stranger and that had concerned her momentarily, especially since from the time her children had been old enough to understand, she'd drilled into them that they shouldn't talk to strangers.

But something about the way the man had been talking quietly to Tyler and more importantly, the way he'd been sheltering her son from the gunfire flying around the bank, had eased her concern.

She wasn't sure when or why Tyler had gravitated toward Agent Thornton. If they'd known then that he was a federal agent, she would have assumed that had been the draw, since Tyler had been fixated on FBI agents for the past month. But since they'd only made that connection a few minutes ago, the only explanation that made sense to Brittany was that Tyler had been drawn by the innate sense of protection and security the distinguished looking man emanated.

Agent Thornton had an air about him that imbued confidence that he wouldn't let harm come to anyone around him. He'd certainly proven himself capable of doing just that with the way he'd helped her and the children. From what the elderly woman had said, he'd apparently taken care of her and others as well.

Obviously she wished none of them had been caught up in the robbery and she wished they weren't locked inside a vault. But if it had to happen, she was glad Gary Thornton was with them.

The way he'd taken care of Tyler during the robbery and the gentle, friendly manner with which he was interacting with her son now, warmed her heart. It was the kind of positive male attention her son craved, but sorely lacked where his own father was concerned.

Brittany knew Tyler was starved for male attention, but she was lost as to how to rectify the situation. She didn't believe in introducing her children to men she dated…on those rare occasions when she even had one. Since the divorce she'd been so busy working and being a single mother, she hadn't had much time to devote to any relationship.

And poor Tyler didn't even have the advantage of a close relationship with a grandfather. Adam's father was as much of a mess as Adam. While her father would be perfect for the job, her parents lived over seven hundred miles away in North Carolina, where she grew up. She'd been thinking about moving back there to be closer to them, but her job was here and it paid well, allowing her and her children to lead a comfortable life.

Still, watching Tyler soak in the attention Agent Thornton was showing him, Brittany realized how much her son needed a positive male role model he could emulate.

She let her mind ponder the federal agent. He was certainly kind and compassionate and seemed to genuinely like children. And based on his reaction to Tyler's offer to have her kiss him, he also appeared to have a good sense of humor. All necessary qualities in a man where she was concerned.

She'd be tempted to ask him to dinner and see where things went from there if it weren't for one very important detail.

The gold wedding band on his hand.

Dang! All the good ones were taken.

# Chapter Seven

Several ulterior motives had driven Gary to use the boy to get the contact information. He'd wanted to encourage Tyler's interest in the Bureau. Gary would never forget Kate's father taking him under his wing and fostering his youthful interest in law enforcement.

The world had lost an honorable man and admirable role model the day Thomas Callahan had tragically been killed in the line of duty…one month before he'd been scheduled to retire. Gary tried every day to live up to the legacy his father-in-law had left behind.

But Gary had also had two selfish reasons asking for Tyler's help. The main one being that every time he moved, pain sucked the air out of his lungs and now that he was semi-comfortable, he wasn't inclined to get up again. He also figured the boy's contagious enthusiasm would help defuse any tension remaining in the room as a result of the confrontation with Ron Chandler.

Gary quickly saw his ploy was working. The women were all making a show of admiring Tyler's pin and although Chandler still shot a periodic glare his way, the manager was at least cooperating.

Satisfied the boy had things under control on his end, Gary's mind returned to the Phantoms.

It was frustrating as hell being locked inside a vault, not knowing what was happening on the outside. Not being out there with his team to help. And with his cell phone useless, he didn't even know if they'd managed to get into position before the Phantoms had hit.

As if his thoughts were heard, the bud in his ear suddenly came to life. The thing had been silent since before he'd entered Chandler's office, but apparently it was working because a second later Zach's worried voice came through loud and clear.

"Dad, talk to me. Please tell me you're okay?"

The question gave Gary a start.

Eight years ago when Zach had joined the Bureau, he'd insisted Gary not use his influence as a senior agent to help him. Zach had been determined to succeed on his own merits without any appearance of favoritism. To that end, Zach had wanted to keep their family connection as quiet as possible.

Within the Bureau, those who needed to know they were father and son, knew. But when they were working, the family connection was left behind and they were strictly on a first name basis. The fact Zach had abandoned all pretense of hiding their relationship over the team's communication system, spoke volumes to the level of his concern.

Resigned to the fact he was going to have to conduct his business with a room full of witnesses within earshot, Gary kept his voice as quiet as possible.

"I'm fine, Zach," he replied simply, wanting to get answers instead of giving them. "How'd it go outside? Did we get them?"

"There was a brief firefight when they came out of the bank. We've got two in custody with one of them wounded. Two are dead but two got away…"

Gary's brow knit as he made a mental calculation. "Wait a minute," he interrupted. "There were only five of them inside the bank. Where was the sixth man? In the car?"

Everyone he'd seen pile out of the car had come into the bank. But the SUV's windows had been so heavily tinted he hadn't seen anyone inside.

"Yeah. When the local cops arrived at the bank they realized the SUV was running. The driver inside was so intent watching the door of the bank he never saw them approaching until they yanked open the car door. They had him in custody before he knew what hit him."

A driver. Interesting. That explained how the bandits had made such quick getaways in previous robberies. "You said two got away?"

"Yes. In the confusion of the firefight, they managed to carjack an unsuspecting motorist. Yanked the woman from her car and got away. We've got an APB out on the car, but I think it's probably been dumped by now. Good news is the woman wasn't hurt and we recovered all the money."

The surge of excitement that coursed through Gary's veins was tempered by the mention of a firefight. "How'd we fare? Anyone hurt?"

"Two local officers were cut by flying glass, but nothing serious. Our team and the state troopers are fine." Zach confirmed.

Gary felt a wave of relief wash over him. Too many people had already died at the hands of the Phantoms. At least this time, they'd come out relatively unscathed.

Obviously his goal had been to capture the entire group, but considering the robbery had gone down before his team was in place, he figured they'd done well capturing anyone. With any luck one of the dead men was the gang's leader and they'd be able to coerce the prisoners into giving up the names of their cohorts.

"I don't want either of the captures questioned until I'm present," Gary cautioned. It wasn't that he didn't trust his team to handle things in his absence; he did. But this was still his investigation and after the events of today, he had too many specific questions he wanted answered to delegate the interviews to someone else.

"Well, the driver lawyered up immediately. He's not talking to anyone," Zach replied. "The other guy is unconscious. Neither of them had identification on them. We're running the driver's prints but we have to wait for the other guy to come out of surgery before we can get his prints. Hopefully we'll get hits on both of them."

All in all, Gary was pleased with the outcome of a day where their original plan had been shot to hell, so he shifted focus. "Good. What's being done to get us out of here?"

"The team just finished securing the building. Give me a second and I'll get someone on site to give you a firsthand update."

Gary took advantage of the brief silence while the communication patch was being made, to shift his position in an attempt to get more comfortable. And by the time the sound of activity filtered through his earpiece again, he'd regained the breath stolen by the move. A second later Special Agent Jim Barrett greeted him.

"You've got quite a crowd in there, big guy. Are you having fun?"

In spite of the pain in his ribs, Gary couldn't help laughing. He'd trained the former All-American quarterback five years ago when the now thirty-two year old lawyer had first joined the Bureau. With the blond good looks of a young Robert Redford, Barrett was a chick magnet, attracting women wherever he went without even trying, but he'd quickly proven himself to be a smart and very able agent. But only Jimmy would find humor in a group of people being locked inside a bank vault.

"I'm glad you're amused. What are you doing to get us out?"

"Well…there's good news and bad news," Barrett answered.

Why didn't that surprise him?

"And?" Gary said, bracing himself for whatever was coming.

"The vault is a dinosaur, Thorny. We've got a locksmith on the way but you're going to be stuck in there for about four hours."

And the day just kept getting better. Definitely not the news Gary wanted to hear, but not unexpected. When he'd been assessing the bank's security, he'd recognized the vault as an old time-locked model and he knew from previous robbery investigations that once they were locked they couldn't be reopened until the pre-set time, which was usually the next morning. And drilling out the lock was tedious work for a locksmith because one wrong move could destroy the lock mechanism and prevent the door from being opened at all.

Gary refrained from blowing out a breath of frustration. "Please tell me that's the bad news."

A small chuckle came through his ear bud. "Yeah, that's the bad news. Good news is, the fire department is here and as soon as they're set up, they're going to drill a hole through the wall so they can pump fresh air inside. And once they're through, they'll also feed a hose in, so everyone has access to water."

Too bad they couldn't feed a bathroom into the vault, too. With two children, a pregnant woman and an octogenarian, not to mention the excitement of the robbery, Gary figured it wouldn't be long before someone needed one of them. But if things got too desperate, people could always use the metal trash can tucked in the corner by the floor vault.

And since there wasn't anything he could do to change the situation, he opted for words of encouragement.

"That's great, Jimmy; they'll both be appreciated."

"Yeah, well, before they can start, you need to get all your playmates to move away from the front wall."

Gary stifled another chuckle and looked around at his fellow captives. "Consider it done. And Jimmy, get Lucas to check outside for family members of the people in here."

Quickly he rattled off their names from memory. "If any of their relatives are there or show up, have him bring them inside and find some place private and comfortable where they can wait to be reunited."

"Will do, Thorny."

Gary knew without being told that Jim had already disconnected his end of the conversation to go back to work.

A team of FBI agents and local law enforcement would be scouring the bank for evidence. Gary doubted they'd find fingerprints since the robbers always wore gloves, but just collecting the shells from all the gunfire would be a time consuming process.

And while the crime scene investigators were busy, another team would be obtaining copies of the bank's surveillance video and also canvassing neighboring businesses looking for other cameras that might have captured anything related to the robbery. Other investigators would be talking to people in the area, searching for anyone who had information of value.

In short, his entire team had their hands full at this point and conversing with a boss who was stuck in a vault didn't accomplish anything.

But the earpiece feed was still live, so Gary knew his son was still there.

"Zach," he called. "My cell phone shattered during the robbery…"

The curse his son uttered echoed Gary's own sentiment. He and Zach had gotten identical phones less than three months ago. Gary had a ton of contacts and personal settings on his and didn't want to lose them. But before he could suggest anything, Zach read his mind.

"Give me a couple minutes to find the phone store in that area," Zach said. "I'll send someone out to get you a new one so you'll be up and running as soon as you're out of there."

That worked for him. "Thanks, Zach."

"No problem." There was a pause for several moments and when Zach spoke again, the efficient federal agent had been replaced by his son. "You had Mom really worried, Dad."

A wave of guilt washed over Gary. As soon as he'd heard a television crew was on its way to the bank, he should have figured Kate would learn of the robbery and he should have borrowed someone's phone to call her. To let her know he was okay. But he'd been preoccupied trying to prevent Chandler's mutiny and making sure everyone was okay, he'd hadn't thought to do it.

"I know…and I'm sorry."

"We're all just glad you're okay," Zach answered. "While you were talking to Jimmy, I called Mom. She said to tell you she loves you."

Gary felt a smile curve his lips. "Thanks Zach. Keep me posted."

"Will do."

Gary heard the line go quiet and blew out a breath of resignation. Nothing to do now, but wait. So he turned to his pint-sized partner who had finished his assignment and was now sitting beside him, staring at him curiously.

"Whatcha doin', Agent Gary?"

Not a bad question considering it probably looked like he'd been carrying on a conversation with himself. The kid probably thought he was nuts.

He pulled the bud from his ear long enough to show it to Tyler and then quickly put it back in place and pointed to the nearly invisible pin on his collar. "There are other FBI agents out in the bank lobby and we can talk to each other using these devices."

"Like a phone?"

Gary smiled. Not a bad analogy for a five year old. "Yes…similar to a phone or a walkie talkie."

A frown furrowed a deep crease in Tyler's brow. "What's a walkie talkie?"

The question threw him for a moment and Gary had to regroup. Talk about feeling old. He and his buddies had thought walkie talkies were the best gadgets ever. But maybe Tyler was still a little too young to have heard of them.

"They're like a phone," he answered. Not a brilliant answer by any means, but he doubted calling it a handheld radio transceiver would clarify anything.

"How'd you make out?" Gary asked, deciding it was time to change the subject. "Did you get the information we needed?"

Tyler's head bobbed. "Uh huh! All finished." He handed back the pen and pad, seemingly oblivious to the fact he was wedged into a space that would barely hold a shoe, let alone a child.

"Thanks, partner."

Moving over to give Tyler more room, Gary picked up on the conversation in the room, quickly realizing the others had been introducing themselves.

"I was born and raised in Charlotte, North Carolina and moved to Hagerstown six years ago. I'm a single mother," Brittany Franks said motioning to her children. "Tyler, whom you already met, is five and Nikki just turned three.

"I graduated from University of Maryland School of Law in December and was fortunate enough to be hired by a law firm here. I'm taking the bar exam next month and when I pass that, the firm has committed to hiring me as an attorney. Until then I've been working as a paralegal to gain some experience in the field."

Brittany took a deep breath and smiled. "How I got caught up in the robbery? Well…my ex-husband wanted me to meet him here this morning to set up savings accounts for the children." With a shrug, she added. "I took a half day vacation to meet Adam here and then I was going to take the kids to their doctor's appointments."

She turned a hopeful look on Gary. "I don't suppose you'd write an excuse for me for the doctor and my boss, so they know why I didn't show up, would you?"

With another wince, Gary chuckled aloud. "I'll not only write a note, but if you'd like, I'll speak to them personally." He glanced at the others. "If anyone else needs me to intercede on your behalf, just let me know."

And while he had the floor, he decided to fill them in on what was being done to free them.

"I'm sorry I missed some of your introductions," he said. "But since you already know who I am, let me give you a little update on what's happening outside."

Seeing eager faces peering at him, he didn't keep them in suspense.

"My team of agents and local police are inside the bank and they're working to get us out of here." Hopefully it would be less than the four hours Jim mentioned, but since there was nothing they could do to speed up the process from inside the vault, he left that detail out and settled for a glossed over version of the truth.

"It's going to take a little while because of the age of this vault."

Chandler heaved a sigh impatiently and shook his head in disgust.

Gary eyed him curiously. Either the man had a hot lunch date waiting for him or he was in serious need of an attitude adjustment. Gary was betting it was the latter.

Ignoring the manager's pique, he continued his update. "In the meantime, the fire department is here and they are going to drill a hole in the wall and pump some fresh air in here for us."

Considering it was already stifling hot, he understood the look of relief that came over most of the adults. His next comment erased the relief.

"But those of you against the front wall need to move away from that area, so they can start drilling."

He chuckled when everyone groaned. "I know we're already packed in like sardines, but the sooner you move away from the front, the sooner they'll get us that fresh air. And they're also going to feed a hose inside so we have access to water."

When people began to move, he noticed the pregnant teller looking for a place to sit. "Ms. Myers," he called to her. "We can make some room for you over here."

Space was definitely at a premium and since Brittany Franks' daughter was on her lap, Gary turned to Tyler and patted his lap.

"How about you sit with me, buddy, so we can make room for Ms. Myers?" he suggested.

The little tyke looked up at the pregnant teller. "You can have my seat. I'll sit wiff Agent Gary," Tyler announced, sliding over onto Gary's lap as if it was the most natural thing in the world to do.

She smiled down at them gratefully. "Thank you, gentlemen, but please call me Jessie."

As soon as she was seated, she turned to study Gary. "I thought you looked familiar when I saw you in the lobby, but until you mentioned the FBI, I couldn't connect why. I've seen you being interviewed on the news."

In all the years he'd been in law enforcement, Gary had been able to go about his business with a degree of anonymity. But since he'd been named to head the task force investigation, every time he turned around, some reporter stuck a microphone in his face and wanted an update on the high profile Phantoms case.

He'd uttered the words *no comment* so often they'd probably carve it as the epitaph on his tombstone someday.

But Jessica's comment sent a ripple of unease through him. Even though Rose hadn't been able to place why, she had recognized him outside the bank. And someone else had obviously known him because the press had been tipped off to his presence at the bank.

But the robbery had unfolded so quickly, he'd barely had time to clear the lobby, let alone consider all the ramifications of remaining there himself.

In hindsight, considering the way the press had plastered him all over the news in recent months, he was damn lucky to be alive because at least two of the gunmen had known he was a federal agent.

He still couldn't figure out the exchange between those two men. Why one had been ready to execute him and the other had stopped it. Hell, he'd thought for sure he was a dead man. When he'd heard that click, he could have sworn his life flashed before his eyes.

He'd never felt so helpless…except perhaps when his old man had been beating him to a pulp in that damn root cellar. And he'd told Tyler he'd been scared, but in truth, those words, *scared* and *helpless*, didn't begin to touch on what he'd been feeling.

Terror was more like it. Definitely not something he ever wanted to experience again.

"How did you get caught in the robbery, Agent Thornton? Do you live here in Hagerstown?" Brittany asked.

Relieved to be pulled away from the disturbing thoughts, he turned to Tyler's mother.

"No, I work out of the Bureau's Baltimore office and live near there. I suppose you could say that like the rest of you, I was in the wrong place at the wrong time."

The comment drew a chuckle from some of his companions.

"Actually, I was meeting with Mr. Chandler when the gunmen arrived. The Bureau had identified this bank as a Phantoms' target and I was warning him of an impending hold-up. But unfortunately for everyone in here, the bandits showed up about six hours before we anticipated their arrival."

"Did they catch the bandits?" Rose asked curiously.

He thought for a moment about how much information to give them and decided he might as well tell them most of it, since the media was already on the story.

"During the robbery, my team and your local and state police were closing in on the bank. The Phantoms ran into them when they got outside. We recovered the money and captured four of them." With children present, Gary saw no need to specify that two of those men were dead.

"That's all I can tell you for now," Gary said when Chandler began a barrage of questions about the robbery. And intentionally changing the subject, he turned to the pregnant teller.

"When's your baby due, Jessie?"

She gazed at him with a dead-panned expression. "Have you ever delivered a baby?"

A chorus of gasps erupted from those who heard her. Gary completely understood their reaction. "Uh…yes," he answered hesitantly, hoping to hell she was joking.

His second year with the Houston PD he'd been dispatched to a car accident and discovered a passenger in one of the vehicles was in the final stages of labor. By the time the ambulance had arrived, he was holding her newborn son. But the delivery had been out of necessity, not choice and considering it had happened thirty years ago, Gary figured it was fair to say his delivery skills were rusty at best.

"But it wouldn't be on my top ten list of things to do, especially here in this vault," he added, just because he thought it needed to be said.

The young teller chuckled. "Don't worry…I was just kidding. I'm not due for another two weeks."

Gary, only half-jokingly, reached for his heart and blew out an audible sigh of relief.

Jessie shot him a worried glance. "I'm sorry. Are you okay?"

He chuckled softly. "I'm fine, but you can't imagine how glad I am to hear that. Hopefully we'll be out of here long before junior decides to make his or her debut."

As if on cue, a loud motor revved to life outside the vault, signaling the drilling had begun.

# Chapter Eight

Not that Gary was counting, but three hours, thirty-six minutes and about fifteen seconds after the vault door had slammed shut, it finally swung open again, freeing them from their captivity.

Standing up, Gary retrieved Rose's walker for her and then slipped back into his suit coat, fastened his top shirt button and cinched the knot of his tie to straighten it. Time to go back to work.

As the others began filing into the lobby where FBI agents waited to interview them, Gary felt a tug on his hand and glanced down to see Tyler gazing up at him.

"Here Agent Gary…dis is yours," the boy said, handing him the pin he'd removed from his collar.

Since Brittany was eying her son carefully, Gary suspected she'd prompted the return. He shot a quick glance at her, then turned his attention to Tyler and shook his head. "No, buddy…that's for you."

Eyes wide as saucers with excitement, Tyler stared at the pin and then looked up at Gary. "It's for me, really? I can keep it?"

With a confirming nod to Brittany, Gary smiled and ignoring pain that sucked the air from his lungs, he knelt down in front of Tyler. "You sure can," he said, re-fastening the pin on the boy's collar. "And when you look at it I want you to remember the good things about today, like the fact you and I met and that you helped me with an FBI investigation."

The boy nodded mutely, clearly in awe of the gift.

Gary gave him a gentle pat on the shoulder. "I'm giving your mother a card with my phone number on it so you can call me whenever you want, okay?"

Tyler's eyes widened even further. "Anytime?"

Chuckling, Gary nodded, wondering if he was opening a can of worms making that offer. But he still figured the boy's infatuation with the Bureau would wane in a couple weeks, so even if he called a few times it wouldn't be a problem.

"Anytime," Gary confirmed. "And when you get older, if you still want to be an FBI agent, I promise I'll help you any way I can."

Without standing, Gary handed Brittany another one of his business cards. "I'll be retiring in a couple years, but my son Zach is also an agent. His contact information is on the back of the card. If for some reason, you can't reach me at one of my numbers, contact him and he'll get in touch with me."

His gaze met Tyler's again. "You take care of yourself, okay?" he said offering the boy another handshake.

"You too, Agent Gary," Tyler said with tears brimming his eyes. Ignoring the offered hand, he threw his arms around Gary's neck and hugged him tightly. "And fank you for protecting me."

Choked with emotion over the boy's show of affection, Gary hugged him back. "You're welcome, son."

Tyler finally released him and sniffing loudly, stepped back beside his mother. Gary slowly got to his feet and handed her the note he'd hand written on her behalf.

"You tell your boss and the doctor to call me if they have any questions about why you didn't show up today. And if they give you any grief, call me and I'll set them straight."

"Thank you," she replied, stretching up and kissing him on the cheek. "Tyler and I will never forget you or the kindness you gave him today."

Gary smiled down at Brittany, then chucked Nikki under her chin causing the toddler to giggle. Finally, he met the boy's gaze again and gave his hair a gentle ruffle. "Take care, partner."

Staring up at him silently, the boy nodded and then took his mother's hand as they headed out of the vault. But at the door, Tyler turned to look back at him and waved. "Bye."

"Bye."

Jim Barrett, waiting by the vault door, smiled down at the young boy, but the moment Gary stepped into the lobby, Barrett's attention turned to him. "A couple things before I get your statement, boss…"

"Gary!"

His name, called with such urgency by a voice he knew as well as his own, caused Gary to spin to his left, his eyes immediately spotting auburn hair in the crowd and locking on the very last person he expected to see.

"Kate?" His wife's name came out in stunned disbelief, but she was truly a sight for sore eyes.

If possible, Katie was even more smokin' hot in her fifties than she'd been in her twenties and she'd been plenty pretty back then. But she had a kind of wholesome feminine beauty that didn't need make-up to enhance her features. Her emerald green eyes sparkled with life, her cheeks held a natural blush and she had the same tall, trim, sexy body she'd had the day they married.

But more than just her looks made her the most attractive woman he knew. Her curiosity for learning had never waned. The woman could intelligently discuss everything from nuclear medicine and world politics to the latest best sellers. Her athletic ability kept him on his toes and her sense of humor could reduce him to laughter faster than most comedians.

Then there was her passion…well, he couldn't imagine ever tiring of making love to her. She was truly his soul mate and right now, there was nothing on earth he needed or wanted more than to hold her.

"She's one of the things I was trying to tell you," Jim uttered. But Gary barely heard him as he took a few long strides to close the distance to his wife. And he'd just barely managed to brace himself before she flew into his arms.

Katie's ardor always managed to steal his breath and this time was no different. But he wasn't sure if it was from the passion behind her kiss or the pain that erupted in his ribs from the impact of her embrace. And even though he tried, he couldn't stop the groan that managed to escape between their sealed lips.

Almost as quickly as she'd wrapped her arms around him, Kate let him go, concern darkening her eyes. The change in her expression and demeanor was instantaneous.

Exit wife; enter doctor. Panicked doctor.

"Oh my God, you're hurt," she cried, running her hands under his jacket gently searching for his injuries. "Let me see. Where?"

Gary gathered her wandering hands and wrapped her back in an embrace again. Holding her in his arms was worth a little pain…well…actually more than a little, but nothing he couldn't handle.

"I'm fine," he lied.

One glance at the skeptical look she gave him and he knew she hadn't fallen for it. "Okay…I'm not fine. I'm pretty sure I've got a couple cracked ribs. But just let me hold you for a minute before you go all doctor on me."

**KATE GAZED UP** at Gary with concern. If his ribs were broken they could puncture a lung. He belonged in a hospital where they could check him out thoroughly. She should insist on it.

But she didn't…and for a very simple reason.

She knew him.

In fact, she'd known him her entire life and jokingly told people she'd fallen in love with him when she saw him in an adjacent bassinet in the hospital nursery. It wasn't far from the truth, but the feeling hadn't been one-sided either.

Gary had first asked her to marry him in sixth grade and had even given her a ring. Granted the diamond had been a fake and the metal on the gum machine prize had turned her finger green, but that treasured keepsake was still stored in their wall safe along with other valuables.

They'd married while she was in med school and knew each other so well they could usually pick up on the other's mood at a mere glance.

But when he'd stepped out of the vault, she'd been so happy and relieved to see him that her sole focus had been getting to him. Now that she truly looked at him, she could see he was in pain.

She saw something else, too. He was shaken.

Oh, he'd never admit it in public and she doubted even Jim Barrett realized it because her tough lawman kept a tight rein on his emotions. But he failed miserably when it came to hiding anything from her. She could read him like a book. And something had rattled him…badly.

Probably the vault. He was usually able to control his phobia of small places, but she imagined being locked inside the confines of a vault would be enough to set it off.

Still, something tickling the back of her mind told her it was more than that and if he needed to hold her for a few moments to gather his composure again, then she certainly wasn't going to argue.

Willingly, she snuggled back into his familiar embrace. "You want to tell me about it?"

Gary drew in a staggered breath. "It was bad."

Kate hadn't really expected an answer because Gary always tried to shield her from the ugly and dangerous parts of his work. So not only did he surprise her by answering, but those three brief words, the last thing in the world she'd imagined he would say, explained his odd behavior. For him to have made the admission, he must have gone through hell.

"Thorny, come on. We've got things to do."

Kate tensed the moment Jim's impatient voice reached them, expecting Gary to pull away from her and go to work. But he didn't.

"Be right there, Jimmy," he replied over the top of her head without releasing her from his embrace.

Instead, he drew back slightly and gazed down at her silently for several heartbeats as if memorizing her features, then gave her the most adoring smile she'd ever seen on his face.

"I love you, Katie," he said softly, tenderly.

He'd never been bashful about voicing his love for her. But it was the way he said it this time, as if he didn't think she believed it or that he needed to make sure she knew it, that scared her. Not for her, but for him.

It ripped at her insides to see him upset, and since she didn't know the reason, she felt powerless to help. But her response didn't take any thought because it came from the heart.

Caressing his cheek, she smiled at him. "I love you, too, darling…always."

And just when she thought he couldn't surprise her any further. He surprised her again. Really surprised her.

He tipped her head up and kissed her.

If she hadn't known before that something was very wrong with him, she would have known then. Gary had always been affectionate, romantic too, but blatant exhibitions in public had never been his thing. Yet here he was, kissing her in a lobby that was buzzing with police activity and full of strangers.

Granted a lot of those strangers were involved in their own reunions with loved ones, but his was no simple kiss. It was the kind of smoldering lip lock that succeeded in curling her toes and igniting a fire inside her that sent heat coursing through every cell of her body. And her head was spinning with thoughts of finding a bedroom where they could be alone for about a week.

Loathe as she was to end it, the doctor in her wouldn't be distracted. With a tortured whimper, she dragged her mouth from his and feeling the heated flush that filled her cheeks, she gazed up at him.

"I want a rain check to finish that when you get home," she said, trying to quell her breathlessness. "But right now, I want to examine your ribs and I also want to look at the knot you've got on the back of your head."

She'd felt the squishy lump and a sticky clump of hair when she'd run her fingers through his hair while kissing him. His head had been bleeding. Not a lot…but enough she wanted to examine it if for no other reason than to clean the wound.

"And if you give me any argument," she continued. "I'm calling the paramedics and taking you to the hospital."

A smile worked its way across his lips and he chuckled, then dropped a light kiss on her lips and released her. "Okay, sweetheart. I'm all yours."

That comment had her mind whirling right back to his searing kiss and she nearly made a suggestive comeback. But she held her tongue figuring it would only lead to a further delay in examining him.

"Thorny, come on, let's go," Barrett called impatiently.

With a sigh of resignation, Gary swept her hand up in his and led her across the lobby toward an office where Jim was waiting. But at the door, Barrett stopped Kate with a hand on her arm.

"Kate, you'll have to wait out here or go back into the lunch room with the other family members," he said, blocking her entry. "It shouldn't take long."

Gary shook his head. "Let her through, Jimmy."

Kate figured her husband interceded more as a favor to Jim than anything else because Gary knew when she was on a mission — and she was definitely on a mission to examine his injuries — nothing was going to stop her.

"Thorny, we can't do that," Jim countered. "We've got protocol to follow."

Gary drilled the younger agent with a glare and when he spoke his voice was unyielding. "I said, let her through."

"Darling get out of that suit coat and unbutton your shirt," Kate ordered, figuring since her husband was Jim's boss the younger man would follow orders and drop his objection. And besides, she was impatient to get started.

When one of her boys was hurt or sick, she was no longer wife or mother; she was their doctor and they knew not to argue with her. And Gary didn't. But when Barrett still didn't release her, the Irish temper Kate had inherited from her grandmother flared to life.

Straightening to her full five seven height, she faced the man blocking her path. "You listen to me Jim Barrett," she said angrily. "I'm a doctor and my husband needs medical attention. Either you get me my medical bag and let me tend to his injuries while you talk to him or I'm calling an ambulance and your questions can wait until the hospital releases him."

Barrett's brow knit and he dropped his hand from her arm, turning to stare dumbfounded at Gary. "You're hurt?"

"Things got rough," Gary answered peeling off his jacket to reveal a streak of dried blood across the top of his shoulder.

Kate barely reconciled her brain to the fact she was looking at a bullet wound, when Gary's shirt disappeared and she spotted an angry red bruise on his ribs, a perfectly horrifying image of a gun butt, so clear the ridge pattern could be seen.

Most of her twenty-eight years as a physician had been spent working as a trauma surgeon or in emergency rooms. She'd seen just about every malady and form of injury known to mankind and out of self-preservation she'd learned to detach herself from the personal nature of her work. It was the only way to maintain sanity when constantly dealing with the pain and suffering of others.

But when her husband or son was involved, Kate lost all traces of detachment.

Shock sucked the air from her lungs. And she was just about to yell at Barrett who stood frozen, staring at Gary's injuries, when Jim suddenly snapped from his trance. A curse flew from his mouth and he spun to look at her.

"Where is your bag?"

"I left it in the lunch room. My purse is there too," she answered, embarrassed to admit she'd left them unattended. Her only excuse was that she'd been so excited and relieved to see Gary emerge from the vault, she'd leaped out of her seat and run to him, without giving any thought to her belongings. But with the massive police presence in the building, she suspected her things were safe.

"Be right back," Jim answered, jogging down the hall.

# Chapter Nine

Late afternoon sun bathed the hospital parking lot when Gary walked Kate to her car. They'd ended up at the emergency room after she'd given him a quick exam at the bank and discovered the blow to his head had caused a more complicated injury than he'd assumed.

The moment Kate had seen a blood-filled hematoma on the back of his scalp she'd insisted he needed treatment in a sterile setting where the injury could be properly treated. So while Kate drove him to the hospital, Barrett had followed them and had taken his statement while Kate hovered over the doctor treating him.

With six staples to close the gash and doctor's orders to go home and rest, Gary was finally released from the ER.

While going home and relaxing was certainly a tempting idea, there was a ton of work to be done in the wake of the bank robbery and it wouldn't wait. His entire team would be going non-stop, running down leads obtained from surveillance footage and from the identities of the dead and captured bandits. Injured or not, as head of the task force he wasn't going to abandon his team without at least helping with some of the legwork, before he crashed for the evening.

Bodies of the two Phantoms killed had already been taken to the Office of the Chief Medical Examiner in Baltimore for autopsy and fingerprinting, and the Forensic Medical Center wasn't that far from his home. It was a stop he could easily make before he even thought about resting. Hopefully the Medical Examiner would have something for him by the time he got there.

But before Gary went anywhere he intended to check on the wounded Phantom, to see if he was out of surgery and awake yet. After all, he was standing in the parking lot of the hospital where the man was a patient. Who better to check on him?

Gary wrapped Kate in a gentle embrace. "Thank you for driving over here today, sweetheart. You were just the medicine I needed when I stepped out of that vault."

It was true, too. He'd held it together through the robbery and being trapped in the vault, but the terror he'd felt being at the mercy of that human refrigerator, unable to defend himself, without endangering a room full of innocent people had been sheer torture. Hell, he'd never felt so helpless in his adult life.

But holding Katie in his arms for those few brief moments in the bank lobby had grounded him again and given him a sense of normalcy he'd desperately needed after the robbery.

Even so, he had a feeling he'd be having flashbacks to the click of that AK-47 every night for the rest of his life.

Kate smiled up at him. "Wild horses couldn't have kept me away."

He dropped a soft kiss on her lips. "I'm sorry I can't go with you now. But I'll be home as soon as possible."

"Go on; do your thing," she said, patting his chest lovingly. "I knew when I drove over here this morning that you'd be busy. But you are injured, darling, so please humor me and take it easy. No leaping over buildings in a single bound."

And that was just one of the million reasons he loved this woman. She might not like his decision, but she understood it and supported him fully…while maintaining her sense of humor.

Gary chuckled. "I promise; no playing Superman. I might be late, though, so if you get hungry don't wait dinner for me," he said, opening her car door.

Kate slid inside and pressed the ignition button, then blew him another kiss. "Love you."

"Love you, too." Smiling, he closed her door and patted the car roof to signal he was clear. As soon as she pulled away, he strode back into the hospital.

The ride up the elevator turned out to be a waste of time. Their John Doe prisoner had come through surgery to remove two bullets from his chest, but he was still unconscious.

The prisoner wasn't going anywhere. They could get his fingerprints later, when he woke up. But before leaving, Gary gave the police officer guarding the man's room instructions. Either he or Mike Devlin were to be notified as soon as the prisoner regained consciousness and no one was to question the man without Gary being present.

His new cell phone rang as he walked out to his car. "Hey Jimmy. What's up?"

Lucas Shaw had picked Jim up from the ER after Gary had finished giving him his statement and the two agents had returned to the bank where Mike Devlin was supervising the investigation.

"The CSI team is finished," Jim replied. "Impound has collected the Phantom's SUV and bank personnel have been given clearance to reenter the building in the morning."

Gary gave a doubtful chuckle. Employees might have clearance to reenter the bank building, but it would take some major restoration before they could reopen for business. So many rounds of ammunition had been fired inside the building that the ceiling, walls and furniture looked like Swiss cheese.

"There's nothing else here for us tonight," Jim continued. "So Mike, Lucas and I are headed over to the P.D. to go through surveillance videos."

The local police department was working hand in hand with the task force on the robbery since it occurred in their jurisdiction. And they'd graciously offered Gary's team the use of their facilities while the investigation was on going.

When Jim finished his update, Gary filled him in on the status of their wounded prisoner. "I'm going to make a stop at the Forensic Medical Center and then I'm heading home. Call if you need me."

"Go home. Rest," Jim countered. "We've got things covered here and anything we can't do can wait until morning."

Jim was right. It wasn't like they were chasing down people who were going to strike again any moment. The bandits planned their robberies well and weeks passed between their hold-ups. Today law enforcement had put a major dent in the gang, eliminating four of the six participants. And Gary would wager that the two who'd escaped were in hiding trying to figure out how to avoid arrest. Since at the moment, Gary's team didn't know the identity of those two escapees, there wasn't much they could do except search for a lead in the evidence they'd collected.

"See you tomorrow," Gary replied before ending the call.

It was nearly seven when he pulled into the parking lot of the Forensic Medical Center and went inside. More familiar with the morgue than he cared to be, Gary pushed the button to open the hydraulic doors and strode inside, immediately assailed by the odorous combination of chemicals and death.

Over the years he'd attended his share of autopsies and the smell was one that still took his breath away until his nose got used to it. And he made a habit of avoiding the place immediately after eating. No sense in tempting a digestive mutiny.

Up to her elbows inside a corpse laid out on the table in front of her, an attractive chestnut haired woman in her forties lifted what appeared to be someone's liver and glanced over at him.

"Well, if it isn't my favorite federal agent," Dr. Georgiana Baker, Maryland's Chief Medical Examiner quipped with a smile, placing the organ on a scale. "It's about time you get here. I was beginning to think you'd forgotten me."

As medically qualified as she was pretty, only an idiot would forget her. The woman had a bubbly personality and seemed to enjoy teasing his fellow agents and him. Gary figured it was her way of dealing with the unpleasant nature of her job and he never took her flirtation seriously.

"I'd be flattered, Georgie, except I happen to know you greet all my colleagues with that same line," he chuckled.

She grinned guiltily.

"But sorry it took so long," he continued. "It's been one of those days."

He made his way around several exam tables to where she was working and stopped beside her. "Is he one of mine?" he asked studying the body of the young man lying on her autopsy table.

"No, I finished the second of yours about an hour ago. Both of them were pretty standard. No surprises." Using her elbow, she motioned to the wall of refrigerated vaults. "One of them is second row from the top, third from the left."

Gary walked across the room and pointed to a door and when she nodded, he unlatched the lock and slid out the long narrow drawer.

"That's Jamal Lewis, age thirty-two," Georgie called from across the room as she extracted a kidney from the body in front of her. "I got a hit on his identity the minute I put his hand on the digital fingerprint scanner. He's got a record as long as your arm."

A surge of adrenaline pumped through Gary's veins. With Lewis' identity known, the task force could run him through their system and with any luck his information would lead them to the other Phantoms.

But Gary wasn't going to be greedy. Whatever they got would be more than they'd already had.

He peeled back a sheet shrouding the body of a short squat man who in life had been built like a fire hydrant, but now lay lifeless on a cold stainless steel slab.

"Cause of death?" he asked.

"Grab a pair of surgical gloves and turn his head," she replied.

Glancing around, Gary found several boxes of gloves and grabbed a pair marked *Large*. He wasn't sure what to expect when he turned the dead man's head, but it certainly wasn't the gaping wound that had blown away a large chunk of the man's skull.

"He died of a catastrophic wound to the back of his head," the medical examiner announced.

*"No shit,"* Gary thought, studying the wound more closely.

He knew of only one thing that would cause that kind of wound. A high-muzzle velocity weapon like an AK-47. The kinetic energy from those things caused wounds significantly larger than smaller caliber weapons and when they hit a body they caused horrendous internal damage, similar to an explosion.

"You recovered the bullet?" he asked.

"Over on the evidence table," Georgie replied from the sink where she was washing her hands.

Gary walked back over to the table beside the main doorway, spotted the evidence bag marked with Lewis' name and studied the slug inside. They'd have to run ballistics on it to be certain, but the large caliber slug looked to him as if it came from an AK-47. The same kind of weapon some of the bandits had been carrying during the robbery.

Had Lewis been killed by another Phantom to prevent him from talking? An interesting concept, but it was just as feasible the man had been killed by heavily armed police. Either way the result was the same. The man was dead.

"So who's his friend and what killed him?" Gary asked curiously as the Medical Examiner joined him at the evidence table.

Dr. Baker walked him back to the wall of compartments. Choosing one several rows away from Lewis, she unlatched the bottom drawer and slid the tray out.

"Meet Daniel Walker, age thirty-five," she said, giving the task force another name to run through the system. "His prints lit up the scanner too."

Based on the build, the average height and weight of the white male Georgie uncovered, Gary was fairly certain it was the man who had tried to knock Rose over during the robbery. And call him jaded, but Gary couldn't work up even an ounce of remorse over the man's death, considering the way Walker had manhandled the elderly woman.

"Cause of death on this one?"

"Exsanguination from multiple gunshot wounds. The fatal one nicked his aorta."

"Any wounds to the back of this one's head?" Gary asked, testing his theory about the other bandit being executed by other Phantoms.

"None," Baker replied. "And before you ask, I recovered all the bullets from this one, too."

"Anything else you can tell me about them?" he asked.

She nodded thoughtfully. "They both have what looks to me like jail house tats," she replied, lifting one of Walker's arms to reveal the ink artwork. "The work is crude and I'm not an expert, but when I compare this one to Lewis', it looks like both of them were done by the same person."

It was no surprise the thugs had served time in jail. People rarely woke up one morning and decided to start a violent spree of bank robberies with a group of friends. But the fact they had tattoos that looked like they'd been done by the same artist could mean they'd served time together or at least in the same prison. That detail could be an important lead for the task force and was one Gary intended to check immediately.

Following the Medical Examiner back to the lab table, Gary signed for all the evidence bags. "Good work, Georgie. And thanks for getting them done for me so quickly."

"I wouldn't have done it for anyone else," she replied with a smile.

Gary shook his head, chuckling. "Yeah…yeah, that's what you tell all of us," he countered. "I'll have someone contact you as soon as we have a disposition for the bodies. And you've got my number. Call if you have any questions or find anything else of interest," he said heading to the door.

"Tell Kate I said *hi*," she called after him.

He turned and gave her a jaunty salute and then stepped into the hallway, immediately hauling in a breath of fresh air.

# Chapter Ten

After a hectic day filled with roller-coasting emotions, Kate was ready to relax. As she sat down in her recliner, she glanced at her watch. Eight o'clock.

Gary had told her he might be late, but Kate thought he'd be home by now. Another half hour and she was going to eat dinner without him. But she wished he'd get home. The emergency room doctor had told him to rest and as a doctor herself, she wished Gary had; he needed it after the injuries he'd sustained. But she'd known it wasn't going to happen; not on the heels of another bank robbery.

Still she couldn't help worrying about his health.

Pushing away the thought, Kate raised the footrest on her chair, reached for the television remote control and burst out laughing.

Her dear husband had painted the master control button bright red, so she knew which button to push. Still chuckling she stared at the thing.

Nothing could ruin a good mood for her quicker than a television clicker….and he knew it.

The blasted thing had more controls than the cockpit of a jet and she never managed to hit the right one which invariably messed up the programming. Something she did frequently.

Kate didn't know when Gary had dabbed the paint on it, but he had to have done it sometime last night after reprogramming the thing for the umpteenth time.

Eager to see how well it worked, she pressed the button and nearly gave a cheer when the screen illuminated and the accompanying sound bar tossed voices into the den. Unfortunately those voices belonged to a string of never-ending ads which instantly lost her attention.

With dinner needing only some last minute touches and the table already set, she picked up the morning newspaper which she had never gotten around to reading at the hospital because her tea break had come to an abrupt end when Zach and Cassie had appeared in the ER.

Kate shivered recalling the wave of terror that had nearly overwhelmed her learning Gary was trapped inside the bank with the Phantoms. Thankfully she and Cassie had barely left the hospital when Zach called to tell them he'd spoken to Gary and that he was okay. Shortly after Cassie had gone home, though, Kate had decided she still wanted to drive over to Hagerstown.

What a day, she thought, heaving a sigh and dropping her gaze to the newspaper.

She was engrossed in an editorial about the political mess in Washington when the voice of a television anchor on the perpetual news channel caught her attention.

"Up next. Some dramatic video footage from a Maryland bank robbery."

Kate stared at the screen in shock. The Phantoms had hit numerous banks over the past five or six months and while the stories and a few still photos had made the news, there had never been actual video released to the public. And she couldn't imagine Gary or anyone on the task force authorizing the release of video so quickly for a robbery they were still investigating.

Since she had no idea how to start the DVD machine to record the upcoming clip for Gary to watch, Kate grabbed her cell phone and got the camera ready to capture the video. Not ideal, but better than nothing.

A few moments later after a series of ads ended, the news anchor's face filled the screen again and aiming her camera phone at the television, Kate pressed the *Record* icon.

"The notorious Phantoms struck again today, this time in Hagerstown, Maryland and we've acquired some exclusive video of the actual holdup. We want to warn viewers this footage is both violent and graphic in nature and may be unsuitable for younger viewers."

The warning filled Kate with trepidation and her breath caught in her chest a second later when Gary's face appeared on the screen. At that moment, she knew she wasn't going to want to see what was about to happen, that she should turn away…but she couldn't.

Still, even though she knew Gary had been caught up in the robbery and had seen and examined his injuries, nothing prepared her for seeing video action of those injuries being inflicted.

Nausea swirled in Kate's stomach and a whimpered cry escaped her throat as she watched a mammoth masked bandit ram his weapon into Gary's ribs and then crack him over the head knocking him to the floor…for no apparent reason other than he felt like it.

Gary was tall, but he was also sturdy and strong. Kate could only imagine the force of the blows that had dropped him to the floor like a sack of potatoes. She'd certainly seen the shocking results.

And if that wasn't horrific enough, she could only stare in disbelief when the bandit pointed his weapon at Gary. But it took her brain several moments to reconcile what she was seeing, a conclusion confirmed by both Gary's and the gunman's reactions.

Tears flooded Kate's eyes.

The man had actually pulled the trigger and apparently only by the grace of God the gun had misfired or jammed.

"Sources have confirmed the man being assaulted is FBI Supervisory Special Agent Gary Thornton, who heads the task force investigating the Phantoms…"

The news anchor's voice droned on in the background of Kate's mind because the only thing she could wrap her brain around was that she'd just witnessed someone trying to execute her husband.

She'd nearly lost him today. Just the thought caused bile to rise in her throat.

No wonder Gary had seemed so shaken when she'd met him in the bank lobby. He'd lived that terrifying moment; she'd merely watched it and she was shaking.

Fighting to keep from hyperventilating, she stopped the recorder on her phone and stared at the television as the news anchor jumped to the next story.

What was wrong with the press? Why would they show that clip? Who had given it to them?

"Hi Sweetheart, I'm home! Wow! Something smells wonderful in here."

Kate gasped at the sound of Gary's voice, quickly using the back of her hand to swipe tears from her eyes before turning off the television.

"Hi!" She hoped he didn't hear the remnants of those tears in her voice. Dropping her footrest, she got up to greet him, spotting him the moment he stepped into the dining room, his tie and collar loosened and his ruined suit jacket draped over his arm.

Kate was sure he'd assumed his casual appearance out of fatigue. But to her it was the sexiest look in the world. All he needed to complete the picture was mussed hair. And the fragment of her brain that wasn't still in shock over the video sent heat skittering through her body, a reaction that had nothing to do with anger, but everything to do with need.

And that need to reassure herself he was alive and safe hastened her to meet him before he got halfway across the room.

"You must be beat." Slipping her arms around his neck, she rose up on her toes and sealed her lips to his, pouring every ounce of her love into her kiss.

When he pulled her closer and drew out the kiss, Kate thought maybe he wasn't as tired as she first thought. But then he lifted his head and grinned down at her.

"If I wasn't afraid I'd fall asleep on my feet, I'd go out and come back in again to get another greeting like that," he teased.

Kate chuckled softly and kissed him again. "I hope you didn't eat because I made Grandma's lasagna. I just need to warm it up a bit and pop some garlic bread in the oven and it'll be ready in a couple minutes."

Her choice of meal hadn't been random. Gary's grandmother had always made the best lasagna Kate had ever tasted and Gary loved it. The dear woman had shared her secret recipe with Kate after she and Gary married.

After what he'd been through today, Kate figured Gary deserved a special treat.

"Mmm! That sounds wonderful," he exclaimed. "The only thing I've eaten since breakfast was that lukewarm soda and pack of stale cheese crackers Jimmy bought for me from the bank's vending machine while you were examining my ribs."

Kate grimaced a chuckle. "You poor baby."

"I'm starved, but I need a shower and a change of clothing first," he admitted. "I feel like a walking HazMat scene and between the bullet hole and blood, this suit and shirt are history." His lips brushed her temple. "Give me twenty minutes and I'll be ready to eat."

Gary's comment about the suit served to sober her mood and remind Kate of all he'd been through. Not that she needed a reminder. The images from the television were still replaying in her head.

She wanted to talk to him about the robbery, needed to talk to him about it. But as much as she wanted him to open up to her, it was more important that he decompress. He'd tell her when he was ready.

"Go take your shower."

With a nod, he vanished back the hall to their bedroom. Several minutes passed when a thought suddenly came to Kate and she rushed back the hall to find him.

The shower was already running when she poked her head into the master bath. "Honey, be gentle with those staples," she cautioned. "In fact, don't wash your hair; I'll do it for you out here in the sink when you're finished."

She'd already begun to close the door when she heard the shower door open and leaned into the bathroom again to see what he wanted.

"How about coming in here to do it?" he asked with a wicked grin.

Apparently, washing his hair was the last thing her dear husband had on his mind. And any other time she'd take him up on the offer, but not tonight. "Need I remind you of all your injuries?" she retorted, trying to stifle a laugh.

"No…that's my point." His grin grew wider and those cobalt eyes of his gleamed with mischief. "I need a doctor."

Tempting as the idea was, she wasn't giving in. "Well…your doctor says you are in no condition to be fooling around. So finish your shower and I'll wash your hair out here. Then we can eat."

"Spoilsport!" he shot back, as he closed the shower door again.

Kate chuckled aloud; she couldn't help it.

**GARY STRODE DOWN** the hall toward his office. His plan to drive over to Hagerstown had been cancelled when he'd called the hospital to check on the prisoner and learned John Doe was still unconscious.

His thoughts focused on wading through a mound of reports from his team, he turned into his office.

The moment he stepped inside the odor registered. His gaze lifted and he skidded to a halt, staring.

What the hell?

An enormous vase holding several dozen roses perched in the middle of his desk.

Curious to know who sent them Gary dug around until he found a plain white envelope bearing his name. But his curiosity turned to concern when he read the typed, unsigned message.

*Our time together was so special. Until the next time…with all my love.*

He glanced at the envelope again in case he'd misread the typed name and the flowers were for someone else. No…there was nothing wrong with his eyes. That was definitely his name on the envelope.

A multitude of questions flooded his brain. The roses, the note…none of them made sense.

Who the hell had sent them? It certainly hadn't been Katie; she knew he didn't like the smell of roses. Sure, he bought them for her and put up with the smell because she loved roses and he loved her. But she'd never give them to him. In fact, in all the years he'd known her she'd only given him flowers twice, both times when he'd been in the hospital and she'd hand delivered those bouquets, none of which had contained roses.

No…these definitely weren't from her.

That left only disturbing possibilities, especially considering the note. Either someone was having some fun at his expense, an expensive joke at that considering the cost of roses…or he'd acquired a secret admirer suffering from a serious delusion. He didn't give a damn which one it was, he intended to find the person responsible and set them straight.

Carrying the vase, he headed out to the bull pen where agents worked and stopped in front of the secretary's desk.

"Linda, who delivered these," he asked, setting the vase on her desk.

Removing her reading glasses, the gray-haired secretary looked up at him. "Aren't they gorgeous? Debbie down at reception brought them up just before you got here. She said a florist from the shopping center dropped them at the guard gate. Is there a problem?"

He shook his head uncertainly. "I'm not sure. The note is unsigned."

She looked at him as if he was completely dense and chuckled quietly. "Kate probably just assumed you'd know they were from her, silly."

The last thing Gary needed or wanted was someone starting unfounded rumors about trouble in his marriage. But while he'd only been working out of the Baltimore Field Office for six months, Linda had nearly as many years' service with the Bureau as he did and she had a sterling reputation for discretion among the supervisory staff. She could be trusted not to gossip.

"That's the problem. They aren't from Kate."

Seeing the perplexed expression on Linda's face, Gary shrugged. "I can't stand the smell of roses and Katie knows it."

"Well, who are they from then?"

He flicked his brow up and shook his head. "That's the million dollar question. And while I try to figure out the answer, the flowers are yours, if you want them."

"Thank you!" she said, smiling like she'd just won the lottery. Suddenly her expression switched to a look of concern. "But won't they bother you out here?"

Gary grinned and shook his head. "No, just don't take it personally if I avoid your desk for the rest of the day."

Leaving her chuckling, he headed back to his office.

A half hour later, heaving a disgusted sigh, Gary hung up the phone and leaned back in his chair. Nothing. He'd come up with zilch.

The flowers had been ordered by phone, from a number tracing back to a disposable cell phone and they'd been paid for by a pre-paid generic debit card. He stared down at the paper in his hand.

*Jane Smith, 123 Main Street, Notown, MD, 21740.*

Hell, even the name and address of the sender was obviously fictional. Seriously. How could anyone look at that and not question it?

Frustrated and annoyed, his fist crumpled the paper into a ball, but suddenly something clicked in his brain. Quickly, he ironed the page out with his palm and gave the address a second look.

A smile curved his lips. Maybe his efforts weren't for nothing.

Checking a hunch, Gary quickly tapped a few numbers into an Internet search. And an instant later his hunch was confirmed.

The address wasn't completely generic. The zip code belonged to Hagerstown, the same place where he'd been caught in a bank robbery yesterday.

Gary didn't believe in coincidences; to his investigative mind that zip code smacked of a clue. Perhaps an accidental one, but a clue just the same.

His business card containing his office address and phone number had been given to everyone in the vault and with the exception of Ron Chandler, all the other adults had been women; any one of whom he supposed may have mistaken his attention as something more than professional concern.

Now all he had to do was figure out which one of them had sent the flowers and find a gentle way of discouraging them from further attention.

Mentally, he placed Rose Eshleman at the bottom of his list of potential suspects. Maybe he was being naïve, but he just couldn't see an eighty-five year old woman who seemed to have her act together, sending such a suggestive note to a federal agent…or any other man for that matter. Flowers maybe…but not that note. That smacked of someone younger.

The other person Gary tentatively crossed off his list was Rachel Washington. While they'd been locked in the vault, the head teller had enthusiastically told the group that she and her husband were flying to Florida that night and leaving this morning on a weeklong Caribbean cruise, a second honeymoon trip they'd been planning for months. She'd clearly been excited by the prospect and nervous about getting out of the vault in time so they didn't miss their flight. And while Lucas had been interviewing Rachel after the robbery, her husband had been waiting impatiently with airline tickets in hand for her to finish up so they could leave for the airport.

No, Gary doubted either Rose or Rachel were behind the flowers and note.

The person at the top of his list was that ditzy receptionist who'd propositioned him. Emma something.

Searching his brain for a moment produced a name. Carpenter. Yes…that was it. Emma Carpenter.

After propositioning him in the vault and being rebuked by her co-workers and ignored by him, she'd gotten quiet. But she'd made no secret of her interest in him. Hell, even Zach had picked up on it.

As he started to go over what he knew about his stalker, which wasn't a whole hell of a lot, his cell phone rang. Gary glanced at the display. Mike Devlin.

"Hey Dev, what's up?"

"Two things. First, we got confirmation from the news network that the video clip they showed last night was sent to them by someone at the bank. They wouldn't give us a name, but we traced it back to Ron Chandler."

Gary puffed out a disgusted breath. Why didn't that surprise him? Probably because the man had been such a pain in the ass while they'd been in the vault.

"How'd you trace it?"

"Well, we stumbled on it. We confiscated cell phones from the two dead guys and the two we have in custody and ran a search on their phone records. We're still checking the records, but we spotted one curious entry right away. Someone using a bank phone called Daniel Walker around the time of the robbery. So we got a warrant for bank phone records and emails. That's when we uncovered an email from Chandler to several television stations sent shortly after he was released from the vault. Our guess is he went into his office where he had access to the video feed from the camera and made a copy of the robbery footage. Chandler isn't talking though and since the video wasn't part of the scope of our search we can't force the issue."

"Good work though, Dev. I know if we keep digging we're going to find there's an inside link to the robberies and Chandler just jumped to prime suspect in my mind.

"Mine too," Mike agreed.

"What's the other thing you have for me?"

"Our suspect is awake."

Hot damn. That was the news he'd been waiting for.

"I'm on my way," Gary replied, pushing to his feet. "See you in about an hour."

He grabbed his suit jacket from the back of his chair, pulled it on and headed out the door, stopping only long enough to tell Linda where he was going.

# Chapter Eleven

Devlin was waiting by the bank of elevators when Gary stepped out onto the hospital's third floor. "Thanks for calling, Mike, Gary said as the tall athletic agent, who like Jim Barrett, had been an All-American quarterback in college, fell into step beside him. Together they headed toward their prisoner's room.

"Do we know anything about our John Doe yet?"

Devlin chuckled. "You're not going to believe this, but he's asking for you."

Caught by surprise, Gary stopped suddenly and looked at Devlin. "Me?"

"Yup. He asked for you by name."

"Who is he?"

"Don't know. He won't talk to anyone but you."

Gary gave the matter some thought. Since his face had been all over the news recently it was no surprise one of the bandit's knew his name. But if the man thought Gary was going to cut him a break, he was sorely mistaken.

His shoulders lifted in a shrug. "Well, let's go see what our mystery perp has to say?"

With a quick greeting to the officer guarding the door, Gary and Mike entered the room. Lying amid machines monitoring all his vitals, and with an intravenous tube snaking into his arm and a chest heavily bandaged from surgery, their suspect didn't look much like the dangerous bank robber Gary knew him to be.

But the moment the man's eyes opened and he saw the two agents his gaze zeroed in on Gary. He lifted his head off the pillow and shook his short spikey dreadlocks.

"Just you and me, man…or get me my attorney," he demanded belligerently.

A chill raced the length of Gary's spine, as a voice he'd never forget registered in his brain.

*This is your lucky day, Fed. Don't do nothin' stupid.*

Slamming the door shut on his emotions to hold back any reaction, Gary silently considered the tall, thin robber who had held his life in his hands and let him live.

If the options were talking to the man alone and possibly getting some useful information out of him versus having him lawyer up and get nothing…it was a no-brainer. Gary had a ton of questions for this particular Phantom.

"You're willing to talk to me alone without an attorney?" he asked just to confirm the man's conditions.

"Yeah man…but the dude's gotta go," the perp said swinging a hostile glare at Mike.

Silently Gary glanced at Devlin and gave an almost imperceptible tip of his head toward the door. With a nod, Mike handed him a camera pen before walking out of the room and closing the door behind him.

Police interview rooms were wired with closed circuit television cameras that allowed other law enforcement to watch a suspect being questioned. The hospital room had no such feature, but the camera pen captured video of the interview. If Zach was at his computer, he'd be watching the interview live.

Might as well get started, Gary thought, slipping the camera pen into the outside breast pocket of his suit jacket so the lens had an unobstructed view of the perp. But before saying anything, he discretely activated his microphone pin, adding sound to the interview record.

"Before we start, I want to remind you that you have the right to remain silent…"

A pair of intense hazel eyes locked on him. "I know my rights, Thornton," the Phantom interrupted. "You wanna talk or not?"

Gary studied him a moment before nodding. "I do. But I need to make sure you are waiving your rights."

"Yeah I'm waivin' 'em," the robber snapped impatiently.

Since the man was obviously anxious to get started, Gary didn't waste any more time. "You have me at a disadvantage. You obviously know my name, but I don't know yours."

After several heartbeats of silence, the man answered. "Jackson. Trayvon Jackson." He spat the name, giving it as some kind of challenge.

Trayvon Jackson. The name rolled around Gary's brain for a moment. It sounded familiar, but he couldn't place why. Rather than dwell on it, he focused on getting an answer to the question that had been burning in his brain for more than twenty-four hours. But first he had to address another issue.

Gratitude wasn't normally something Gary would express to any criminal, as it showed a potential sign of weakness to the perp. In this instance though, his conscience demanded he acknowledge the man's actions.

"Thank you for saving my life yesterday. But I have to ask why you did it, considering one of your cohorts was hell bent on executing me?"

Jackson stared at him hard, his eyes black with intensity and for several moments Gary thought he wasn't going to answer. But then the man blinked and dropped his head back on his pillow.

"I don't like owin' debts to no one, 'specially no Fed. And I figger now we're even."

Gary keyed on one word. "Debt? What debt?"

Again the intense stare bore into him.

"What's it to you?" Jackson spat angrily. "You lived and now we're even."

Gary gave a sarcastic chuckle, intentionally trying to rile Jackson into answering. "You're afraid aren't you? Afraid to give me a straight answer," he shot back in a tone full of attitude.

When Jackson jerked toward him, rattling the handcuff chaining him to the bed rail, Gary knew his challenge had gotten to the man. Since there was no way Jackson could reach him, Gary didn't move a muscle in response to the outburst.

"Son of a bitch, I ain't afraid of nothin'," Jackson retorted dropping back on his pillow. "You wanna know. I'll tell you. You saved my kid brother's life a few years back."

Gary schooled his expression to remain neutral. The answer was one he hadn't been expecting, but it served to jog his memory and suddenly an image of another male flickered through his mind. A younger man also named Jackson.

Before he continued though, Gary noticed pain contorting Trayvon's face. The angry move had cost Jackson dearly. Considering his own ribs protested his every move; Gary could sympathize with his prisoner.

"Do you need me to ring for the nurse?" he asked.

Jackson cursed under his breath, apparently annoyed with himself. "No, man. But can you get me some water?"

His tray had been moved over to the window so he couldn't reach anything to use as a potential weapon. And Gary walked over to it, poured some water into the glass and handed it to Jackson.

Trayvon took a long draw on the straw, draining half the glass in one swallow.

"You're Marcus' brother?" Gary asked as the man handed the glass back to him.

The perp snorted a chuckle. "You ain't as dumb as you look, old man."

So much for gratitude for the water. Gary couldn't help the thought, but he held any reaction to the taunt instead focusing on one of the many dichotomies of his job. Yesterday Rose Eshleman had called him young man and today he was an old man. He supposed it was all in the perspective. But considering he felt about a hundred years old today, he was inclined to go along with Jackson's age assessment.

"I'll take that as a yes," Gary replied calmly, setting the glass back on the tray.

"Yeah," Jackson added when he saw his insult hadn't bothered Gary. He heaved a deep breath and his hardened exterior cracked. "Marcus got the brains in the family; he was a smart kid and my momma always said he'd go far someday. I tried to keep him from becomin' a loser like me, but the army messed him up big time. And if you hadn't helped him, he'd probably be dead or in prison by now. I owed you for that."

Well, that was an interesting twist. Gary remembered well the day five years ago when twenty year old Marcus Jackson had been arrested by the drug task force. The raid on a warehouse on the docks in Baltimore had targeted a large drug delivery from Luis Santos' South American cartel and had rounded up over a dozen major drug dealers. But while Marcus was present when the raid took place, it had been the young man's first brush with the law.

In talking to Marcus after the arrest, Gary had learned the young man had enlisted in the Army right out of high school and been wounded in action while serving in the Middle East. Like so many other veterans, treatment for his injuries had resulted in an addiction to pain meds. Too proud to ask for help, Marcus had started a downward spiral that had led him to get mixed up with the wrong crowd.

Gary had sensed that given the right motivation, Marcus would be able to turn his life around. And he'd taken a chance on the young man, making arrangements for Marcus to be accepted into Maryland's Veterans' Court, where his jail time had been replaced by mandatory counseling for drug abuse and post-traumatic stress disorder, both of which had been problems for Marcus.

"How's your brother doing?" Gary asked. "Last I heard he'd graduated from the Veterans Court and had gotten a full scholarship to attend Towson."

If a hardened criminal could look like a proud parent, Trayvon succeeded. His face literally beamed a smile. "He done good. He graduated Towson last month with a degree in molecular biology…whatever the hell that is…and he just got a good job with some research firm out in California."

"That's great news." Gary meant it too. In his line of work success stories like that were a rarity.

His train of thought was interrupted when his cell phone vibrated against his hip indicating an incoming text. Pulling the phone from its holder, Gary glanced at the screen.

Apparently Mike had cued Zach to begin monitoring the communication device because the information on his cell phone screen was timely.

With a rap sheet a mile long, Trayvon Jackson had been in trouble his entire life, with crimes dating back to elementary school. Most of the early offenses were petty theft arrests, but by his teens he'd graduated to more serious crimes to support a drug habit and had served hard time for several of those offenses. The drug habit was apparently history since there was no indication Trayvon was going through withdrawal, but his life of crime had continued until yesterday.

But what caught Gary's attention and piqued his interest was the location of Jackson's last incarceration. ECI.

Rap sheets they'd already accumulated for Lewis, Walker and Pennell indicated those three men had recently served time at Eastern Correctional Institution on Maryland's eastern shore, too. And all of them had been paroled shortly before the time the robberies began.

Now they could add Jackson to the mix.

Although no solid evidence had been uncovered yet to prove the men knew each other in prison, their sentences had overlapped and they'd been in the same cell block.

Gary's gut told him the task force had uncovered the link between the Phantoms.

Pulling a chair over to Jackson's bed side and sitting down, he paused for several moments before shifting gears, trying not to wince when pain shot through his ribs.

He caught his breath and then met Jackson's gaze. "Let's talk about the Phantoms."

"What about 'em?"

Without breaking eye contact Gary answered him. "Rob Pennell was captured during the hold up yesterday and he's cooperating with us, providing information about the robberies."

In fact, Pennell had clammed up and was hiding behind his attorney, still refusing to answer any questions. But Gary used the bluff to raise a cloud of suspicion in Jackson about what his cohort was saying. Letting the seed of doubt fester, he continued. "Daniel Walker and Jamal Lewis were killed in the shootout outside the bank…"

"Danny is dead?" Jackson asked and from his expression the news had shaken him. Clearly he hadn't known.

While Gary felt compassion for the man's sense of loss, he wasn't losing any sleep over the dead men. "That can't be much of a surprise. Your group opened fire on federal agents as well as local and state police," he stated bluntly. "What did you guys expect? We'd just let you go?"

When Jackson didn't respond, Gary pushed for more information. "It's just a matter of time until we catch up with the two who got away. But you could help your case by telling us who we're looking for."

Jackson folded his free arm across his chest defensively. "I ain't no snitch."

"Well, Trayvon let me tell you something," Gary replied patiently. "Not being a snitch might be an admirable position in some circles, but in this situation it doesn't get you any points and might just be considered stupid."

He paused to let the man think about it for a moment, then continued. "You're facing multiple…let me repeat that…multiple…first degree murder charges…"

"I ain't never killed no one," Jackson protested. "Never shot no one neither. They was killed by others in the group."

Gary shrugged nonchalantly. "Maybe so, Trayvon. But in the eyes of the law, that doesn't matter. When someone dies during the commission of a crime, anyone involved in that crime is equally responsible for that death. You were present for the robberies, so according to the law you are just as guilty as the person who pulled the trigger."

"Well, Maryland ain't got no death penalty," Jackson countered arrogantly.

"You're right; they don't." Gary stared at Jackson for a heartbeat, pausing just long enough to lure him into a false sense of security. "But the federal government does and the banks you've been hitting are national banks, which means all…those…murders…fall under federal jurisdiction. So, make no mistake, you are facing lethal injection or the electric chair."

"I saved your sorry hide," Jackson shot back. "Don't that count for nothin'?"

"I wouldn't say that," Gary replied casually. "I certainly appreciate your moment of conscience and so does my wife. But saving my sorry hide means nothing to the courts when weighed against the cold blooded murder of four police officers who just happened to walk in on your robberies or the three bank guards who were murdered simply because they wore uniforms."

Jackson's smirk vanished along with the color draining from his face.

Taking advantage of his momentum, Gary pressed forward. "So I suggest you ask yourself this question. Will any jury find you a sympathetic character whose life deserves to be spared?"

Offering his own answer, Gary shook his head. "I don't think so. And that means your only chance to avoid the death penalty is to help us locate the others who got away."

When Jackson still didn't say anything Gary met the light hazel gaze of the prisoner. "Look, we know you were all incarcerated at Eastern Correctional Institution and it's only a matter of time before Pennell gives us the information or we figure out the identities of the others on our own. Once that happens, you lose any leverage for a deal. So, be smart and do yourself some good while you can."

"How do I know you won't double cross me and let 'em shove a needle in my arm anyway?"

"You don't," Gary answered bluntly. "All I can give you is my word that I will personally speak to the US Attorney who will be handling your case. I'll do everything I can to convince him to take capital punishment off the table for you. But only if you give me the names we need…now."

Jackson let loose a string of curses vitriolic enough to ignite a wet campfire. "Matt Sawyer is one of them. Him and Pennell were cellmates at ECI."

The task force had accounted for all but two of the bandits Gary had seen inside the bank. Sawyer was one of those two men…but which one? *Refrigerator Man*? Or the guy who'd told him to shut Patti Henderson up?

Gary thought about it for a moment. Jackson had seemed hostile toward *Refrigerator Man* during the robbery, as if he didn't like the man, but just now when he'd said Sawyer's name he'd been hesitant to give him up, as if the man was a friend.

His gut told him Sawyer was Patti Henderson's tormenter. Gary went with the hunch. "Sawyer is about six two, two hundred pounds?"

Jackson nodded. "Yeah. Why?"

Gary ignored the question, certain that Zach would initiate an immediate search for Sawyer. Instead, he pushed for more information.

"Who's the other one? The big guy who tried to kill me?"

Jackson muttered another curse. "He told us to call him *Tiny*. Don't know his real name and don't care. The dude's crazy."

"He's part of your group and you don't know his name?"

Jackson straightened belligerently. "The dude was a friend of Jamal's. Yesterday was the first time he went with us. Wouldda been his last, too. Idiot wouldn't follow orders. He was shootin' at customers instead of focusin' on the money. Hell, you saw what he tried to do to you."

Gary considered the lead silently. Knowing his would-be executioner was someone named *Tiny* would get them nowhere fast unless the man had a record and the alias showed up in that. Hopefully Zach was already running the name against that of recent parolees from ECI.

Another hunch formed in Gary's brain. He'd watched footage of all the Phantom's robberies so often he knew them by heart. And the men he'd seen yesterday, with the exception of *Refrigerator Man* were the same height and build of the men in the other robberies. But without the Phantoms' faces being visible on any of the bank robbery surveillance videos, the only way the task force could identify them was by their masks. He needed Jackson to tell him the masks were unique to each bandit.

For a moment Gary played with how to word his question for maximum effect. He decided to appeal to the man's ego.

"The disguises you wore were intimidating. Very effective. I don't know where you found them, but did you just have a pile of masks and grab whatever was on top when you left for a bank job?"

"No man…we each had our own individual mask." Jackson grinned as if the masks were something to admire. "Me and Danny were the leaders and those masks let us know who we was givin' orders to."

"You never swapped them with each other?" Gary asked, making his voice curious rather than interrogative and hoping Jackson didn't realize where the question was leading.

Jackson shook his head. "Nah…oh wait…this last time *Tiny* wore Rob's mask."

"Why was that?" Again Gary kept his voice curious and Jackson fell for it.

"Rob sprained his ankle bad two days ago and so Jamal got *Tiny* to go with us. He didn't have no mask so he wore Pennell's."

It took every ounce of Gary's control to keep his expression neutral, but Jackson's candor surprised him. Unwittingly the bandit had just given the task force a crucial piece of evidence. With the admission that the masks were unique, they could use Gary's descriptions and the men's rap sheet descriptions to positively place each of the Phantoms inside the banks that had been robbed.

On a roll, Gary continued to press. "What about outside help? How did you pick the branches you hit?

Jackson's brow suddenly knit, the frown quickly turning to a glare. "Man, you're squeezin' my balls. I think it's time for me to talk to my lawyer."

Gary stared at him hard for a moment and then nodded and pushed to his feet. "Fine, but just remember. You have one shot at saving your sorry hide from a lethal injection…and that shot is now. I walk out that door and the offer expires."

He waited for a reply and when none came, Gary nodded. "Okay…we're done," he said and turning, he strode to the door.

"Wait," Jackson called as Gary swung the door open.

Gary turned slowly and drilled Jackson with an icy glare. "The clock is ticking."

Jackson cursed again and glared back at Gary. "Hell, you'll figger it out anyway when you start diggin'. Might as well save my own ass."

"Smart move," Gary quipped as he walked back over to the bedside, but this time he remained standing. Impatient, he motioned with his hand for Jackson to start talking.

Begrudgingly, the prisoner obeyed. "Danny had connections at Armored Steel and the bank. His brother Richie drives for Armored and Ron Chandler is related to him somehow. Don't know exactly. But Ron was pissed off when he got demoted, so Danny, Richie, Ron and me came up with our plan to hit their banks. Ron's been tippin' us off to big cash deliveries at their branches. And Richie was able to confirm delivery times for us even if he wasn't doin' the drivin' that day."

Controlling any reaction to the case breaking news, Gary pushed again. "Who changed the delivery yesterday morning?"

The question tipped Gary's hand, acknowledging the task force knew the bandits' pattern. But they had enough information now they'd be able to figure out the rest of it on their own if Jackson clammed up.

But Trayvon was apparently in a talkative mood because he didn't even hesitate in his answer.

"We was already plannin' to hit that branch in the afternoon, but when you showed up, Ron recognized you and got nervous. He called Danny and wanted to call off the heist. But the haul was too big to give up, so me and Danny came up with another idea. Richie was drivin' the truck yesterday, so we just called him and he changed the delivery time to the morning. We figured it would throw off any plans you had for us. Guess we was wrong."

Gary found himself momentarily speechless. He'd wanted names, but he'd never expected to get them that easily. And even though the task force had suspected the robberies were inside jobs, they'd had nothing concrete. But now, with a few more warrants, they should be able to piece together the solid evidence they needed to close the case.

After several more questions to fill in some missing details, Gary wrapped things up. "Someone will be in shortly to book and fingerprint you. And, I'll talk to the US Attorney on your behalf."

His only reply was a hostile nod from Jackson. As Gary left the room, the man dropped his head back on his pillow, no doubt seeing his future going down the drain.

Stepping into the hallway, a grin spread across Gary's face. Mike greeted him with a high five, both of them momentarily at a loss for words in the wake of the windfall that had been delivered to them, gift wrapped by Trayvon Jackson.

But the afterglow faded quickly under the weight of the work still to be done. As the two men left the hospital, they were both on their phones firing off orders for the rest of the task force, assigning agents to pick up Ron Chandler and the armored car driver for questioning and to obtain search warrants for the confiscation of cell phones and computers for all the identified bandits and accomplices.

By the time they reached the parking lot, the only loose end was trying to identify *Refrigerator Man.* Parting company, they each headed to their own car.

Gary was several yards away from his SUV when he spotted something white tucked behind the driver side windshield wiper. Instantly on alert, his mind went back to the roses and a sinking feeling settled in his stomach.

Before he even freed the envelope, instinct told him he'd heard from his stalker again. With a blend of anger and curiosity, he slipped a typed note from an envelope, again marked with his name.

*I feel you are mine already. But be patient, my love, it will happen soon.*

Gary stared at the note for only a heartbeat and then looked around. He didn't give a damn if someone watching thought he was looking for them; he wasn't. He was looking for surveillance cameras that might have caught the culprit. And there it was. On a light pole two rows away.

Turning, he headed back into the hospital.

"Where's your security office?" he asked, flashing his credentials at the receptionist.

With a questioning glance the woman pointed to her right. "Follow the hallway and take your second left. The office is first door on the left."

He found the office easily and had his identification ready as he walked through the door. "I need to check footage for the past two hours for the security camera on pole twenty in the parking lot," he said when the guard on duty greeted him.

Ten minutes later, Gary blew out of breath of frustration and thanked the guard for his help. A kid. A damn kid…blond haired; about twelve and definitely someone he'd never seen in his life, had placed the envelope under his wiper.

None of his suspects had a child that age, which meant they'd most likely given the kid a couple bucks and told him what to do. In other words, Gary had nothing.

Cursing silently, he headed back to his car.

# Chapter Twelve

Two days later, Ron Chandler, Matt Sawyer and Richie Walker were in custody, but they were no closer to identifying the mysterious *Tiny*. No one except the deceased Jamal seemed to know the man's identity. If that wasn't frustrating enough, Gary was no closer to learning the identity of his stalker than when he'd started. And another love note had turned up on his car at the bank parking lot. But again, a kid he'd never seen before had placed it there.

Heaving a weary sigh, he pulled into his garage and cut the engine of his SUV. A few moments later when he walked into the kitchen, he found Kate standing at the island with her back to him, an envelope in her hand and a large box sitting on the counter in front of her.

"Hi sweetheart. What's in the box?" he asked, slipping his arms around her waist from behind and peering over her shoulder.

Kate glanced around at him and shrugged. "I'm not sure. It was sitting on the front doorstep. I don't remember ordering anything, but it's addressed to me. Did you order something?"

"No," he answered, trying to convince himself he was jumping at shadows when concern blossomed inside him. But his gaze dropped to the envelope she was opening and he noticed immediately the typed address. Just like the others, only this one had her name on it, not his.

A moment later, his anger turned to shock. Not even the flowers and notes he'd already received could have prepared him for the graphic photo that fell onto the counter when Kate pulled out another typed message.

He heard her gasp and dragged his eyes from the photo long enough to scan the note.

*It's time for you to go away. As you can see; he's mine.*

Cleverly worded, the typed note was designed to infer the woman performing the explicit sexual act in the photo was performing it on him.

Anger, frustration, concern and embarrassment whirled through Gary.

Fresh air. He needed fresh air. Turning, he shoved through the back door. He walked out on the deck and sucked in several deep breaths to clear his head. But all he succeeded in doing was sending a shaft of stabbing pain through his ribcage.

Cursing, he leaned his forearms on the railing and stared out across their yard.

He prided himself on his ability to bring criminals to justice; his record of cleared cases with the Bureau was far above average and included several cold cases that had previously been unsolved by others.

So why couldn't he solve this one? Why couldn't he find the person behind these sick messages? The person now trying to destroy his marriage.

He heard the door open and felt Kate's presence behind him, but when she didn't say anything, a feeling of dread settled over him.

Law enforcement played havoc with relationships, but he and Kate had always had something special. An unshakable relationship built on love, respect, trust and the depth of their intertwined past.

They'd been there for each other through good times and bad. And they'd weathered some incredibly long separations during their marriage, like the nearly five months he'd been at the FBI Academy at Quantico, Virginia while she'd been finishing up her medical residency back in Dallas, Texas.

Katie meant more to him than anyone or anything in the world. He tried hard to shield her from the ugliness of his work and made an effort not to bring his job home. But that photo and note were more than even he could digest and he could only imagine what she must be thinking.

"Katie, I…I don't…" he stammered, at a loss for words.

"You don't honestly believe that I think that's a photo of you, do you?"

Her quietly spoken question was the last thing he'd expected to hear and he spun around searching her face for any hint of doubt. The breath he'd been holding ever since he'd seen the photo, rushed from his lungs in a gush of relief when he saw nothing but trust in her eyes.

"I'm so sorry you had to see something like that," he uttered, pulling her into his arms and holding her tightly. "But you don't know how badly I needed you to believe in me."

"Darling, I don't know what that photo is all about," she murmured against his chest. "But I knew the moment I looked, that the man wasn't you."

As elated as he was, he notched a finger under her chin and tipped her head up to see her face. "Don't get me wrong, I'm glad you have faith in me," he said, confusion knitting his brow. "But from the camera angle there's no way to identify the people in that photo. How could you be so certain?"

Kate glanced up at him in all seriousness. "First of all, Mr. Modesty, I can't imagine you ever allowing a camera anywhere near you in that kind of situation."

Gary chuckled softly. She had a good point about the camera. With scars from childhood beatings covering his torso and limbs, he hated having his picture taken and Kate knew it. But he knew by the grin suddenly curving her lips and the twinkle in her eyes that she had more to say.

"And after all these years, darling, I know exactly what you look like naked." She wiggled her brows suggestively. "And to put it delicately, that man can't hold a candle to you."

He bellowed a laugh, then groaned in pain. But still grinning, lowered his head to drop a kiss on her lips. "God, I love you!"

"And I love you," she murmured, pulling him back down for another kiss. But when it ended, she gazed up at him again. "Now would you mind telling me what you've been keeping from me? What's that picture all about?"

Gary heaved a resigned sigh. "A couple days ago roses were delivered to me at the office along with an unsigned note indicating the person thought we were having some kind of a relationship. The same person has put notes under my windshield wiper the past two days, once while I was parked at the hospital in Hagerstown and the other when I was inside the bank arresting Ron Chandler."

He and Kate didn't argue often, but watching her expression darkening, Gary knew he was in trouble. His hunch was confirmed when she shoved against his chest, freeing herself from his embrace.

"You've had a stalker for three days and it never crossed your mind to tell me about it? Or that it was something I should know? That I had a right to know?" she asked with a healthy dose of incredulity in her voice. "What were you thinking?"

Clearly she thought he hadn't been thinking. And when she phrased her questions like that he wasn't so sure he had been either.

"Sweetheart..."

"Don't sweetheart me; just answer me. Why didn't you tell me?"

Gary rammed fingers through his hair and shook his head. Yup...she was definitely ticked off. And in truth, he couldn't blame her.

"Kate, you're right. I should have told you." He shrugged slightly. "But I thought I could find the person responsible and stop her attention before it escalated to anything that would affect you or our marriage. And I didn't want to upset you. Clearly I failed on both counts. But I swear to you, I'm not involved with anyone. Whoever is behind these incidents is deluded thinking there's something personal between us."

Some of her anger faded and the rigid set of her shoulders eased. "Gary, I know that. I trust you. And I also know you didn't tell me because you were trying to shield me. But I'm not a fragile doll. This wasn't just one of the ugly parts of your job; it's someone trying to take you away from me and that makes it my concern, too."

Gary captured her shoulders, forcing her to look at him. "First of all, I love you and no one is ever going to change that…or take me away from you. And second, I know you aren't a fragile doll. You're an incredibly sexy, smart woman whom I adore." Unable to stop himself, he caressed her cheek. "I was wrong, sweetheart; I should have told you. I'm sorry."

For a moment, Kate didn't say anything and Gary searched his brain for something else to say to make things right. But then she glanced toward the kitchen.

"What do you suppose is inside the box?" she asked.

The box. He'd forgotten all about it the instant the photograph had hit the counter. "I don't know, but I can almost guarantee it's not going to be something we like."

"Let's go look." Kate gently nudged him toward the door and he held it open to let her enter first. "The sooner we find out what's inside, the sooner we can get rid of it," she said over her shoulder. "And then I want to know how you plan to stop this idiot."

Good question. Gary wished he knew the answer.

He also wished he knew how the hell the person had learned where they lived. For more than twenty years he and Katie had lived in McLean, Virginia, but last fall, they'd lost their home and everything in it to an explosion. After that deliberate and revengeful attempt by the drug cartel to kill Kate, she'd agreed to go into temporary hiding for several months. Her relocation had only ended when the men responsible for the contract on their lives were dead.

Out of continued concerns for their safety though, the Bureau had transferred the entire drug task force to other field offices and in January, Gary had joined the Baltimore office. But he and Katie had been living in a furnished apartment for several months while getting familiar with the area and looking for a house. They'd only moved into the new home three weeks ago.

So how had his stalker found their address? It wasn't something he or the Bureau revealed to anyone.

That left the disturbing probability the stalker had followed him or put a tracking device on his car. How else would they have known he was at the hospital or bank? And how else would they have found his home? A tracking device seemed a little drastic for a deluded stalker, but he'd have to have his car scanned to make sure. But if they'd tailed him, they'd been damn good at it because he hadn't spotted them and he'd been looking.

As a federal agent, he'd made his share of enemies over the years and he'd developed certain routines to ensure his personal safety and that of his family. One of those routines was to check and make sure he wasn't being followed. But somehow, somewhere his stalker had managed to circumvent his caution and that disturbed him greatly.

Lost in thought, he looked up to see Kate using a pair of scissors to slice open the top of the box.

"Something just moved inside this thing," she exclaimed staring down at it warily.

Alarm bells went off in Gary's brain immediately, escalating when he noticed a series of tiny pin holes perforating the sides. A heartbeat later he heard a bone-chilling noise, a hiss that sounded like a growling dog.

Anger bordering on fury swept through him along with a wave of fear.

"Don't open that," he ordered, slamming his hand on top of the box and accidently catching her fingers beneath the heel of his hand.

"Ow!" Kate snapped, yanking her hand free and scowling at him. "What's wrong with you?"

It wasn't what was wrong with him; it was what was inside the box.

"Sorry about that. But trust me; you don't want to open that. It's a snake."

Kate hated snakes as much as he hated small closed in spaces. He knew this because they'd grown up in rural Texas where slithering reptiles were an unavoidable fact of life and he'd witnessed her reaction to them more times than he could count. It didn't matter to her if they were a poisonous rattler or a harmless garter snake. She freaked out regardless.

And what was inside that box was more deadly than any rattler.

He'd heard that same hissing growl only once before in his life and it had been during the arrest of a group illegally smuggling exotic animals into the country. Among the contraband the FBI and Customs had confiscated was one of the most deadly snakes in the world and it had escaped its crate. Fortunately no one had been bitten, but Gary would never forget the angry noise that thing made while experts were trying to corral it.

"I'm pretty sure it's a king cobra," he added, keeping his hand firmly planted on the lid while praying the reptile couldn't bite through the cardboard.

Kate's face contorted with a look of horror and a shudder raced through her, vibrating her body from head to toe. "A cobra!"

Gary had no idea how she'd managed to get the box into the house without realizing there was a snake inside — maybe it had been asleep — but it was definitely awake now and it was royally ticked off.

Nodding, he tilted his head to motion her away. "Get me the roll of packing tape in the pantry."

A few moments later he had the package secured again, but it was over an hour before Kate stopped shaking and that was only after agents from US Customs arrived to remove the snake from the house.

For flowers, notes and photos he might have settled for giving his stalker a harsh warning amounting to little more than a slap on the wrist. But considering the venom in a single bite from a king cobra could kill about twenty people, there was no question about the stalker's intent. With the same premeditation as if there'd been a ticking bomb in that box, someone had tried to kill Kate. And when Gary found the woman, he'd intended to arrest her for first-degree attempted murder.

But first he had to make sure Kate was okay.

He found her in the den, nervously fidgeting with a remote control she'd plucked from the end table between their recliners. That concerned him almost as much as the cobra.

Kate never fidgeted; she was a surgeon for God's sake. She had the steadiest hands of anyone he knew. And she hated remote controls. In fact, nothing was a bigger threat to their happy home and marriage than those little devices.

They were a problem because he loved electronics and had created a sophisticated stereo surround sound system throughout the house, linking every conceivable device…laptops, televisions, DVD player — if it was possible to connect; he'd linked it…to the system. To him it was the coolest thing in the world to be able to walk from one room to another and not miss a second of a football or hockey game he was watching or to hear music in every room of the house. He loved it.

Kate on the other hand hated it, mainly because she'd never mastered all the clickers for the various pieces of equipment. She'd once threatened to divorce him if he brought one more remote into the house.

She'd been joking of course…or at least he hoped she had…but on the chance she hadn't, he'd whittled the number of remotes down to a bare minimum.

Still, she invariably picked up the wrong one and when it wouldn't turn on the television or mute the sound…or do whatever she was trying to do…he could feel her displeasure before she said a word.

She had that look about her now.

Scrambling to defuse the situation, he walked over to her, plucked the remote from her hand and gave her a quick kiss. "Let's go out for dinner and then go miniature golfing."

The diversion worked and her scowl turned to a smile just before she laughed aloud. "Are you feeling okay?" she asked, standing up and caressing his cheeks and then putting a hand on his forehead checking for fever.

"I feel fine," he answered, knowing full well why she asked, but playing along. "Why?"

She scoffed another laugh. "You're really challenging me to a game of miniature golf?"

"Sure…why not. It'll be fun."

Grinning, she patted his cheek gently. "You're on, darling and no backing out after we eat."

Gary had no delusions about the outcome of the evening. He was going to lose; there was no question about it. Give him a football to throw or a baseball to hit and he'd match his skills with the best of them. And on the shooting range his skill was undeniable. But when it came to golf, he was hopeless. His drive and fairway shots were good, but once he got a putter in his hands, he couldn't hit that damn tiny hole if his life depended on it.

On the other hand, it usually took Kate an extra shot to reach the green, but once she did, she nailed her putts with such surgical skill he'd once accused her of having been a professional golfer in a previous life.

Since miniature golf was pretty much all about putting, he had no doubt he was in for another dose of defeat. But if the game erased the worry line between his dear wife's brows it would be worth every minute of the humbling experience. And Gary figured he could always blame his score on sore ribs.

"Me, back out? No way. I'm feeling lucky," he replied with feigned cockiness.

Kate dissolved in laughter.

Some men might have taken exception to their wife laughing at them, but not him. In fact, seeing her reaction made him laugh too. And still chuckling, he draped an arm around her shoulder and turned her toward the door.

"Come on, ace; let's go."

# Chapter Thirteen

Fresh on the heels of his latest golfing humiliation, Gary walked into his office the next morning determined to learn who'd sent the cobra to Kate. But within moments his plans were derailed when reports came in that the downtown post office had been leveled by an explosion of suspicious origin.

Gary's Criminal Investigation Division had responded to the site immediately, but late afternoon when a previously unknown terrorist group claimed responsibility for the blast, he turned the investigation over to the Bureau's Joint Terrorism Task Force. By the time he arrived home, Gary was looking forward to spending a quiet weekend relaxing.

"Hi honey, I'm home. How was your day?" he called as he opened the door from the garage and entered their kitchen.

The lack of any aroma wafting from the oven and nothing on the stove immediately caught his attention. He chuckled at Katie's not-so-subtle hint she wanted to go out to dinner again.

She worked long hours just as he did and many were the nights when they were both too tired or just didn't feel like making dinner and having to clean up the mess afterwards. If a dinner out was what she needed or wanted, dinner out it would be.

"Where do you want to go for dinner?"

Waiting for her to either appear or call back to him, he shuffled through the small stack of mail on the island, grateful to see there was nothing from his stalker. Tossing the junk mail into their recycle bin, he glanced up and looked around for Kate wondering why she hadn't answered.

From his vantage point at the kitchen island, he could see into the living and dining rooms. He didn't see her anywhere, but he'd learned early in their relationship that Kate hated being startled or scared, so he always yelled a greeting when he came into the house so she knew he was there. He tried again.

"Katie, I'm home!" he hollered louder, heading to his home office with his briefcase and two utility bills in hand. "Where are you?"

She had to be here; her car was in the garage and her pocketbook was sitting on the kitchen counter right by the door where she always dropped it.

Detouring away from his office, Gary headed back the hallway to their master bedroom, thinking maybe she was in the shower and didn't hear him.

The room was empty.

A wave of concern built inside him. Where the hell was she?

"Kate! Where are you?" he called again, giving into the urgency he felt. Quickly checking the rest of the house and finding no trace of her, he went out the back door to search the yard. Still no sight of her.

Mentally, he ruled out the neighbors. Between their crazy work schedules and getting settled, they hadn't had time to do more than wave to their new neighbors, let alone get to know any of them. And in his line of work, he took a cautious approach to making new friends, preferring to get a feel for people before getting too chummy. Kate had adopted that approach too, so it was highly unlikely she was visiting anyone on the block.

But it disturbed him that he couldn't find any sign of where she'd gone.

Pulling his cell phone from its waist clip, he pressed Kate's speed dial, but it went directly to her voice mail. Trying to contain his concern, he left a message.

"Hi honey. It's me. Just checking to make sure you're okay and when you'll be home. Call me."

Slipping the phone back into its holder, he scratched the nape of his neck where his internal radar had suddenly kicked to life with an annoying crawling sensation.

It wasn't like Katie to disappear like this.

The thought stopped him dead in his tracks and he realized the reason for the radar. His stalker! Hell, the person had sent Kate a cobra. Anyone twisted enough to do that was capable of just about anything.

Was it possible the lunatic had come after her?

The idea terrified him. Frantic, he hollered her name again while sprinting from room to room, this time checking the attic and basement as well as closets and the trunk of her car. But the house was just as empty this time as it had been before.

He stopped in the front entry trying to collect his thoughts and noticed something he'd missed before.

The front door was unlocked.

Before they'd moved into the house three weeks ago he'd had a security system installed and he'd been pestering Kate ever since to set it when she was home alone. But she rarely did, so he hadn't given thought to the alarm being off when he'd first come inside.

But now, with the front door unlocked, the wave of concern inside him escalated to full-fledged worry. She came into the house through the door from the garage to the kitchen. The only reason that front door would be unlocked is if she'd opened it. And she was nowhere to be found.

Grasping at straws, he grabbed his cell again and punched in Zach's speed dial. In addition to loving their new home, one of the reasons he and Kate had chosen it was because their son and daughter-in-law lived only two blocks away.

Maybe Kate had walked over to their home for some reason and hadn't left a note figuring she'd be home before Gary would miss her. But that didn't explain the unlocked door.

"Hi Dad. What's up?" Zach greeted cheerfully.

"Is your mother over there?"

"No."

"Do you know where she is?" Gary asked, pacing back and forth in the front entry, trying to stay calm.

"No, why? Isn't she home?"

A curse rattled silently through Gary's head. "No. Is Cassie there?"

"Yeah."

"Ask her if she knows where your mother is?"

"Dad…what's going on?"

Zach knew about the stalker and the concern apparent in his voice indicated he'd begun to worry, but Gary was beyond explaining; he wanted answers.

"Just ask her!" he demanded.

While he waited impatiently for Zach to come back on the line, Gary checked his text messages to make sure he hadn't missed one from Kate, but he knew before looking that he hadn't. Her texts and calls had a unique vibration and tone so he'd recognize them. He hadn't heard or felt anything from her since he'd gotten a text telling him she'd just gotten home from work and wondered when he'd be home.

That had been at five thirty, over an hour ago. Surely if she'd decided to go somewhere with a friend or been called back to the hospital after sending the message, she would have texted or called him with an update. And she would have locked the door.

"Dad, Cassie talked to Mom around lunchtime today to invite you two over for a barbeque tomorrow night, but she hasn't seen or heard from her since. What's going on?"

All the air seemed to rush from Gary's lungs. He'd been hanging onto the hope Kate's disappearance was all some innocent mix-up in communication, but Zach had effectively severed that hope. And every sinister possibility filled the gap in his mind.

He blew out a deep breath to steady his voice before answering. "I got home a few minutes ago. Your mother's car is in the garage and her purse is in the kitchen, but she's nowhere to be found and the front door is unlocked."

As he started to take another step his gaze landed on the rug and he froze, cursing aloud.

"What the hell is going on?"

Zach's question caught him as he was dropping to his knees. And before answering, Gary touched the spot he'd seen. It was still damp so it wasn't that old.

Another curse flew from his mouth, but the investigator in him took charge.

"Zach…I just spotted blood on the rug by the front door. I want a crime scene team here pronto and then see if you can trace her cell phone using the GPS."

Normally Gary wouldn't jump to such a rush decision, but while he'd searched the house, he'd not only been looking for Kate, he'd been searching for clues as to where she could be. If there'd been blood in the bathroom or kitchen, he would have seen it. And the carpets throughout the house were light colored; blood would have stood out immediately. But the only place he could see any was right by the front door.

He'd almost missed the stain because it was on a multi-colored braided rug covering the hardwood floor entry. And if Kate had been injured badly enough she needed an ambulance, there would have been some evidence an emergency crew had been in the house. There was none.

"I'll take care of everything, Dad. Cassie and I will be there as soon as I run the trace on Mom's phone. Try to stay calm."

Yeah…like that was going to happen. He was scared to death thinking of what had happened to Kate, of where she might be. But Gary had no doubt who was behind her disappearance.

His stalker. And dammit, he still didn't know who she was. But he damn well knew where she lived and the first chance he got, he was going to Hagerstown. And he'd interrogate every person in the town until he found Kate and had the demented woman who'd dared to hurt her in handcuffs.

Unfortunately, he couldn't go anywhere until he was cleared by the detectives who'd arrived minutes before the crime scene team descended on the house.

Two hours later, Gary walked out of his home office, hauled in a deep breath, blew it out in a gush, and shook his head. He was used to being the one asking the questions, not answering them. But that's exactly what he'd been doing for the past hour. His head was spinning.

With his law enforcement background, logically he knew when someone disappeared, the spouse was always the first person suspected. But damn, it was unnerving being on the receiving end of that suspicion.

Thankfully the hospital had verified Kate had been at work until a little after four o'clock and Gary had the most impeccably airtight alibi possible. Namely scores of FBI agents and half the Baltimore police department. But none of that had stopped the two detectives who'd been grilling him for over an hour.

They were just doing things by the book, though, and since the victim was his wife, he was glad for their thoroughness. He didn't want anyone leaving any stones unturned. Still, he was glad to be cleared.

As soon as he reached the living room, he waved Zach aside.

"What did you find with the phone trace?" he asked anxiously.

"Mom's phone is pinging off a tower near Hagerstown, but that's the best I can give you right now."

Unless or until Kate or someone else used her phone, Gary knew it would be impossible to get a more accurate reading on her location. But at least they knew she was headed for Hagerstown. He wished that gave him a sense of relief, but it didn't. The only thing it did was confirm his suspicion that Katie had been kidnapped by his stalker.

"Have they found anything?" he asked, turning to watch the investigators spraying Luminol on the rug to search for hidden traces of blood.

Zach nodded. "They lifted a set of prints from the table in the entry way. I told them we wanted them processed immediately and to let me know what they find."

With the same air-tight alibi Gary had, Zach had already been cleared by the detectives. A good thing too, since Gary intended to head to Hagerstown and needed Zach to stay behind and oversee the activity at the house.

"Thanks. I'm out of here," Gary said. "Keep me posted."

"Consider it done, Dad." Zach heaved a worried sigh and hugged him. "We'll find her. I know we will."

Swiping away moisture gathering in his eyes, Gary nodded. "I'll talk to you later," he said, grabbing his keys and the overnight bag he'd already packed and heading directly to the garage. But as he backed his car out of the bay, an SUV swung into his driveway, blocking him in.

Cursing, Gary swung open his car door and got out, ready to peel a layer of hide off the person detaining him. Two hours had already elapsed and he was in a hurry.

To his surprise, he came face to face with Mike Devlin and Lucas Shaw.

Before he had a chance to process why they were there, movement caught his attention and he noticed Jim Barrett sprinting around the corner from the back of the house.

For a moment Gary was too stunned to say anything, but then he found his voice. "What the hell are you guys doing here?"

"We were still at the office finishing up some paperwork when Zach's call came in requesting a crime scene team. When we found out what happened, we high-tailed it over here," Jim explained.

"You didn't think we'd let you tackle this by yourself did you, Thorny?" Lucas added.

Devlin nodded. "No one messes with Kate and gets away with it. She's family. When we arrived, detectives were busy questioning you and Zach, so we decided to talk to your neighbors."

"The lady over there," Lucas said pointing to his left. "Saw a dark blue van over here around five-thirty. Unfortunately, she didn't pay much attention to make and model and didn't get the plate number. None of the other neighbors saw anything."

Not that it brought Gary any pleasure to be right, but it helped to know for sure that a stranger had been at their home. And with a stalker looming around them the past week, he was more certain than ever that person was responsible for Kate's disappearance.

"We checked Maryland DMV for the registrations for all our suspects and none of them own a van of any color," Jim added. "So we're probably dealing with a rental."

Damn! A rental wasn't much of a lead in finding Kate.

Mike planted his hands on his hips. "Thorny, we know you. You aren't going to sit back and wait for an answer, so, whatever you have planned, we're in on it."

When Jim and Lucas nodded agreement, a lump of emotion clogged Gary's throat and he had to swallow a few times before it dislodged.

"I don't know what to say." And it was true.

Ever since he'd walked into the house and realized Kate was missing, his sole focus had been on finding her. He'd never given thought to asking for help from other agents, especially since he had no proof this whole thing wasn't some colossal error on his part, that Kate and he weren't just experiencing a breakdown in communication of some sort.

But the blood on the rug told him that wasn't the case and the willingness of his friends to help humbled him.

"I was planning to drive over to Hagerstown and get a hotel. And I'm not coming back until I either find Kate or have substantial evidence she's not there," he said.

"Count us in, Thorny," Mike said.

Lucas nodded. "Yes, we're in this together…to the finish."

Jim held out his hand. "But you aren't in any condition to be driving anywhere, so give me your keys. I'll drive you wherever you want to go. Mike and Lucas can follow and we'll have two cars to conduct the search."

Regaining his composure, a tight smile tugged at Gary's mouth. Jimmy was right; he wasn't in any condition to drive. He handed Barrett his keys. "Okay, then…let's go find Katie."

# Chapter Fourteen

Kate struggled against bindings on her wrists and ankles, trying to loosen them any way she could. But it was useless. They were too tight.

From the motion and noise she could hear, she was inside a moving vehicle, but the blindfold covering her eyes kept her from seeing anything. And her kidnapper hadn't said a word to her.

In fact she'd never seen the person and had no idea if it was a man or woman. All she knew was the doorbell had rung and when she hadn't seen anyone, she'd opened the door. She'd been hit by something that had sent excruciating pain through her body rendering her powerless. Then everything had gone black.

She wasn't sure how long she'd been unconscious but other than a headache, she didn't think she had any lasting damage from whatever had happened.

Motion beneath her indicated the vehicle had slowed and suddenly it came to a halt, rocking her unsteadily. A moment later a door slid open and she felt warm fresh air surround her. From the noise of the door, she thought she was probably in a van. It was the only vehicle she could think of that had a sliding door.

"You're awake. Good," said the strangest voice she'd ever heard. It sounded unearthly and definitely not human. Which was impossible so it had to be a machine disguising the voice.

But why? Was this someone she knew?

While she was still trying to decide the answer, hands grabbed her ankles and yanked her forward, sliding her along a surface that scraped uncomfortably against her back. When something touched her chin, Kate jerked away, startled and more than a little afraid.

Something hard slammed into her cheek. Not that she'd ever been hit by one, but it felt like a two by four.

Pain radiated through Kate's face and tears sprang to her eyes, but she refused to give the person the satisfaction of knowing they'd hurt her. While she tried to unscramble her brain from the impact, she heard a noise that sounded strangely like typing. After a pause, the demonic voice spoke again.

"Hold still, bitch. Scream and you are dead."

With her head swimming from the blow, she was unprepared for the piece of tape covering her mouth being ripped away, feeling like it took several layers of skin with it. But again, Kate bit back a whimper.

She heard the typing noise again just before a hand grabbed her arm roughly, yanking her upright. "Drink this!"

It was a demand not a request.

Terror threatened to overwhelm her, but Kate reached deep inside for a healthy dose of anger and used it to control any quiver in her voice. "What is it?" she asked.

The hard object delivered another brain jarring blow, this one to the other cheekbone. And almost immediately the odd typing sound preceded another unearthly order.

"Drink it."

From all the tapping of keys she heard, Kate deduced the person was entering commands into an electronic device that put voice to whatever was typed. Whatever the machine was, it had the most fiendish voice she'd ever heard.

Drawing on more of that anger still roiling inside her, Kate wasn't about to comply meekly. "No, not until you tell me what it is."

"Drink it or I will kill Gary," the voice stated with demonic calm.

Gary? Dear Lord, was he in the van with her? When had they kidnapped him? And why hadn't she known he was there? He hadn't made a sound. Was he hurt? Unconscious?

"Drink it or he dies now."

The electronic command was emphasized by an ominous sound. Kate might not be the weapons expert in her household, but she knew the sound of the slide on a gun being racked when she heard it.

"No! Don't!" she cried, unable to hide the panic in her voice. "I'll drink it. I'll do whatever you want, just please don't hurt Gary."

No response came, but a cold glass brushed her lips and liquid splashed against the seam. Against her better judgment Kate opened her lips and cold liquid filled her mouth. Fully expecting something rank to assail her taste buds, she was surprised to recognize the flavor of a Coke.

Common sense told her to spit it out, but she was terrified if she did, the person would shoot Gary. Still, instead of swallowing, she held the sugary liquid in her mouth, hoping she could get rid of it when she was alone again.

"Swallow it or he dies," ordered the fiendish voice.

The menacing warning erased any lingering thoughts Kate had of defying the order. Reluctantly, she swallowed, trying not to think about what drug or poison she'd just ingested.

"Gary?" she called out, praying he'd answer her.

An object rammed into her face again, snapping her head back and nearly knocking her over. More key tapping signaled she was about to get another command.

"Forget him and drink it. All of it," the voice demanded when she made no effort to drink more.

Resigned to the fact she had no choice, Kate obeyed. It took her several more swallows to finish the drink, but even before it was gone, she began to feel light headed and numb. And the last thing she remembered before her mind went blank was being shoved back inside and her prison doors slamming closed.

**BY THE** time the agents reached their first destination, the summer sun was sinking, painting the sky over Hagerstown in gorgeous shades of pinks and blues. But the beauty of the sunset was lost on Gary. He was too worried about Kate.

Finding two hotel rooms late on a Friday night had proven to be a challenge, but they'd finally found a place with vacancies for the weekend at a rate that didn't require a second mortgage on their homes. After checking in, Gary had initially suggested that they divide up the list of suspects so they could go through it quicker, but Mike suggested trading speed for strategy, countering that if Gary's stalker was in fact one of the women, having him present during the questioning might trip her up.

Gary liked the idea, figuring it just might work. He also liked the idea of the other agents being there to stop him from wringing his stalker's scrawny neck when he found her. He was wound so tightly, he didn't trust that he'd be able to stop himself, which was the main reason Mike had insisted on driving to the interview. Gary suspected Dev was afraid that in the state he was in, he'd wrap the car around a tree and kill them all. So they'd left his SUV in the hotel parking lot and climbed into Mike's. Using his seniority and his size, Gary had claimed dibs on the front passenger seat, though. No sense in being a nervous wreck and uncomfortable.

Waiting impatiently for someone to answer the door, Gary took a deep steadying breath. A click signaled the front door being unlocked, a moment before it swung open.

And every word in Gary's head abandoned him. The same affliction apparently hit the other men, too, because none of them uttered a word.

They were all too busy staring, slack-jawed.

Seriously, who answered their door wearing nothing but a skimpy bath towel?

"Agent Thornton, what a pleasant surprise," Emma Carpenter exclaimed with a bright smile.

Blinking his eyes back into their sockets, Gary managed to find his tongue and flipped open his credentials. "Hello, Ms. Carpenter. I believe you already know Special Agents Devlin, Barrett and Shaw."

She'd met them in the bank lobby as Kate was getting ready to take him to the hospital and Gary was certain she remembered them.

If he'd expected her to be embarrassed by her lack of clothing or intimidated by the presence of four federal agents on her doorstep, he'd have been sorely disappointed. But true to her character, she hadn't batted an eyelash in surprise.

After a lustful appraisal of all four of them, her gaze settled on Gary. "This has to be my wildest fantasy. Four gorgeous hunks on my doorstep." She wiggled her brows suggestively and ran a finger down Gary's chest. "You can frisk me if you want…but only if I can frisk you too." she giggled as if she'd just made the funniest joke in the world.

It took every ounce of Gary's self-control not to grab her hand and fling it away from him. He'd met a lot of flakes during his career and this one ranked near the top of his list. Even on a good day he'd be hard-pressed to tolerate her behavior, but with Kate missing he wasn't in any mood for it. And if she made one more suggestive comment, he wouldn't be responsible for his actions.

Standing his ground, Gary glared at her until she removed her hand from his chest, then dropping all traces of civility, he spoke.

"This isn't a social call; we're here on official business. And before we begin, I have to advise you that you have the right to remain silent…"

Miranda wasn't necessary at this point in their investigation, but he gave it for effect and it worked. As he recited the warning, Emma's gleeful expression melted to confusion. As far as Gary was concerned, it was a welcome change and about damn time she got serious.

When she'd acknowledged her rights, he shifted his gaze past her to look into her apartment. "May we come in?"

She shot a quick glanced behind her and shrugged. "I suppose so," she replied, stepping back to let them enter. In the living room, she motioned for them to sit down, but all four men remained standing.

"Perhaps you'd like to go put on something more appropriate," Gary said in a tone that made it more an order than a suggestion.

"Okay," she answered, her voice finally showing some signs of concern.

The moment she was gone, the agents looked at each other and shook their heads. The receptionist had been the butt of several task force jokes ever since they'd watched video of her attempting to entice Gary into her bed prior to the robbery. This time it was Jim who voiced what they were all thinking.

"She's a piece of work," he said quietly, before following her down the hallway to make sure she didn't try to bolt.

On the fourth floor of the building, there were only two ways out of Emma's apartment. Through the front door or off the balcony. But just to cover all bases, Mike walked over to the sliding balcony door to make sure she didn't try to go out a window while Lucas discreetly wandered the apartment searching for any signs of Kate.

For his part, Gary tried to control his temper and the acid churning in his gut.

When Emma returned a few minutes later, she'd traded the towel for a pair of jeans. But she'd either been in a hurry to get back to them or she was still holding out hope for some action because she wasn't wearing a bra beneath a skin-tight tee shirt that left nothing to the imagination.

Thirty minutes later, as Gary slid into the passenger seat of Mike's Bureau-issued SUV, he heaved a deep sigh. Nothing. They'd learned nothing from her. Either she was the coolest liar ever born or she wasn't his stalker. And they'd uncovered absolutely nothing to indicate her involvement in Kate's disappearance.

Frustrated and worried beyond belief, Gary waited anxiously for them to reach their next stop.

When they arrived, lights still glowed from inside the home. But even if the place had been completely dark inside, Gary would have rung the doorbell. They were investigating a kidnapping, not conducting a routine interview, and every second counted. He didn't give a damn that it was nearly eleven at night.

"Agent Thornton! This is a pleasant surprise," Brittany Franks greeted as she opened the door to them. "Tyler's going to be so upset that he missed you. He's done nothing but talk about you ever since the robbery. But Adam picked him up from school and they're spending the weekend together. Tyler won't be back until Sunday afternoon."

Under other circumstances, Gary would enjoy seeing Tyler again, but he wasn't looking forward to interviewing the mother of a boy he knew idolized him. No matter how it ended, it was likely to sour Tyler on FBI agents in general and Gary specifically. And Gary truly liked the child; he hated to disillusion him, so he was just as glad the boy wasn't home.

"Ms. Franks, I'm not here to see Tyler." Gary directed her attention to the other agents. "I believe you met Special Agents Devlin, Barrett and Shaw the day of the robbery."

"Yes…it's nice to see you again. What can I do for all of you?"

Gary heard the door behind them open and turned to see one of her neighbors, a thirty-something body-builder peering at them from his doorway.

"Is everything okay, Brit?" the young man called, obviously concerned by the presence of four suited men at her door at that late hour.

She gave him a friendly smile. "Everything is fine, Ted. Thanks for checking."

As soon as he shut his door, she motioned them inside her apartment. "Please, come in…and have a seat. Can I get anyone anything to drink? It would just take a minute to brew some coffee."

"No thank you," Gary replied, lowering his tall frame into an easy chair, while Mike and Jim took chairs flanking her television set. Confusion knitting her brow, Brittany sat down on the sofa beside Lucas, and immediately leaned forward, lacing her fingers together.

Her gaze bounced between the four of them before settling on Gary. "What's this about, Agent Thornton?"

"Brittany, we're here on official business. And before we go any further, I have to advise you of your Miranda rights." he answered, again watching carefully for any hint of guilt.

A look of worry replaced her confusion, but her steady gaze looked him right in the eyes.

"Why did you read me my rights?" she asked the moment she'd acknowledged understanding them. "Has something happened? Am I in some kind of trouble?"

All very reasonable questions. And asked without a trace of guilt.

Gary couldn't help noticing the profound contrast between her demeanor and Emma Carpenter's. And mentally he crossed Brittany off his list of suspects before ever asking her a question. Still, he had to eliminate her with more than a hunch and proceeded to do just that.

With a few well-chosen questions he quickly established she had what appeared to be a solid alibi for her whereabouts that afternoon. She'd been at work until five; something the agents would easily be able to confirm by a quick call to the law office. And after picking up Nikki from daycare, the two of them had stopped at the grocery store and then gone to a fast food restaurant for dinner before coming home. The time stamped on the dated receipts from both the grocery store and restaurant, effectively eliminated her as a suspect.

She couldn't possibly be in two places at the same time and she'd clearly been in a Hagerstown grocery store when Kate was being kidnapped an hour away.

As much as Gary hadn't wanted Brittany to be involved, clearing her didn't get him any closer to finding Katie. And blowing out a breath of frustration, he sagged back into the chair, trying to determine their next step.

"Why did you want to know where I was?" she asked.

Again, there wasn't an ounce of guilt or nervousness about her question, just pure confusion.

Lucas shot a look over at him and Gary gave him silent permission to explain. "Agent Thornton's wife was kidnapped this afternoon."

Brittany gasped in horror before he even finished, her eyes matching her shocked reaction and her gaze flew to Gary.

"Oh my God! I'm so sorry," she exclaimed.

Gary didn't want her sympathy; he wanted to find his wife. But he'd had enough experience dealing with suspects to recognize a genuine reaction when he saw one. Hers was completely bona fide.

"We believe the person behind her kidnapping is the same person who has been stalking Agent Thornton ever since the bank robbery," Mike Devlin added, quickly ticking off the stalking incidents.

Mention of the snake, pulled another sincere reaction from her.

"A cobra!" she echoed, horror twisting her face while a shudder vibrated her entire body. "I'd have a heart attack if someone did something like that to me."

Gary saw Jim glance his way and knew Barrett had crossed her off his list, too. But leaving Mike and Lucas to conduct the rest of the interview, Gary remained quiet.

"We're trying to identify the stalker," Devlin continued. "And to that end, we're talking to everyone who was present the day of the robbery."

Brittany listened with obvious interest to what he said and just as candidly answered all his questions, maintaining eye contact throughout.

But when Mike and Lucas finished with her, she turned back to Gary again. "Agent Thornton, I wish I could help you, but I don't know anything about your wife's disappearance or who might have been stalking you. It certainly wasn't me, though, if that's what you want to know."

She shook her head with obvious concern. "And I hope and pray you find your wife safe. I only met her briefly that day, but she was so nice. I can't imagine anyone wanting to hurt her."

A few minutes later, as they left Brittany's apartment building, Gary sighed heavily. Another damn dead end. He wanted to scream his anger and frustration. But instead he gazed up at the stars twinkling in the moonlit sky and made a silent vow.

*Hang in there, sweetheart. I'll find you. I promise.*

# Chapter Fifteen

Her limbs were numb and heavy, as if they were weighted down and no matter how hard Kate tried, she couldn't move them. But as paralyzed as they seemed, her head felt as if it was floating in the surf, bobbing along on the waves. Prying her eyes open, she gazed into a total, disorienting darkness, where every shallow breath pulled stale, musty air into her lungs.

For several moments she let her head float above her body in a kind of psychedelic disconnect, but too tired to keep her eyes open, she let the floating euphoria carry her away.

Her eyes slit open again and swamped by confusion, Kate glanced around again at the total darkness surrounding her. Had she fallen asleep? Or had she only imagined it?

Licking her parched lips, she tried to lift her arm, but a spasm sent the arm sideways, colliding with a barrier beside her. She tried again and the same thing happened. It was as if her brain had turned to mush and her body was unable to follow even the simplest of commands.

What was wrong with her? And where was she?

She'd been in dark rooms before, but once her eyes adjusted, she'd always been able to make out shapes. Not here. It was so dark she doubted she'd be able to see her hand in front of her face. That is…if she could lift her hand. So far she'd had little luck getting spastic limbs to cooperate.

The air around her probably wasn't helping either. It was so stale it felt too thick to inhale, like a cold, damp locker room full of sweaty clothing. And breathing it weighted her eyelids until they were too heavy to keep open.

Kate jerked awake with a start. She must have dozed off again, though she didn't remember doing it. Why couldn't she stay awake? And where was she?

Determined to find out, she tried to lift her arms again. And failed.

Her mind, mired in sludge, tried unsuccessfully to make sense of the mutiny. It made no sense. She'd been an athlete in high school and kept herself physically fit. She'd never had trouble with coordination. But now her limbs refused to cooperate at all.

Mustering every ounce of her concentration she tried again. And this time she was finally able to move her right arm, but within a few inches it bumped into a barrier. She pulled the arm back and fought with the other arm for several minutes before convincing it to cooperate. But the result was the same. Another barrier.

Was she wedged between two walls?

And what was above her. Another barrier? Whatever it was, it had two faintly glowing eyes staring down at her. Unnerved, she blinked, hoping to make the eyes go away, but a wave of nausea suddenly washed over her. As much as she could in the confining space, she turned to her side just before she got sick.

When the nausea passed, she rolled to her back shivering against the cold and closed her eyes so she couldn't see the demon staring at her.

**A GRIN CURVED** Jessica Myers' lips the moment she saw Gary. But from the urgent expression on her husband's face and the overnight bag in his hand, they were on their way out the door, not answering the FBI agents' early morning knock.

"Agent Thornton! Did you change your mind about delivering my baby? If so, you're just in time, because I'm in labor and we're on our way to the hospital."

Gary's stomach did a little flip in response to a curve ball. According to what Jessica had told him in the vault, she wasn't due for another week. But he supposed babies had minds of their own and when they decided it was time to join the world, there was no stopping them.

"No…that's not why we're here," Gary assured her. "And we'll get out of your way. Best of luck with the delivery," he added, motioning Mike, Jim and Lucas it was time to leave.

Jessica grasped his arm, "Wait…"

"Jessie, come on," her husband interrupted, clearly in a hurry to get her to the hospital.

Gary couldn't blame him. Jessica had told him the baby was their first child and while he'd never been an expectant father, he could imagine how anxious her husband must be.

Hell, he was anxious too. Anxious for her to leave. Delivering a baby wasn't on his agenda of things to do today or any day, for that matter.

But Jessica kept her hand on his arm and gave her husband a reassuring smile. "Clint…I'm fine," she called to him calmly, as if they were just making a trip to the grocery store, instead of on their way to the hospital to deliver a baby.

She shifted her focus back to Gary. "Why are you here?"

As he'd done with Brittany, Gary got right to the point, asking a few pointed questions about her whereabouts the day before.

Satisfied with her answers, Gary deferred to Jim when she asked for an explanation.

"Someone has been stalking Agent Thornton since the bank robbery and whoever that person is, kidnapped his wife last evening." Barrett explained, adding that they were interviewing all the robbery victims, hoping to get a lead on Kate's whereabouts.

Clint Myers jerked away from the car where he'd placed the overnight bag, his head snapping up and immediately locking angry eyes on Gary. "You're crazy if you think Jessie has something to do with the kidnapping," he shouted furiously, charging toward the FBI agents with his fists tightly clenched.

While there was no sign of a weapon, Gary wasn't taking any chances. Making no effort to hide what he was doing, he slipped his hand inside his jacket, ready to pull his service weapon if necessary. In his periphery, he noticed Mike and Jim doing the same thing just before Lucas subdued the husband with a restraining hold.

Alarmed by three federal agents reaching toward their weapons and another with an iron grip on her husband, Jessica stepped in front of her husband and placed a firm hand on his chest.

"Clint, calm down!"

The young man's anger was unmistakable, but his wife's plea seemed to work and when he settled down, Lucas eased his hold and slowly let him go. And when in lieu of any threatening moves, Clint slipped a protective arm around Jessica's shoulders, Gary dropped his hand away from the butt of his gun and visibly relaxed his stance. But he didn't drop his guard.

"Agent Thornton didn't accuse anyone," Jessie said, trying to further calm her husband. "He's just trying to find his wife."

Again her gaze swung back to Gary. "I am so sorry about your wife. You've got to be worried sick about her. But I can't imagine who would have kidnapped her."

Like with Brittany Franks, Gary had gotten the immediate sense that Jessica wasn't his stalker. Sure she enjoyed teasing him about the baby, but there was nothing in her demeanor to indicate she was anything more than a fun-loving young woman. And from the protective way Clint Myers was hovering over her and the adoring looks he gave her, Gary's gut told him they were happily married.

Disappointment pressed down on him like a weight, threatening to crush him. Sure he was glad he could scratch Jessica's name off his list of suspects; he liked her, he didn't want her to be involved. But eliminating her didn't get him any closer to finding Kate and she'd been missing for more than twelve hours. Time was slipping through his fingers.

"Okay. Sorry to delay you," Gary said, trying to control the emotion rising inside him.

"I hope you find your wife quickly and that she's okay," Jessica offered.

Gary nodded and without another word, spun on his heel and headed back to the car. Apparently worried about him, Lucas hastened after him. Shaw, who had lost his wife to cancer ten months ago, knew better than anyone except Zach, the emotional hell Gary was going through. While the circumstances were different, Lucas had lived through the nightmare of losing someone he adored.

Whatever Mike and Jim said after they left didn't take long and within minutes they were back in the car and headed to their next stop.

**SHE MUST HAVE** drifted off to sleep again, but Kate didn't remember doing it. And if she'd been asleep, it might have been seconds or hours. Swallowed by pitch darkness and in a vacuum of silence, time had no point of reference.

Taking a mental inventory of her condition, she found her arms and legs still felt sluggish and heavy. Her mind was still mired in fog, but at least her head no longer felt as if it was floating above her body.

Kate still couldn't see anything though, and that concerned her because she knew her eyes were open and she couldn't feel anything covering them. It was as if she was in a complete void…if that was even possible. But she'd rather think that, because the alternative was even worse. The mere thought she might be blind scared her to death.

Forcing away the depressing idea, she moved her arms away from her sides again, checking if she'd been mistaken about her surroundings.

She hadn't. She was definitely lying in a very narrow and very solid enclosure. The walls felt cold to the touch — no surprise there, wherever she was, it was cold — and the air was stale at best. The surface beneath her was hard, too…and decidedly uncomfortable.

The only explanation that made any sense to Kate was that she was hallucinating. Because what she was feeling couldn't be real. Could it?

A sliver of concern worked its way through the fog in Kate's brain as she tried again to process her surroundings. Tentatively she lifted her arm, surprising herself that it actually cooperated. But she'd only gotten it about eight inches or so above her body when she encountered another barrier.

Her concern escalated to alarm. And in an almost desperate attempt to refute her findings, she pushed at the walls and ceiling again.

Nothing moved.

Pushing away her growing panic, she tried to concentrate. Where was she? What had happened to her?

The last thing she remembered was leaving work. She's been looking forward to a quiet weekend at home with Gary. But where was she now? And how had she gotten there?

Questions ricocheting through the fog in Kate's head slowly dispersed some of the mire. And a flash of memory materialized in her brain.

The fleeting thought she'd been on her way home from work hadn't been completely wrong. She'd actually made it home and remembered walking into the kitchen. She'd set her purse down and…what then? The doorbell? Yes, that's right. The doorbell had rung and she'd…oh no!

She'd opened the door.

Everything after that was a blur, but images from a nightmarish dream floated in and out of her head. Lying on a floor listening to crying while evil swirled all around her, pummeling her repeatedly, threatening to kill Gary unless she drank a steaming potion. And then after she'd swallowed the poison, being led to a precipice and pushed over the edge.

A shiver raced the length of Kate's spine, recalling the horrid nightmare.

She couldn't be certain what, if any, of it had been real or even what had happened after she'd opened her front door. Someone must have overpowered her; that much was obvious. And if she took an educated guess, she'd been drugged into oblivion.

Kate wanted to kick herself for being so stupid. After the incident with the cobra and knowing Gary's stalker had begun focusing on her, Kate couldn't believe she'd made what could very well have been a fatal error in judgment by opening the door to a stranger.

Still, what was done was done; she couldn't undo it. What she had to do now was figure a way out of the infernal box holding her prisoner.

But how?

Concentrating was no easy task, but she fought back another wave of nausea and stared into her inky abyss.

Something caught her eye and she blinked to make sure it was really there. Yes…it was. Curiously, she stared at what looked like a thin line between the roof and the wall. After not being able to see anything for what seemed an eternity, she was elated to finally see something.

What was it, though? Curious, she reached up to touch it, but the moment she did, it disappeared.

Her mind still clouded by drugs, she tried again and the same thing happened. And for several minutes she entertained herself playing with the disappearing line until fatigue made her eyelids too heavy to stay open and she drifted off again.

**"GARY THORNTON, YOU** handsome devil, you! To what do I owe this unexpected pleasure," Rose Eshleman asked opening the door and motioning for the four agents on her doorstep to come inside.

Gary knew this visit was an exercise in futility before they'd even set out, but in order to be thorough, they had to interview everyone present during the robbery.

No matter how he considered it, though he still couldn't wrap his brain around the idea of an eighty-five year old woman stalking anyone, let alone a federal agent thirty-one years her junior. And besides that, Rose didn't own a gun…he'd checked…and she was too small to force Kate to do anything without the deadly force threat a weapon would have provided.

He supposed if Rose was desperate enough she could have obtained one illegally or hired someone else to kidnap Kate, but Gary's gut told him the odds of one of those scenarios playing out were infinitesimal.

Still he had to rule her out officially, and in truth seeing her again brought a smile to his face. Those had been in short supply since Kate had disappeared.

"Hi Rose! How have you been?"

"Fine," she replied. "But if you don't mind me saying so, you look like hell. What's wrong?"

To his surprise, another dose of her frank assessments pulled a chuckle from him. But it was short-lived when Lucas answered the question for him.

"Mrs. Eshleman, we're actually here on official business," Shaw explained. "Agent Thornton's wife has been kidnapped and we have reason to believe she was taken by someone connected to the bank robbery. We're interviewing everyone who was there that day, hoping to get a lead on where she is."

As Gary had expected, Rose's reaction was one of horror, mixed with compassion.

"Oh, Gary…I'm so sorry," she exclaimed, rising up on her toes and tugging him down until she could hug him. "A blind person could tell how crazy you and Kate are about each other. This must be tearing you apart."

Since he was too choked up to do more than murmur agreement, Gary deferred to the other agents, letting them handle the rest of the interview. But as Gary had suspected from the start, Rose didn't know anything about the kidnapping or who might be stalking him.

"I wish I could say I was shocked to hear Ron Chandler was involved with the robberies," she said. "But I'm not. I've known him and his family for decades and he's always been a schemer, trying to get something for nothing." Rose thought a moment and then gazed at Gary. "Perhaps he's behind Kate's disappearance as some kind of revenge. That would be just like him. After all, you ruined a good thing for him."

The speculation gave Gary pause. He'd never even considered Kate's kidnapping could be related to the Phantoms instead of his stalker, that the two incidents might not be related. But the idea had merit.

Instead of being relieved at the prospect of a new avenue to investigate, Gary groaned silently. Their list of potential suspects just doubled in size. And since there was nothing more to learn from Rose, they ended the interview quickly.

As she walked them to the door, she hugged Gary again. "Take care dear. I hope you find Kate soon."

# Chapter Sixteen

Gary's cell phone buzzed as Mike pulled to a stop in the parking lot of the greenhouse.

A glance at the display lifted Gary's brows. Chuck Clark, the Special Agent-in-Charge of the Baltimore Field Office. His boss calling him on a Saturday morning? This couldn't be a good thing.

"Hi Chuck. What's up?"

Gary glanced over at Mike and shook his head in disbelief to what he was hearing. "We're on our way," he said to Clark before ending the call.

"You're not going to believe this," he said, tossing a glance back to include Lucas and Jim. "The Phantoms just struck another bank here in Hagerstown."

"What?" Jim bellowed.

"You're kidding!" Lucas added.

"Dammit!" Mike exclaimed at the same time.

Gary was thinking of something a lot stronger than *dammit* to describe his feelings. Giving Mike the address, he shook his head in disgust as the car pulled away from the curb again.

"Drop me back at our hotel first," Gary instructed Mike. "I want my own car so I can leave if I get any leads on Kate."

He didn't have time to deal with a robbery today. Kate needed him and if he didn't find her soon, it might be too late. And that outcome was not only unacceptable to him, it scared him to death.

How the hell had the Phantoms struck? All of them were either behind bars or in the morgue, except for the elusive *Tiny*. Had the task force missed some major clue indicating the gang was larger than six members? Had Trayvon Jackson misled them?

Shaking away the questions, Gary stared out the car window, torn for the first time in his life between his job and family.

Two hours later, Gary and Lucas climbed into Gary's car and pulled out of the parking lot, leaving the robbery scene behind.

With Mike and Jim perfectly capable of wrapping up the loose ends before turning the scene over to local police, Gary figured getting back to his search for Kate was a more effective use of his time.

While this hold-up would be chalked up as part of the Phantom case, Gary considered it to be a lone wolf robbery. What had surprised him was the identity of the perp. Video surveillance had clearly shown the bandit to be *Tiny*, alias *Refrigerator Man,* the newest member of the Phantoms with only one robbery under his belt, acting alone this time.

Although *Tiny* had worn his borrowed Phantoms' mask and carried the same AK-47 he'd used for his attempted murder of Gary, the robbery had definitely been carried out in a haphazard manner that had little resemblance to previous, well-organized hold-ups by the Phantoms. There'd been no ties to a cash delivery, the hostages weren't locked inside a vault afterwards, the uniformed guard was unharmed and the haul had consisted of exactly one teller's cash drawer before something spooked *Tiny*.

If justice had a sense of humor, it was exercised today. As *Tiny* had dashed out the bank door, he'd stuffed the money bag into the front of his pants and he'd barely made it to the parking lot when the dye pack in the bait money he'd grabbed had exploded, staining his pants with red dye. Gary got some perverse pleasure thinking about the burns on the man's genitals.

Served him right for robbing the bank in the first place.

**THE MOMENT GARY** Thornton walked through the door of the greenhouse, Patti Henderson's heart did a crazy little flip inside her chest.

Her family and co-workers thought she lived in a fantasy world of made up romances. And maybe in the past she had, but not this time. What she felt for the tall federal agent wasn't a figment of her imagination.

At first, she'd tried to convince herself the attraction she felt was only because he'd saved her life. Sure that was part of it. It's how they'd met. But it was so much more than that.

He was everything she wanted in a man…tall, handsome, strong, honorable, intelligent, kind and just about the sexiest man she'd ever met. The zap of electricity she'd felt race up her arm, the moment she'd linked her fingers with his during the bank robbery, was like nothing she'd ever felt before, had made her want things she'd never wanted before.

Those urges had been so overwhelming, that once they'd reached the vault, she'd intentionally stayed away from him, trying to convince herself that she was only imagining the feelings swirling inside her. But when he'd shown such a tender, understanding and compassionate side interacting with that small boy, she'd been unable to help herself and had found her eyes continually wandering over to watch him.

For the last couple years she'd been feeling her biological clock ticking away at an alarming rate. Her hope of ever having a child of her own was slipping away because she hadn't found the right man, someone who would be good husband material for her and a good father for their children.

But that endless waiting had come to an end the fateful day of the robbery, because in the midst of that nightmare, she'd miraculously found the man of her dreams. Gary. And it wasn't like there was no connection between them. After all, he'd risked his life to save her. No one did that if they didn't care. And the way he'd smiled at her, she was sure he'd felt the connection too.

She'd never in her life so much as flirted with a good-looking man. Okay…she'd never flirted with any man…but she'd found the strength to reach out and grasp him that day. And now she had no intention of letting go.

Everything about their encounter had been a sign…an omen that he was the one. She'd been in misery the past week, aching to see him again, to hear his voice or have him touch her. And she'd been subtly trying to let him know they were meant to be together, even going so far as attempting to remove a major obstacle in her way.

And now he was here.

Was it too much to hope that he'd realized they were meant to be together? That he wanted her as much as she wanted him?

**WHEN KATE AWAKENED** again the numbness was gone and her nerve endings were working overtime. She hurt all over. Her face felt like it was swollen and bruised. Her left ankle throbbed and every muscle in her body ached. But she had no idea why.

And if that wasn't bad enough, it felt like she was lying on a bed of lumpy sticks and rocks.

The good news was some of the fog had cleared from her brain. Based on what she remembered of her symptoms — distorted perception, no sense of time, the out of body head floating sensation; not to mention her nausea, memory problems and impaired motor functions — Kate figured she'd been injected with Ketamine or something similar. And the way she felt, there was a good possibility she'd been given some kind of double whammy of Ketamine and something else.

Whatever she'd been given, Kate prayed there were no lasting effects. As a doctor, she knew only too well that some drugs could have devastating and permanent effects if used improperly or given in too high a dosage.

Even at proper dosages, without food or water to help dissipate the effects, drugs like Ketamine lingered in the body for hours, sometimes days, which explained why all she'd wanted to do was sleep.

But she was awake now and more alert than she'd felt before, so it was time to figure out where she was and come up with a plan of escape.

Shifting to get comfortable, her right arm thunked against something hard in one of her pockets. Feeling around, she realized she was still wearing the cargo style scrub pants she'd worn to work.

Trying to control her excitement, Kate dug into the thigh pocket praying she was right about what she'd find. The moment her hand closed around the object, she gasped aloud.

Her cell phone!

Kate held her breath and prayed harder than she'd ever prayed in her life as she powered the phone on. Several agonizing seconds later the screen came to life.

Tears of relief filled her eyes as Gary's face smiled down at her from the phone wallpaper. But she tried not to get her hopes up too high. Only one bar of service lit on the display, so God only knew if she'd have enough reception for a call to go through. But she had to try.

She knew she should call 911 for help, but first she wanted to call Gary. He had to be frantic by now and she wanted to let him know she was alive. More than that, she needed to hear his voice, because he was the only person in the world who could convince her she wasn't going to die inside this box.

Pressing the speed dial for his phone, Kate held her breath, praying it didn't go to his voice mail.

---

**GARY SLAMMED HIS** car door and heaved a frustrated sigh, as he and Lucas walked over to where Mike and Jim were sitting in their Bureau SUV.

He couldn't decide if he was lost in the twilight zone or mired in quicksand…maybe both.

The interview with Patti Henderson had been bizarre, to say the least. But at least his stalker was now in custody.

She'd almost proudly admitted what she'd done and had seemed truly perplexed that he was upset she'd tried to kill Kate with the cobra. What shocked him almost as much as her admission was the fact the snake was hers. The woman had an extensive reptile collection which she'd inherited from her father and had owned for several years. And she'd made no secret that she'd delivered her pet to Kate, fully intending the cobra to bite and kill Kate so she could have Gary for herself.

When Lucas had asked how she'd found Gary's home address, she'd unrepentantly admitted rifling through Kate's purse in the bank lunchroom. She'd found their address on Kate's new driver's license.

Patti's admission of those crimes had given them probable cause for a search of her home. Thankfully the reptiles were all securely caged. But while Gary's hopes of finding Kate there had been dashed, what they'd discovered at the home had been thoroughly unsettling.

The woman had photos of him all over her home. Photos she'd apparently taken while they'd been in the bank vault or while she'd been stalking him in the days afterwards.

The Henderson woman was seriously delusional, but she'd adamantly denied having anything to do with Kate's kidnapping. And the more he and Lucas had talked to her, the more Gary had been inclined to believe her. Frankly, he didn't think she had the mental wherewithal to pull off a kidnapping.

Which meant Kate's kidnapper was still out there somewhere and his list of suspects had just exploded in size. Hell, if his stalker wasn't behind the kidnapping, the list of people with possible grudges against him grew to include everyone he'd ever arrested during his thirty-one years in law enforcement.

The scope of the investigation was mind boggling and Kate was running out of time.

But while Gary had called in favors with fellow agents to check on several of the more probable suspects from previous cases, he was still convinced Kate's disappearance was tied to the bank robbery. And when Zach had tracked the GPS on Kate's cell phone the ping had originated from a tower near Hagerstown.

That coincidence reinforced Gary's belief she was somewhere in or near that town.

But he and the guys had been from one end of Washington County to the other, conducting interviews of people related to the Phantom investigation and were no closer to finding Kate now, then when they'd begun.

Not only was it discouraging and depressing, it was downright infuriating.

Someone, somewhere knew something about Kate's disappearance, but every person they'd contacted claimed to know nothing about the kidnapping.

Jim Barrett lowered the front passenger window as Gary and Lucas approached their car.

"Unless someone has a better idea, I suggest we go upstairs and review what we've got," Mike Devlin said, his own frustration evident. He shot a glance across the car's interior to where Gary stood to get his decision.

As much as Gary hated to quit for the day, they'd hit a dead end and Mike's idea made the most sense. It would give them a chance to begin the process of verifying the alibis they'd heard from all the suspects and setting up surveillance of them to see if any of them tipped their hand.

"Yeah…let's go," Gary agreed resignedly.

Before Mike opened his door, Gary's cell phone rang and his breath hitched in his chest. The ringtone was the one he'd been praying he'd hear.

"Wait," he demanded, tugging the phone from the clip at his waist and flicking on the speaker in case it was the kidnapper.

"Katie?"

# Chapter Seventeen

Until the moment she heard Gary's voice, Kate had held it together. But the worry in his voice and just hearing him say her name shattered her tenuous hold on composure and before she could say a word, she burst into tears.

"Katie...Dear Lord...are you okay? Sweetheart...talk to me?"

Trying to suck in a breath to regain control took another few seconds and she could hear him trying to soothe her.

"Calm down, honey. Tell me where you are."

It took every ounce of her shaky self-control to tell him the fragments of what she remembered. "It's my fault. I opened the door..." the tears started flowing again as her terror won out over her tenuous control.

Her loving husband's voice suddenly became that of a stern federal agent. "Kate! Pull yourself together. Talk to me. Where are you? Who kidnapped you?"

To a stranger his tone would have sounded heartless; she knew better. Gary was as far from heartless as a man could be. He was only trying to shock her and it worked.

She sucked in a breath of courage, swiping the tears from her eyes with the back of her hand, trying not to think about how filthy it probably was. There were more important things to worry about, like her phone battery dying or the signal dropping her call.

But all her thoughts and words were jumbled in her brain. Frustrated, Kate fought to organize them logically, praying she made sense. "I'm drugged. In a box. I don't remember a face. It's so dark…and cold. Can't see anything. Am I underground?" she asked, unable to stop the tremor of fear in her voice.

"Someone get a trace on her GPS, quick," Gary snapped to someone.

"I've already got Zach working on it."

She recognized Jim Barrett's voice immediately and excitement surged through Kate. If Jim was there, so were Mike Devlin and Lucas Shaw. She'd known in her heart that Gary and Zach would be looking for her and that they wouldn't stop until they found her, but knowing all of them were searching gave her renewed hope they'd find her before it was too late.

"Honey, are you bleeding? Or hurt?"

"My ankle hurts…maybe broken. Don't think I'm bleeding." She didn't bother telling Gary she hurt all over. Her brain might not be working properly, but she was coherent enough to realize there was no sense in worrying him any further than she imagined he already was.

A moment of silence greeted her. When Gary spoke again his voice was tight, but steady.

"Do you have enough air?"

"Yes." At least she hoped she did. The quality of what was there was less than inviting, but at least it wasn't toxic and she wasn't struggling to breathe.

"But I'm so thirsty," she added, as an afterthought. In fact her mouth felt like cotton, a symptom she knew from experience was an after effect of the drugs. Though why she told Gary, she wasn't certain. It wasn't like he could magically make a bottle of water appear.

"How's the battery charge on your phone?"

She'd noticed when she turned it on that the battery reading showed ten percent. "It's low."

She heard him mutter a curse.

"Okay…when we hang up, I want you to leave the phone powered on. The GPS will help us find you."

Hearing Gary's voice, just talking to him, gave her renewed courage, but the thought of disconnecting the call and going back to the terrifying silence of her prison, scared her to death. "Please hurry."

"We will, sweetheart and I'll make sure you've got something to drink as soon as you're out. Just stay calm and try not to worry." He paused for a heartbeat. "I'll worry for both of us."

Kate heard the teasing tone in Gary's last comment and sputtered a chuckle. Given the circumstances, she wouldn't have thought it possible for her to find humor in anything, but he'd managed the impossible. And he'd done it intentionally. She knew darn well he didn't think her situation was the least bit funny, but he'd made her laugh just to convince her everything would be okay.

Still, they only had a few seconds left to talk and she needed to tell him something. "Gary…I love you and if I don't make it…"

Emotion tightened her throat and she couldn't go on.

"Don't even think like that, Katie."

All traces of humor had vanished and she could hear the strain in his voice. As terrified as she was, her heart ached for him, for what he was going through, searching for her. She knew how panicked she'd been when he'd been trapped inside that bank with the Phantoms.

He hauled in a deep breath that steadied his voice. "I love you too, sweetheart and I want you to hang in there for me. We're doing everything we can to find you as quickly as possible."

**DISCONNECTING THE CALL** was one of the hardest things Gary had ever done in his life. More than anything, he'd wanted to keep talking to Katie until they found her. But if her battery was low, they couldn't afford to waste it by idle chatter, no matter how comforting both of them may have found it.

Relief didn't begin to describe what he was feeling knowing she was alive, but just thinking about what she'd been through, what she was still going through nearly reduced him to tears. He knew all too well the terror of being locked beneath the ground, but it made him sick to think of Kate in such a nightmare situation.

He felt her terror as clearly as if it was his own. She'd sounded so lost and scared it tore at his heart. But something else worried him more than her mental state.

Whatever drugs she'd been given were playing havoc with her speech. Her words had been slurred; her thoughts disjointed. And that was so atypical of Katie, he had no doubt she needed medical attention and needed it quickly.

The problem was he had no idea where the hell she was.

"Where are we with the trace of her phone?" he asked no one in particular.

"Dammit!" Jim Barrett's oath drew his attention and Gary turned to look at him.

"Zach was pinging her phone, but he lost the signal again. He thinks her phone went dead."

Gary echoed Jim's curse. "Either that or she lost her signal. Did he get anything?"

"Only that it came off a cell tower somewhere south of town," Jim said.

It wasn't much, but it was more than they'd had before. The signal Zach had picked up the evening Kate had vanished had confirmed she was in Hagerstown, but they'd lost the signal completely before he'd been able to pinpoint anything.

"Tell him to keep trying," Gary instructed, praying for a miracle.

A moment later Barrett spoke again. "Zach said to tell you the Bureau didn't get a hit on those prints found in your entry hall. So that's a dead end until we have someone in custody we can run them against."

Another curse rattling around in Gary's brain worked its way free and flew from his mouth.

**SLIDING HER PHONE** back into her pocket so she wasn't tempted to call Gary again, Kate resigned herself to the fact she just had to wait and be patient and pray they found her quickly.

The thin line above her caught her attention and Kate studied it, trying to figure out if it was brighter or if her mind was simply playing tricks on her again. The last few times she'd checked, the line was nowhere to be seen.

But, no…it wasn't her imagination; it was really there and much brighter than before.

Was that daylight?

Adrenaline poured into every cell of her body. If it was light, that meant an opening. And if there was an opening it could lead to escape.

Concentrating to pour all her strength into her arms and shoulders she pushed at the ceiling above her head. But nothing budged.

The exertion exhausted her sluggish muscles and after several attempts to dislodge whatever was above her, her arms dropped back onto the hard unforgiving surface and she forced her breathing to slow.

But then her gaze landed on the sliver of light and she realized there were other areas where light filtered into her prison as well. One in particular caught her eye.

On the wall near her head was a ragged hole about the size of a half-dollar. Kate's nerves battled with her courage. She wanted to look out, but part of her was terrified of what she'd find.

Deciding she'd rather know than not, she rolled toward the hole and pressed her eye to the opening. Pulling back, she blinked to clear her vision and then peered out again at her surreal surroundings.

Two strange looking boxes were piled on top of each other along the wall of a long narrow room that looked like concrete or stone. And far above her on the ceiling was a large cockeyed tile with a thin ray of light filtering around the edges. The entire room was cold and smelled damp and musty as if it had been closed up for a long time.

The temperature oozing through the holes explained why she was so cold.

Glancing around again her gaze landed on the stacked objects. They appeared to be made of concrete and had some faded carvings on them. They were an interesting shape, though. Broad at one end, narrow at the other.

What are they?

She studied them a moment. Her brain must be playing tricks on her again because they looked like old sarcophaguses.

The thought sobered her and she blinked and then hesitantly, looked again. And froze.

Dear God, it wasn't her imagination. They were burial vaults.

Trying to convince herself she was wrong, she dropped her hand to the floor of her prison. But feeling around her, brought about another terrifying reality. She wasn't alone in her box. The crunching she'd heard when she moved hadn't just been sticks and stones…it was bones.

Alarm turned to panic as she came fully awake and realization slammed into her.

Dear God! She'd been buried alive!

A scream echoed through her brain, but Kate managed to squelch it before it reached her lips. Every instinct told her to yell, to try to attract attention and to shove and push at the walls until she freed herself, but she managed to suppress the urge.

If she was right, if she really was sealed inside something, panicking and screaming would only use up whatever limited supply of air she had. She had to remain calm, had to control her breathing in order to conserve the oxygen as long as possible.

And what if the person who'd put her here was within earshot? If she screamed, they might hear her and come back to finish what they started.

There was a thought she didn't want to consider. At least as long as she was alive, there was always the chance someone would rescue her.

The deafening silence of her surroundings was broken only by the wild pounding of her heart and the untimely rumbling of her stomach. She'd sell her soul for a chocolate bar…and a drink of water. Her mouth was so dry it felt like her lips were stuck to her gums.

Desperate to do something, she reached for her phone again. Gary. She had to tell him what she'd discovered. And even if her battery went dead sooner as a result of the call, at least he'd have a clue that might help him find her more quickly.

She pressed the power button again, waiting impatiently for the screen to illuminate. Several moments passed and nothing happened. Unwilling to accept defeat, she tried again.

Nothing.

The phone was dead. Not only couldn't she call anyone, the GPS wouldn't work, which meant there was no way to use it to find her.

A shiver rattled through her body and this time she knew it wasn't just due to the cold. Taking a deep breath of the stale air, she willed her pulse to slow down, but it didn't work. How could it? She was petrified.

But if she had any chance of survival, she had to get hold of herself. To think. If she could do that, maybe she could figure a way out of her tomb.

The walls and roof of her prison were so solid though, they hadn't budged at all when she'd pushed at them. The lid was either too heavy or she was too weak to move it. Either way, she was trapped.

Pushing away her negative thoughts, Kate gave herself a mental pep talk. She was a doctor; she knew what the human body could endure. People survived for weeks without food and she'd be fine for a couple days without water, too. After that dehydration would set in.

A flicker of doubt worked its way into Kate's brain.

The nausea. She'd gotten sick at least twice that she remembered. Had it happened more than that? If so, she was already in danger of dehydration. And once that set in, she wouldn't stand much of a chance.

She shook away the depressing thought.

If she could just figure out how long she'd been trapped. It felt like days, but that could just be her imagination. Without knowing, though, she couldn't calculate how long she'd already been without water. She might already be running out of time.

Fear clouded her thoughts, tangling together until they were nearly impossible to decipher. But one thought in particular wouldn't be ignored.

Ever since she'd first learned of the abuse Gary's father had inflicted on him…the beatings, locking him inside a root cellar…she'd been horrified that anyone could do such a thing to another individual. But she'd never completely understood the terror he must have felt.

Until now.

Suddenly, every instance where her husband had flinched or hesitated before entering a confining space made perfect sense in her muddled brain.

Now, faced with that same terrifying situation, fear of the inevitable turned to a surge of anger. Anger at the injustice of it all, anger at herself for letting her emotions nearly get the best of her and anger at the person who'd concocted this insane scheme.

Well, she damn well wasn't going to just lay here waiting to die; she refused to let her kidnapper win.

Ignoring the fact her hands were pressing into someone else's disintegrated bones, she squirmed and moved until she could leverage herself to shove with all her might against the lid to her box, struggling to free herself until screaming muscles and excruciating pain in her ankle forced her to stop. But after only a few moments of pause to catch her breath, she tried again.

Finally, exhaustion won out and she fell back against her bony companion. Tired, but not defeated she lay there contemplating her strategy. If she could get out of her box, all she had to do was use the sarcophaguses as steps and perhaps she could reach the top and climb out of her tomb.

In theory it seemed easy; putting it into action would be an entirely different ballgame. Especially since her ankle hurt so bad she was certain it was broken and she hadn't been able to budge the lid to her box even a fraction of an inch.

It was as if something was holding it down.

She'd give anything for one nice big gulp of fresh air. Maybe then she could muster the energy to dislodge the lid. The air was so stuffy though, whenever she exerted herself, it was difficult to recapture her breath or her strength. But with the lid at the top of the crypt askew and holes in the top of her coffin, there had to be fresh air seeping inside, even if it was only seeping slowly.

At least that's what she was going to tell herself because suffocating slowly was a terrifying death she didn't want to contemplate.

She just had to stay calm and try to conserve her air until Gary found her. Closing her eyes, she prayed he'd been able to pinpoint her location before the GPS had died along with her battery.

Kate awakened with a start sometime later to find all traces of light gone again. But more terrifying than the darkness was the realization that instead of feeling rested; she felt sluggish, her muscles weak. The worst part was, she knew exactly why she felt that way.

Dehydration had set in. On top of that, she was using up oxygen faster than it was seeping into her prison, which meant she was breathing in carbon dioxide she'd exhaled.

Suddenly, that stale air seemed to press in on her, making it impossible for Kate to deny what she'd been trying desperately not to admit.

She couldn't free herself or call for help. And no one was going to find and rescue her, because no one knew where she was. She was going to die right here in this Godforsaken hole and there was nothing she could do to prevent it. She was going to end up like those people she read about in the newspaper who vanished without a trace, never to be seen or heard from again.

Angry and terrified, she tried again frantically to dislodge the lid above her, this time screaming at the top of her lungs. If she was going to die, she was going out fighting and she didn't care if her kidnapper heard her or not. Maybe, just maybe, someone else would hear her.

But finally the hopelessness of her situation slammed into her; it was no use; the lid wouldn't budge. And the air around her felt too thick to breathe.

Collapsing from exhaustion, tears flooded Kate's eyes and she hiccupped trying to hold them back. But that was a hopeless cause too and unable to stop herself, she began to sob.

# Chapter Eighteen

Gary glanced at his watch, trying desperately to contain the overwhelming sense of panic that had taken root in his brain. More than forty-eight hours since Kate had vanished and no solid leads on finding her had his stomach tied in knots and his emotions raw.

Kate's call had been like a shot of pure adrenaline. Hope had surged into every cell of his body, only to vanish a few minutes after the call ended when the signal had been lost. The reason they'd lost the signal didn't matter; it was gone…useless to them. And that had been more than twelve hours ago.

He only prayed Kate wasn't aware the signal had been lost because he didn't want her losing hope and giving up.

Some luck; that's what he needed. Some damn luck. A dose of that would go a long way toward restoring his confidence that things would turn out okay, but so far that commodity had been non-existent.

"Dad…what are you doing?"

His daughter-in-law's voice and a soft caress along his shoulders brought Gary's gaze up from the pile of files he was reading.

Following Rose Eshleman's suggestion he and his team had interviewed the captured Phantoms regarding the kidnapping. And several agents around the country were interviewing people who potentially held grudges against Gary related to previous cases.

He'd been studying all those interviews and been over everything so often he knew every detail by heart.

And he hadn't learned anything he hadn't caught in the first reading. He couldn't help himself though. He had to be missing something, overlooking some tiny detail that would help him find Kate.

"I thought you were going to try to get some sleep," Cassie persisted. "You're going to collapse from exhaustion if you don't."

First, Mike, Jim and Lucas had been acting like mother hens, pestering him to take care of himself and now that Zach and Cassie had joined them in Hagerstown, he was getting pressure from all sides.

*You need to rest. You should get some sleep. You need to eat.*

Like any of that was going to happen.

Sure, he was tired, but going without sleep was nothing new to him. When investigations began, he often went a couple days without stopping, while running down initial leads. But he was smart enough to know this was different.

The victim in this crime wasn't some stranger; she was his wife. A person he'd gladly give up his own life to protect. And his emotions were tied into so many knots he'd probably never unravel them all.

The only other time in his life he'd experienced anything comparable was when as eighteen year old high school seniors, Katie had been diagnosed with cancer. He'd been as terrified of losing her then as he was now.

Surgery to cure her of the cancer had left her unable to bear children, but it had given them a chance for a lifetime together. Years Gary wouldn't trade for anything.

He wished to hell this situation could be resolved by surgical skill. But he didn't have the emotional reserve to waste on wishful thinking. Adrenaline that had seen him through the first thirty-six hours was long gone and fatigue tugged at every muscle. But he couldn't stop; he wouldn't stop.

Sighing heavily, he reached back and patted Cassie's hand. "I'm okay. I'll get some sleep when I find Katie."

Leaning down, Cassie pressed a kiss on his cheek and walked over to the living room of the suite she and Zach were sharing with him. And although she sat down beside her husband who was searching Bureau files on his computer, Gary could feel her peering over at him with concern.

She'd let his lie slide, but Gary knew he wasn't fooling anyone. He was about as far from okay as a person could be. In fact, he was as close to losing it as he ever remembered being in his life.

And he truly appreciated everyone's concern and the emotional support they offered. They were the only thing keeping him from falling apart.

At this point, Gary was struggling to convince himself that they still had time to find Kate alive. But his years in law enforcement made that a difficult sell. Every cop worth his salt knew the best chance of solving a case happened in the first forty-eight hours. After that the trail began to grow cold and the chances of solving it deteriorated significantly.

But, hell, if Kate's trail was any colder it would be glacial.

And he didn't need his imagination to conjure up ideas of where she was or what had been done to her; a whole career of caseloads had been rerunning through his mind since the moment he'd first realized she was missing. Remembering the outcome of many of those cases had been enough to wipe away any thoughts of sleep as well as his appetite, not to mention send his thoughts to a dark place he didn't want to visit.

He felt like time was slipping through his fingers and he was powerless to stop it. He'd thought he'd felt helpless facing an AK-47 in the bank, but that had been a picnic compared to this. And his grief at the thought he might never see Katie again warred with his anger over a situation he couldn't seem to get a handle on, couldn't fix. It gave a whole new meaning to the word *helpless*.

The unexpected tone of his cell phone ringing caused him to jump. He gave the display a quick glance and didn't recognize the number. The possibility it might be the kidnapper put him on immediate alert and he quickly connected the call.

"Thornton," he answered curtly.

"Hi, Agent Gary!"

The sound of Tyler Franks' small voice popped Gary's ballooning hope in an instant and as much as he liked the child, the last thing he felt like doing was making small talk. Still, he didn't have it in him to be short with the boy. After all, he'd told Tyler he could call any time.

But what the hell was a five year old doing up at eleven o'clock at night? Gary had been in high school before his grandparents had let him stay up that late and then it was only on weekends. That was ancient history though. Might as well find out what his pint-sized friend wanted.

"Hi, Tyler," Gary replied, trying to sound like he was pleased to hear from the boy. "It's awful late. Is everything okay? Where's your mother?"

"I was crying and she told me I was having a nightmare. And when I stopped, she went back to bed. But I know it was real."

Gary scratched his head. Maybe he was more tired than he thought because the explanation lost him completely. "What was real?"

"Agent Gary…dis is important. FBI important. My daddy did sumping really bad."

Gary wasn't sure what to make of that announcement either. Probably just Tyler's imagination running wild. But during his interviews with Brittany, Gary had learned her ex-husband's physical abuse of her and his verbal abuse of her and the children had led to their divorce.

After his own childhood, Gary couldn't conjure up any positive sentiments toward a bullying husband and father. If Adam Franks had truly committed a crime, Gary wasn't about to ignore it.

"What did he do?"

"He hurted Dr. Kate…da lady who gives you magic kisses and he made her go away wiff him."

Breath caught in Gary's throat and he nearly dropped his cell phone.

After all this time he finally knew who had kidnapped Kate. Adam Franks.

But it didn't make sense. Gary didn't even know the man; neither did Kate for that matter. Why would Franks want to kidnap her?

Gary shook away the thought. Questions and reasons didn't matter at the moment; he had his first lead and it was a solid one.

Tyler was definitely talking about Katie. Gary had introduced her to Brittany and her children in the bank lobby before they'd left for the hospital and Tyler had asked if she was the lady who gave him magic kisses. Kate had told Tyler he could call her Dr. Kate and she'd gotten such a chuckle over the magic kisses comment, she'd been teasing Gary about it ever since.

Snapping his fingers to get Zach's attention Gary switched the phone to speaker. And as Zach vaulted from the sofa and made it to his side in a heartbeat, Gary prompted the child.

"Tell me that again, partner." Gary wanted Zach to hear Tyler's answer, mainly because he was so tired he was afraid he might be imagining the entire conversation.

"I said my daddy did sumping bad. He hurted Dr. Kate and took her away from your house."

When Zach and Cassie both sucked in startled breaths, Gary knew he hadn't imagined anything. When he'd spoken to Kate she'd mentioned that her ankle might be broken, but was it possible she had other injuries? "What did he do to her, Tyler?"

"He zapped her and tied her up and carried her to da van."

What the hell did the kid mean by *he zapped her*? Had Adam Franks knocked her out or what? "Son, what do you mean by *zapped*?"

"His gun made a funny noise and it shot string dat made Dr. Kate wiggle on da floor. And when she stopped moving Daddy tied her up and took her to da van. Den he putted her under da ground."

Anger ignited in Gary, making his blood boil. That bastard had used a Taser on Kate and she'd collapsed. Sure she was healthy and had a strong heart, but if the voltage had been too high or delivered too prolonged, it could have killed her.

Controlling his anger, he focused on getting as much information as possible.

If Adam Franks kidnapped Kate and Tyler witnessed it, Gary needed a parent present to question the boy further. The logical choice was to talk to Brittany, but what if she was involved? He could jeopardize Tyler's safety if she discovered the boy had talked.

If Gary had more time he'd investigate Brittany further, but he didn't have the luxury of time. Katie was out there somewhere, possibly hurt and if Tyler was right that she was underground, she could be running out of air.

He needed answers and he needed them now. Unfortunately, there was only one way to get them. And his gut told him Brittany wasn't involved. He just hoped to hell he was right.

"Tyler, does your mother know what your father did?"

"I tried to tell her, but she said I was just having a bad dream."

The story was bizarre enough to be a nightmare, but at this point Gary wasn't willing to assume anything. "Well I need you to wake her up and get her on the phone so I can talk to her for a moment."

"Okay. Don't go away."

Gary almost laughed at that one. No way in hell was he going anywhere until he had the answers he needed to find Kate and slap handcuffs on Adam Franks…if Tyler's story was correct.

He turned to look over his shoulder into the living room where Zach had returned to his laptop.

"Get me every scrap of information you can find on Adam Franks. I want everything down to what he had for dinner tonight."

Information on Franks had been negligible in the background report they'd compiled on Brittany because the couple was divorced and they'd been focused on her. Pretty much all Gary knew about Adam was his name and without more details, they'd be looking for a needle in a haystack.

"I'm already on it, Dad," Zach replied, continuing to tap the keys on his computer, as the printer in the room kicked to life.

Several agonizing moments passed before Brittany Franks' sleepy voice came over the phone. "Agent Thornton, I'm so sorry if Tyler got you awake. He had a nightmare and I thought he went back to sleep. I never expected him to bother you."

"He didn't bother me, Brittany. Did he explain to you what upset him?"

"No…not really…just that someone was in a dark hole underground."

Gary nodded to himself. He could understand why she'd think it was just a nightmare.

"You mentioned before that Tyler was with your ex-husband for the weekend. When did he get home?"

"I think it was around five. Why?"

Ignoring Brittany's question, Gary continued to press. "Did you see or talk to your ex-husband at all this weekend?"

"No. He picked Tyler up from daycare around four on Friday afternoon while I was still at work. And when he dropped Tyler off, Adam waited in the car until I opened the door; then he drove away."

"What was Adam driving?"

"A blue van. It looked like one his father owns," she answered with a slight hedge to her reply. "Why?"

Gary's gut told him Tyler's story was true, but he still wanted to make sure he hadn't overlooked any obvious holes in it. "Was Tyler acting normal when he got home?"

"He was quiet…a little withdrawn and didn't eat much of his dinner. And then he had the nightmare. But none of that is particularly unusual after visits with Adam and it's why I'm trying to get the court to make those visits supervised." There was silence for a moment before she continued. "Now that I think about it, though, Tyler wanted me to leave his bedside light on tonight when he went to sleep and he's never asked that before. Agent Thornton, what's going on? Why all the questions?"

Gary blew out a breath. "Brittany, I don't think Tyler had a nightmare; I think he saw something that scared him when he was with your ex-husband."

Brittany's gasp filtered through the phone. "Like what?"

"That's what I'm trying to determine," Gary told her. "I want you to put your phone on speaker and ask Tyler to explain again what he told me. And based on what he says, I need your permission to question him further."

"Okay. Sure." Her tentative voice replied. Gary heard the phone switch to speaker and then Brittany spoke again, this time to her son. "Sweetie, explain to me what you told Agent Thornton."

For the third time the boy repeated his story and no major portion of it changed from his initial telling. No embellishment, no addition, no retractions. Gary would bet his pension the kid was telling the truth.

"Oh my God! It wasn't a dream, was it? Your father really kidnapped Agent Thornton's wife."

"Uh huh," the boy agreed. "He tooked Dr. Kate away."

With Brittany's consent, Gary took charge of the conversation again. "When did all this happen, Tyler? Was it today?"

"Uh uh," the boy answered without hesitation. "Daddy got me da utter day and we went right to Dr. Kate's house."

Gary hadn't intended the question as a trick; he'd merely wanted to test the boy's perception of time. But Tyler's answer erased any doubt about there being some mistake. Brittany had told him Adam picked the boy up at four, directly from daycare on Friday and Kate had been kidnapped between five thirty when she'd texted him to ask when he'd be home and six thirty when he'd arrived home. That fit with the hour drive time between Hagerstown and Baltimore.

"And what happened when you got to my house?"

"Dat's when Daddy zapped Dr. Kate."

"Okay. After he took Dr. Kate to the van. What did he do then?" Gary pressed; terrified of the answer he'd receive.

"When she woked up, Daddy hit her and made her drink sumping. She didn't wanna do it, but he got mad and hit her again and said he'd kill you if she didn't. So she drinked it."

Kate had clearly been drugged and Gary was betting that whatever that drug was had been in the liquid Franks had forced her to swallow. "Tyler, do you know what your father made her drink?"

"Uh uh…but it made her go to sleep."

"And after Dr. Kate was asleep. What did he do? Did he take her back to his house?"

"Uh uh. He took her to some building and put her under da ground."

Against a wave of bile rising in his throat, Gary managed to continue to press for information. "You saw all this happen?"

As farfetched as the story sounded, there was too much detail for it all to be nothing more than Tyler's imagination.

"Uh huh!"

Gary's mind whirled back to the small fingerprints that had been lifted from the entry table in their foyer. It hadn't matched anything in the Bureau's extensive fingerprint files. All along, investigators and Gary had been operating under the assumption the small sized prints belonged to a female…specifically Gary's stalker. But they hadn't matched Patti Henderson's prints either. From what Tyler had just said, he'd been inside the house and Gary was willing to bet if they fingerprinted the boy, the prints would match.

Shaking away the immaterial thought, he focused on Tyler's voice as the boy continued to talk.

"…Daddy said Mommy is babyin' me and I needed to learn to be a man. He said he was teachin' me to be tough."

Rage roared through Gary so hard and fast he had to bite his tongue to keep from unleashing a string of curses. And his hand began to cramp from the stranglehold he had on his phone. What parent would subject a child to something that twisted?

"But what he did to Dr. Kate scared me," Tyler continued. "And when I cried and told him not to do it, he yelled at me and said he'd put me under da ground too if I told anyone. But I had to tell you, Agent Gary. You made me a junior FBI agent and what he did was wrong. Wasn't it?"

So many emotions hit Gary at once, he didn't know how to process them all, while trying to make sense of Tyler's explanation. It sounded as if Franks had buried Katie.

God, he didn't even want to consider that possibility. It took every ounce of his control to clear his thoughts when he noticed Zach walking toward him.

"Yes it was, Tyler and I'm glad you called me. But I need you to hang on a minute, buddy. Don't go away," he said repeating Tyler's warning to him."

"'Kay."

The innocence of the reply caused an inadvertent smile to tug at Gary's mouth. But it vanished as he muted the call and met Zach's gaze. "What do you have?"

Zach dropped several sheets of paper into Gary's hand, but briefly summed up the content. "Franks is a paradox. He's college educated but never held a job for more than a couple years. He's been fired four times for punching his boss or a co-worker and arrested several times for assaulting his wife. He's also been involved in a couple barroom brawls. Nothing major, though and he's never served more than a few days in county lock up."

None of that gave Gary any clue as to why the man would target Kate. He glanced down at a mug shot of a nice looking man. But good-looking or not, a guy with a hair trigger temper would be one dangerous bastard, which meant Kate was in serious danger.

Gary nodded. "Get the others over here. We need to move on this now."

"I'll get them," Cassie said, hopping to her feet and crossing the room to rap on the connecting door between the two suites, as Gary returned his attention to the boy.

"Tyler, you've been a huge help, but I need some more information. Do you know where your father took Dr. Kate? Can you take me to her?" Gary asked, holding his breath, praying the answer was *yes*.

"I don't know its name or how to get dere," he said, causing Gary to sag in defeat

"But you do, don't you, Mommy?" The question snagged Gary's full attention again.

"It's where Poppy works," Tyler said.

Brittany gasped aloud and Gary's hope soared again.

"Oh my God," she exclaimed. "Adam's father, Wayne is the caretaker at a cemetery south of town."

Gary hauled in a deep breath to quell the surge of nausea that rolled through his stomach. Kate missing and hurt, somewhere underground and now in a cemetery…this nightmare just kept getting worse. The bastard really had buried her alive.

Another deep breath centered his thoughts again and grabbing a piece of paper, Gary scrawled the directions Brittany rattled off, then repeated them back to her to make sure he'd gotten them correct.

"Thanks. We'll find it," he said, as Mike, Jim and Lucas filed into the suite.

Tyler piped up again. "Take me, Agent Gary. I can show you where she is."

As much as Gary hated to involve the boy any further, they needed his help, but ultimately that decision lay with Brittany, so Gary made his request to her.

"Brittany, take your phone off speaker for a minute," he advised her, waiting until she gave him the go-ahead. "I would never allow

Tyler to see anything traumatic, but if Kate is alive and underground, she may be running low on oxygen and without his help, we could waste precious time trying to locate her in the dark."

Brittany never hesitated. "I just need to get my neighbor to watch Nikki and then Tyler and I will meet you at the cemetery. We should be there in a half hour."

Gary blew out a silent breath in relief. Their hotel was on the opposite side of town from Brittany's apartment. Not having to drive out of their way to pick up Tyler would save valuable time.

"Thanks Brittany. See you soon. But don't alert Adam that we're on to him. If you get to the cemetery before us and see him, stay out of view and don't confront him. If he thinks he's about to be caught, he could be dangerous."

Gary heard the quiver of nerves in her voice when she replied. "Okay…we'll see you there shortly."

On his feet and moving before he even disconnected the call, Gary remembered his promise to Kate and grabbed several water bottles from the refrigerator before snagging his jacket from the entry closet and heading out the door. He didn't have to look to know the others, including Cassie, were right behind him.

# Chapter Nineteen

The time it took to reach the cemetery was the longest twenty minutes of Gary's life and the emotional rollercoaster he'd been on since Kate disappeared showed no signs of slowing down. As eager as he was to find her, he was terrified of what they'd find. The thought she might be dead was more than he could bring himself to consider, let alone accept. But the rational part of his brain wouldn't let the idea go and it was torturing him.

The sound of gravel beneath Mike's tires pulled Gary's thoughts back from the dismal track they'd been on. He looked up in time to see Devlin pulling his SUV beside the three police cruisers and ambulance which had already arrived at the cemetery.

Gary swung open his door, his feet hitting the pavement the moment the car stopped. Pulling on his FBI windbreaker against a chill he rationalized was more nerves than temperature, he flipped open his identification. He introduced himself to an officer with sergeant's stripes on his sleeves, whose name plate identified him as Sgt. K. Brooks. Gary quickly filled him in on what was happening.

Brooks nodded and motioned to three of the five officers with him. "Get some lights ready to set up as soon as we locate her."

While the officers began pulling lighting equipment from the trunks of their squad cars, Brooks turned back to Gary. "We've got the APB out on Adam Franks, as you requested. But we're having trouble ascertaining where he lives. So far the addresses we uncovered are dead ends."

"His ex-wife will be here shortly," Gary offered. "She might be able to shed light on where he's living." He thought a moment before adding, "I'd appreciate if you could put a couple officers on Ms. Franks and her children until Franks is in custody. With his history he's capable of anything and I don't want anything happening to the family."

"Consider it done," Brooks replied.

Brittany and Tyler arrived just then and as soon as the car stopped, Brooks sent one of his officers over to get information on Adam. While Brittany was occupied, Tyler released himself from his seat belt and booster and bound out the car door.

The boy rushed over to greet Gary as if this was all some grand adventure. When he skidded to a halt at Gary's feet, he stuck his hand out. "Hi Agent Gary!"

Where the kid got his energy at this hour of the night, Gary didn't know, but he took the offered hand and shook it.

"I'm proud of you, Tyler. Helping me find my wife is a brave thing for you to do. And I promise you, I won't let your father hurt you…or your mom and sister."

"Dat's good, 'cause he's gonna be really mad at me for tellin' on him," Tyler replied. "But he shouldn't have hurted Dr. Kate. She's a nice lady; I like her."

Gary had a sneaking suspicion part of the boy's infatuation with Kate had to do with the ever present chocolate she carried in her purse, candy she'd shared with Tyler and Nikki when she'd met them at the bank. But whatever the reason, Gary was grateful Tyler possessed the moral compass to defy his father and had called him.

Anxious to find Kate, he handed a flashlight to Tyler. "Lead the way, partner."

"'Kay." Tyler looked all around for a moment and then grabbed Gary's hand. "Dis way," he said, moving off to their left.

Footsteps crunched across the gravel drive, quieting as they entered the grass, but there was no hesitation in Tyler's step as he made his way through the darkened cemetery, guided only by the beams of several flashlights and the headlamps Gary and the other agents wore.

Gary had no idea what Tyler was doing, but periodically he lifted his flashlight and aimed it into the distance and then resumed trudging along.

Far off the beaten path, the boy suddenly stopped as if hesitant to go any further. "She's in dere," he said, pointing at what at first glance appeared to be an enormous rock about twenty feet away.

Immediately every flashlight aimed its beam at the object, illuminating a mausoleum surrounded on three sides by large shrubs. Over a hundred years ago the building had probably been quite ornate, but now it sat dilapidated by time and the elements.

Gary took it all in with one sweeping glance and what he noticed immediately was a shiny new padlock on the ancient iron door, a lock completely out of place for such an old structure.

"How did you ever remember where this was?" Gary asked, amazed the child had been able to find it in the dark. He wasn't sure he'd be able to find it again in broad daylight. The cemetery was huge and had multiple sections to it.

Tyler tugged on his arm and Gary knelt down on one knee, realizing the boy wanted to tell him something he didn't want others to hear.

On cue Tyler cupped his hands around his mouth and whispered into Gary's ear. "Daddy was mad when I started to cry and he made me come outside by myself. I was scared bein' in da dark all alone, but I did what you told me. I tried to make it not scary. I pretended dat lady over dere was my mommy," he said pointing to a large angel, adorning the top of another mausoleum. "She's waving at us."

Gary looked at the angel whose right arm was extended with her hand pointed directly toward the clump of bushes. It was the perfect landmark.

His gaze dropped to Tyler and he found himself smiling. "You've got a sharp set of eyes, young man. You're amazing." The kid was a born detective and if he didn't end up working for the Bureau someday, it would be the FBI's loss.

Gary bracketed the boy's shoulders with his hands. "Tyler, you've been a big help and I really appreciate everything you've done, but now I want you to go over with your mother and Mrs. Taylor."

Standing, Gary motioned to Brittany and Cassie to come get the boy. "I'll talk to you again as soon as we get Dr. Kate out of there."

Tyler gazed at him somberly. "I asked God for her to be okay."

Gary's throat tightened so badly it hurt to swallow, but he managed to croak out a reply. "Thank you, son," he said, giving the boy's head a gentle caress.

As the other agents and officers began setting up spot lights to illuminate the mausoleum, Gary turned his attention to the lock.

Nearly beyond rational thinking, he was tempted to shoot the damn thing off, but enough common sense prevailed that he resisted the urge. Kate was on the other side of that door somewhere and since he refused to believe she was dead, he couldn't chance her being hit by a ricocheting bullet.

"Do your men have bolt cutters?" he asked the sergeant.

"Yeah," Brooks replied. "I sent an officer back to the cars to get them."

A few agonizing minutes later the officer returned and made short work of removing the padlock, bagging it for evidence. As soon as two officers swung open the heavy iron doors, a bright spotlight was aimed at the interior, giving them a clear view of any awaiting ambush. But it was empty. Adam Franks was nowhere to be seen.

Gary stepped into a musty smelling room that had once held an intimate family chapel, but which had long ago been stripped of any creature comforts, leaving the altar and benches in disrepair.

There was no sign of Kate, but before disappointment had a chance to take root, something else snared Gary's attention and he caught himself before stepping on a large piece of fresh plywood that lay crooked on the floor at the center of the room.

The anomaly immediately registered in Gary's brain.

A mausoleum this old would have had a slab of stone or marble covering the entry to an underground crypt. But from the scenario forming in his head, the plywood made sense.

Adam Franks would never have been able to lift or move the original slab that had covered the opening, so in all probability he destroyed it and replaced it with something he could move in a hurry. And since this mausoleum, secluded in an old section of the cemetery, obviously hadn't been used or visited for years, Franks had been able to make his preparations without anyone being the wiser. And as Tyler had confirmed, he'd used cover of darkness to move Kate inside.

"Watch your step," Gary cautioned as the others piled in around him. "Everyone back up."

Pulling on a pair of latex gloves, Gary waited for them to get out of his way and then slid the plywood aside opening a gaping hole. "Get this wood dusted for prints," he ordered to no one in particular.

Gary angled the beam of his headlamp downward into a large crypt easily ten feet deep, where chunks of marble and marble dust were strewn across the floor. Remnants of whatever had once covered the crypt entrance, Gary figured. His light beam illuminated two burial vaults, both clearly more than a century in age, stacked atop each other. The ornate artwork on the top one had been severely damaged by the marble that had cascaded from above. But it was the vault sitting alone on the floor on the other side of the crypt that caught and held his attention.

Instead of the kind of neatly fitting lids sealing the other vaults, this one was covered by what appeared to be hastily positioned slabs of stone in varying sizes. More remnants of the crypt cover, no doubt.

Staring down into the crypt, Gary knew he was looking at what Franks had intended to be Kate's grave.

"Kate!" he hollered into the hole. Holding his breath, he prayed he'd hear her voice, but even if she had answered there was too much noise surrounding him to hear her. He needed to get down there.

Brooks seemed to read his mind. "Someone find a ladder," he hollered to the officers he'd posted outside for safety. "Check the caretaker's shed. Hurry."

Gary couldn't bring himself to admit Kate could be dead, but the terror tightening his throat was excruciating. If she was down there…and he was sure she was…she'd been trapped for too damn long already. No way in hell was he waiting for someone to find a ladder or call the caretaker.

In fact, he wasn't waiting another minute.

Ignoring the flashbacks and nightmares that had chased him his entire life and the pain he knew would erupt in his ribs; Gary grabbed onto the edge of the crypt and swung down into the small dark hole. As tall as he was, it wasn't a long drop, but even if it had been, he wouldn't have cared. Katie needed him.

"What the hell are you doing?" Brooks hollered after him.

"He's rescuing his wife and my mother," Zach answered bluntly. "And if you're smart you won't interfere."

The soft soles of Gary's shoes slapped the stone floor lifting a cloud of dust as he landed on his feet next to the vault he suspected held his wife. And the small fragment of his brain that was able to process anything except the coffin urged him to proceed cautiously.

Sweeping the area with his gaze, he ensured there was only one way in or out…the hole he'd dropped through. Satisfied there was no way Adam Franks or anyone else could ambush him, Gary shifted his gaze back to the coffin in front of him and took a steeling breath.

"Kate!" he called again, while lifting one of the rocks away.

Again, nothing; just dead silence.

So many emotions whirled inside him, Gary couldn't have identified them if his life depended on it. He dropped the rock on the floor beside him as Zach and Lucas scrambled down a metal extension ladder. A heartbeat later the crypt was flooded by bright lights aimed from above.

"Dad, why don't you go back up and let us do this," Zach suggested softly, squinting against the sudden assault of light.

"Yeah, Thorny…let us handle this. You don't need to be down here," Lucas agreed.

While Gary appreciated that they were trying to spare him from whatever they were going to find, there was no way he was leaving. Not now.

But unable to speak through the fear and emotion clogging his throat he merely shook his head and yanked off his head lamp, pocketing it before beginning to lift away more of the rocks that had been piled on top of the vault. The others immediately began grabbing them too and in only a few moments they'd uncovered three large flat slabs of stone that lay atop the burial vault.

Without waiting for help, Lucas tossed aside one of the slabs.

The sight that greeted them stole every molecule of oxygen from Gary's lungs and he was sure it would haunt him for the rest of his life.

Lying motionless with her eyes closed and dried tears staining her bruised cheeks, Kate appeared to be sleeping. But her face was void of any color except for the bruises.

A tsunami of fury surged inside Gary. Adam Franks was lucky he wasn't there because Gary wasn't sure he'd be able to restrain himself from killing the man. But his fury was eclipsed by fear.

Terrified of what he'd find, he checked the pulse at Kate's carotid.

"Please God!" he uttered on a choked sob when he felt only cold clammy skin and no sign of life beneath his fingertips.

"Katie!" Her name came out on another choked breath as unwilling to accept she was gone, Gary shifted his fingers against her neck again.

Anxiously Zach put a hand on his shoulder. "Is there anything?" he asked in a voice tight with fear.

At first Gary thought he only imagined the rapid thready pulsation, figuring it was a case of wishful thinking. But a slight adjustment of his fingers erased any doubt.

Tears flooded his eyes and the grief pressing down on him lifted suddenly on a surge of hope. "She's alive," he managed to choke out around the bowling ball clogging his throat.

"She's alive!" Lucas Shaw hollered to those above. "Get the medics and a stretcher down here now."

"And a blanket for her!" Zach added. "It's cold down here."

Zach was right. The crypt was cold and damp; the temperature alone would be enough to compromise Kate's system and throw her into shock. And God only knew what had actually been done to her that could have added to the risk.

Hurriedly Gary shucked out of his jacket and draped it over Kate. "Katie, sweetheart, can you hear me?" he asked, tenderly tucking the jacket around her shoulders.

"Come on, Mom. Wake up," Zach added. "Show me those pretty eyes of yours."

While they tried to rouse her by talking to her, Lucas shoved away the two remaining large slabs, letting them crash to the floor with loud bangs that echoed through the small chamber.

"Dad, she moved!" Zach cried excitedly, grasping Gary's forearm. "Mom moved her leg. Did you see it?"

No, he hadn't. He'd been too horrified by the vision of Kate in that damn coffin. It had been bad enough when all he could see were her head and shoulders. But now that she was completely uncovered, it was worse.

He fought to suck air into his lungs, trying desperately to contain the bile rising in his throat.

The deep purple discoloration on Katie's cheeks, bruises Gary recognized as those caused by brass knuckles, were enough to make him want to pummel Adam Franks in retribution. And her nails were broken, her fingers bloody and her arms bruised. Matching those injuries to images of her frantically trying to claw her way free did nothing to quell the nausea in his stomach.

He gulped in another lungful of the stale air and blinked back tears, while continuing to gaze down at his wife.

She'd put up one hell of a struggle before she'd been imprisoned here because her blouse was torn and the knees of her pants were stained by grass and a gray dust that looked like it came from the floor of the crypt. And her left ankle, bent at an odd angle was clearly broken, an injury Gary didn't even want to contemplate.

But it was the disintegrated remains of another human being lying beneath her that made Gary want to scream in rage.

How could anyone do this to Kate? To any living being, for that matter?

What kind of sociopath was Adam Franks that he could concoct such a diabolical scheme?

Only the ill-fitting slabs of stone over the coffin had prevented her from suffocation, but the combined weight of those slabs had been so heavy she'd never have been able to budge them.

Gary took a quick glance around him. Even on the million to one chance she could have gotten free of the coffin, with her ankle so badly broken there was no way she could have ever gotten out of the crypt. She would have had to climb up on top of the two sarcophaguses. And even if she could have done that, which didn't seem likely, the piece of plywood that had covered the crypt opening would have been out of her reach by a good foot or more.

Only boiling anger kept the nausea swirling in Gary's gut from winning the battle of emotions waging war inside him.

No matter how he looked at it, he didn't see how Kate ever could have gotten free if they hadn't found her. So it wasn't like Franks had intentionally given her a chance of survival.

How could he have done that? Katie had devoted her whole life to helping others, to saving lives. How could Franks have left her to die of dehydration or starvation in this godforsaken hole?

It seemed impossible that someone capable of doing this could function normally on a day to day basis. Did others realize the malevolence in his character? Had Brittany ever seen any hint of him being a monster capable of this kind of evil?

Gazing down at Kate, Gary took her hand, caressing it between his. His breaths came in short spurts as he fought unsuccessfully to stop more tears from rolling down his cheeks.

She'd gone through hell and he ached to wrap her in his arms, to pick her up and get her out of the disgusting deathtrap, but he was afraid to move her. If she had other broken bones besides her ankle or internal injuries, moving her could cause irreparable damage.

Angry and frustrated, Gary cursed aloud.

Nothing about this situation made sense. Kate didn't even know Adam Franks. Neither did he. So what could Franks possibly have against them that would cause him to do this to her?

A hand touched his back gently. "Sir, your son and the other agent have gone top-side and we need you to move out of the way."

Gary swiped away his tears and glanced around to find the ambulance crew standing behind him. He'd been so lost in thought he hadn't heard them enter the crypt or the others leave.

The petite young brunette smiled sympathetically when his gaze met hers. "We need to check your wife's vitals and get her stabilized and then we can get her out of here."

Now that he'd found Kate, Gary didn't want to leave her, but she needed medical attention and that was something he couldn't give her.

Nodding, he turned back to Kate and tenderly caressed her cheek. "You're safe now, sweetheart. The medics are going to take care of you and we'll get you out of here soon." He waited several heartbeats hoping for a response or some signal Kate heard him, but when there was none, he reluctantly released her hand and backed out of their way.

What seemed like hours to Gary passed in a blur as the medics took Kate's vitals, started an intravenous, fitted her ankle with an air splint and checked her for other visible injuries.

Following the medics' lead, Gary helped them slide a large sling beneath her which they then used to lift her out of the coffin and onto the basket stretcher that had been lowered to the floor. And when the medics climbed up the ladder, one carrying their gear and the other holding the bags of intravenous fluids, Gary used the advantage of his height to balance his wife's stretcher from below as it was pulled out of the crypt by the men above.

Gary scrambled up the ladder after Kate, but when he realized the medics were stopping to check her vitals again and that it would be another few minutes before they loaded her into the ambulance, he decided to get a breath of fresh air.

**SEETHING WITH FURY,** Adam Franks watched the bustling activity around the mausoleum from the shadows of the cemetery.

All his careful planning was unraveling and the traitor was his own flesh and blood. He couldn't believe it. His kid was a stool pigeon, a rat who'd sold him out. And he'd lay money on his bitch of an ex-wife being behind it. Her and that damn Fed.

It was bad enough Brittany was trying to convince the court to take away his visitation rights, but Thornton had been interfering where he didn't belong, sticking his nose into Adam's business and turning his son against him.

Tyler had developed such a serious case of hero worship, Thornton was all he talked about. Hell, even Brittany acted like Thornton walked on water.

But to Adam's way of thinking, Thornton was an interloper who needed to be removed. Nobody messed with him and got away with it.

Thornton had emotionally stolen his son, so Adam had returned the favor.

He should have killed the old man instead of toying with him, instead of playing his elaborate scheme. But Adam firmly believed in the *eye for an eye* brand of justice. He'd wanted to give Thornton a taste of his own medicine. Let the man suffer by losing something important.

He'd hit Thornton where he knew it would hurt most by kidnapping his wife and he'd enjoyed watching the big tough Fed being reduced to an emotional wreck, worrying over her fate.

His original plan had been to kill the woman outright, but then he'd decided it would torture the Fed even more to know he hadn't been able to find and save her. It's why Adam hadn't taken the woman's cell phone away from her. He'd figured she'd eventually come to and find it. But that far underground, it would have been virtually impossible for them to pinpoint her location before she suffocated or died from lack of food and water.

His plan would have worked too, if his son hadn't ruined everything.

And dammit, from all the activity, it looked like the woman was alive. Just the fact Thornton and the cops had shown up meant Adam better lay low because he was sure there was an APB out for his arrest by now. They probably had every cop in the state looking for him.

But that was okay. He'd managed to stay under the radar so far and he had no intention of getting caught. At least not until he got revenge on everyone who'd crossed him.

**THE MOMENT GARY** stepped out of the mausoleum, he saw Brittany and Tyler waiting anxiously back by the ambulance with Cassie. Two of Sergeant Brooks' men were standing guard beside them, something Gary was pleased to see. Anyone capable of doing the things Adam Franks had done to Kate, was capable of anything.

Gary didn't want to take a chance the man would go after his ex-wife and children.

As Gary headed their way, his gaze locked on Tyler and he smiled. It didn't take a medical degree to know Katie wouldn't have survived much longer in that death trap.

How did he thank the child for giving him his wife back, for literally saving her life? Somehow a handshake or a pat on the head just wouldn't cut it.

Following his gut, Gary knelt down and hugged the boy. "Tyler, you are my hero!" he said, meaning every word. "I don't know how I can ever repay you for helping me find Dr. Kate…except to say *thank you*."

Tyler grinned back at him, clearly pleased. "Partners help each utter. Right, Agent Gary?"

"Right, son…and you are the best partner ever," Gary replied humbled by the boy's modesty. And because he couldn't think of anything else to do, Gary lifted his FBI ball cap off his head and plopped it on Tyler's head.

"I'd give you my jacket too," he said gazing at the dirty windbreaker draped over his arm. "But I think it might be a little big for you, buddy. When I get back to my office, though, I promise I'll send you one you can wear."

Somewhere among all the FBI apparel agents handed out to family and friends, there were children's sizes and if he couldn't find a jacket to fit Tyler, he'd damn well have one tailored for the boy. For that matter, he'd send the kid one of everything he could find that had the Bureau logo on it. Let him wall paper his room with FBI paraphernalia. Gary didn't care if it cost him a small fortune; Tyler deserved it.

Tyler's eyes, already wide with awe over the hat, widened like saucers. "Really. My own FBI jacket?"

"You bet! I can't think of anyone who deserves to wear one more than you, partner. You're the best junior agent ever."

"Agent Thornton, it looks like they're getting ready to take your wife to the hospital," Brittany interjected, brushing tears from her eyes.

Gary shot a glance over his shoulder and saw Kate's stretcher moving across the grass toward them.

"Thanks again for everything…both of you," he said before sprinting over to the ambulance and hopping inside.

# Chapter Twenty

The black hole of death gaping open before her beckoned to Kate, malevolence forcing her toward the edge and in the blink of an eye, she was falling into the abyss. The bottom rushed up to meet her, slamming into her unyieldingly. And pain…excruciating pain erupted in her ankle.

She collapsed in a heap as hideous laughter rained down on her, mockingly. And while she struggled futilely to stand, footsteps descended into the hole and a one eyed demon loomed over her, the glow from his eye illuminating a surreal windowless gray room.

From somewhere above her, a child's voice cried out.

"No Daddy, don't. Stop!"

"Shut up or I'll kill you too," the demon raged as he forced liquid into her mouth until she nearly choked on it.

Kate's head began to swim and her body levitated off the ground. But a moment later, she felt herself falling again, this time into an inescapable prison. Her heart pounded uncontrollably, but she was unable to move and could only watch in helpless terror while the demon entombed her, one block at a time, until even the evil glow of his eye disappeared and she was swallowed by blackness.

A scream ripped from Kate's throat.

"HEELLLPP!"

"Kate!"

The deep voice seemed to rock her entire prison, causing it to roll beneath her and sending a new wave of panic surging through her. Had her killer returned? Kate's heart jack hammered in her chest and she flailed her arms blindly, landing a solid punch against a body.

"Ow! Katie…wake up."

Warm hands closed on her shoulders, delivering a gentle shake that succeeded in registering the voice in her brain. Another scream rising in her throat died on her lips.

"Sweetheart, wake up. You're having another nightmare."

With a gasp, Kate's eyes flew open and she jerked upright. In the dimly lit room, she saw Gary gazing at her with concern darkening his cobalt eyes. But the nightmare had been so real, so terrifying, she didn't trust what she saw. Like a deer caught in headlights, her first instinct was to escape. But a heartbeat later she recognized their bedroom from the soft glow of the electric candles in their windows. Her gaze drifted back to Gary's.

The fragment of her brain that was processing reality told her she wasn't buried beneath the ground slowly suffocating to death; that she was safe inside her home. And that she was no longer lying atop the remains of some long deceased stranger, but rather sharing a comfortable bed with her husband. She also realized it was the middle of the night and she'd awakened Gary from a sound sleep.

But none of that reality stopped the tremors of fear rattling her body or the tears that chose that exact moment to erupt and roll down her cheeks unchecked.

"You found me." She wanted to snatch the words back, but she couldn't. They'd just sort of slipped out of her mouth on their own. It wasn't like she'd just been pulled from the crypt. The rescue had taken place three days ago. And after two nights in the hospital, she'd convinced her doctor to let her come home. Still, every time she looked at Gary she knew she'd have died in that hole if he hadn't found her when he did.

"Aw, Katie," Gary said in a voice laden with pain as he gathered her in his arms and lifted her onto his lap. The warmth of his hand permeated through her silky nightgown, heating a soothing path as he gently stroked her back while she cried away the remnants of her nightmare.

"Shh," he murmured. "It's all over and you're safe now, honey."

Craving the shelter of his broad chest and the strength of his arms, Kate buried her face against his neck, letting his comforting embrace and his familiar masculine scent calm her. But letting him go wasn't an option, not yet.

"I'm sorry I got you awake, but it was just so real," she uttered several minutes later when she could finally speak.

He gave her a patient look and touched his index finger to her lips. "Katie, don't apologize. You've been through a horrific experience. It's going to take time to recover. But you're not alone; we're in this together. No matter what you need, we'll do it or get it."

If she didn't already love this man with all her heart, the tenderness in his voice, his understanding and compassion would have won her over. But she was already hopelessly in love with him and had been for as long as she could remember.

Mustering a smile, she slipped her arms around his neck and pressed a kiss on his lips. "Thank you."

For several quiet moments she merely savored being in his arms. But slowly the ache in her ankle turned to a mild throbbing sensation, one she didn't want to get out of hand.

Pulling back, she eased out of his embrace.

"Are you okay?" he asked with concern when she slid to the edge of the bed and picked up her crutches.

She shot a smile back at him. "Just going into the bathroom. My ankle is throbbing and I need a pain pill."

Gary stopped her with a gentle hand on her arm. "Stay here. I'll get it for you."

She turned a questioning gaze on him. "Can you go to the bathroom for me, too?"

Her feigned seriousness drew a chuckle from him. "Uh…that would be a *no*, but if you need help while you're in there, just holler."

When Kate returned a few minutes later she thought she'd find him asleep, but instead he was sitting up propped against the headboard, clearly waiting for her.

The adrenaline that had pumped through her system in the wake of her nightmare had fled once she'd awakened and moved around. The pain medicine couldn't possibly be working this quickly but she was actually tired. Crazy as it seemed though, she was half afraid to fall asleep again, scared that if she did, the nightmare would return.

Rather than climb back into bed right away, she merely stood staring down at it as if she expected it to morph in to the burial crypt. Finally she mustered her courage and slipped back beneath the covers beside Gary.

She couldn't seem to relax though, her tense muscles making her body rigid.

"You want to talk about it?" Gary asked softly as if he'd read her mind. And he probably had. He knew her that well.

"I'm tired…but I'm scared the dream will return." Her gaze slid up to meet his. "Will you hold me?"

He chuckled softly. "As if you have to ask."

He leaned over her, dropping a tender kiss on her lips and then laid down and opened his arms to her. The moment she snuggled against him, his arms encircled her. And cocooned in the safety of his embrace, she felt her tension slowly drain away until her eyelids grew heavy and drifted closed.

**WRAPPING KATIE IN** his arms was an easy thing for Gary to do. Hell, he'd hold her as long and as often as she needed him to, if it would relieve her pain and suffering.

He had no idea what time it was and with his arms wrapped around Kate he couldn't see his watch, but he figured it was well after midnight.

He'd barely left Kate's side in the two days she'd been in the hospital and between the bank robbery, his stalker and her kidnapping, the house had been neglected. Even the fingerprint dust from the crime scene team was still on tabletops. So when Kate had gone to bed around nine, he'd straightened up the house and made some minor furniture adjustments in the den to accommodate her injuries.

Tired, he'd finally fallen into bed around eleven and crashed as soon as his head hit the pillow.

Kate's shrill scream had jumpstarted his heart, snatching him from the depths of sleep. Terror had filled his entire being; panic that someone was harming her again. But then he'd realized she was having one of the nightmares that had plagued her since she'd regained consciousness.

It took little effort to draw down on the pool of fury boiling in his gut at the thought of what Adam Franks had done to her, but he thanked God she was alive.

He could only imagine the terror she must have felt, realizing her life was ebbing away as the oxygen in her tomb grew scarce and dehydration began taking its toll on her body.

How someone ever got over that kind of trauma was something Gary couldn't fathom. There was no telling what damage had been incurred or if it would be lasting.

*You found me.*

He'd had to clench his jaw to keep from coming unraveled at the relief in her voice because he knew how close he'd come to losing her. A few more hours and he would have been arranging her funeral instead of comforting her nightmare. Doctors had confirmed that fact.

As the ambulance had pulled away from the cemetery, Gary had climbed into the back with Kate and had been there when she'd regained consciousness during the ride to the hospital. And he wasn't ashamed to say tears of happiness had streamed down his face when she'd opened her eyes and smiled at him. By the time they'd reached the hospital, the IVs the paramedics had inserted had begun to reverse the effects of her dehydration. And fortunately the numerous tests doctors had run on her had all come back showing her systems were operating normally.

Miraculously, the combination of Ketamine and Rohypnol Franks had given her, hadn't caused any lasting damage and in spite of the presence of those date rape drugs in her system, there'd been no evidence of sexual assault.

Gary shook his head, filled with a mix of relief and concern. Kate's physical injuries would heal. The psychological effects; those were a whole different ball game. No telling how long they would take to heal.

Guilt gnawed at him. If it weren't for him and his job, none of this would have happened to her. And to make matters worse, it was the second time in less than a year that a case of his had brought violent danger to their home and both times Katie had nearly been killed.

Nothing he could do in the aftermath of those two incidents would change or lessen the trauma they'd inflicted on her. All he could do is give her whatever support she needed. And he was prepared to do just that.

Gary had already cleared taking two weeks' vacation with the Bureau. And he had more time coming to him if needed. When that was gone, he'd play it by ear. Retirement was always an option, but he'd cross that bridge if and when he got to it.

**GLANCING AROUND AT** her surroundings in the den, Kate swallowed a healthy dose of guilt.

From the moment she'd awakened in the ambulance Gary had been by her side, solicitous of her every need as well as those he anticipated. And nothing had changed now that she was home.

This morning, she'd awakened to the enticing odor of bacon and opened her eyes to find her dear husband standing beside the bed with a food tray balanced in his hands and the morning paper tucked under his arm.

She'd been almost as surprised at being served a meal fit for a queen while still lying in bed, as she'd been seeing Gary wearing jeans and a polo shirt on a weekday morning. And when she'd questioned him about it, she learned he'd taken vacation time to care for her.

She hated being sick; hated feeling helpless and having inactivity forced on her was intolerable. And after only three days it was driving her crazy. Then again, after her behavior this morning, maybe she'd already gotten there.

She supposed the old saying was true about doctors making the worst patients. But intelligently Kate also knew her injuries were nothing to take cavalierly.

Confined inside the coffin, she hadn't been able to move much and hadn't realized the extent of her injuries. But in the light of day, it was horrifying to see the array of colors covering her body. Some of the bruises, like the ones on her cheeks and arms had been inflicted by Adam Franks when he'd beaten her into submission. But the more serious of her injuries had been incurred when she'd fallen or been pushed into the burial crypt.

In her hallucinogenic memory of that nightmare, she felt herself being pushed into the hole. Gary and her doctor believed her recollection was correct.

The ankle she'd broken in that fall had actually been minor compared to the internal injuries she'd sustained. Bruising to her heart and spleen had led doctors to keep her in the hospital for two days while they satisfied themselves she wasn't bleeding internally.

But even then, doctors had only released her from the hospital after she'd agreed to complete rest for the next two weeks. And apparently Gary was intent on seeing she followed those instructions, anticipating her every need to minimize her movement and discomfort.

As she slowly made her way into their den, she couldn't believe the effort he'd gone to on her behalf…especially after the way she'd taken his head off earlier. But he'd thought of everything.

The television remote had been set within arm reach of her recliner, as had a glass of water and her pain medication. A carafe of water on a warming plate, a small basket of her favorite tea bags and a fresh mug sat on the table as well.

On the floor beside her chair she found a cooler stocked with a soda and several bottles of water, along with a variety of anything she might want for lunch. And adding to her guilt, she discovered Gary had even included a chocolate bar to satisfy her sweet tooth. If he was trying to spoil her, he was doing a good job of it and she adored him for it.

But she was also extremely sore and cranky about being confined and unable to do simple things she always did for herself.

Rationally she knew none of that was Gary's fault. But a half hour ago, in a moment of complete irrationality while he'd merely been trying to help her get dressed, she'd taken her frustration out on him. She still couldn't believe she'd flipped out and gone into a crazed tirade. She'd actually told him to leave her alone and get out, that he was driving her crazy and if he didn't stop she was going to scream.

In hindsight, she'd been screaming like a banshee when she'd hurled ludicrous barbs at him as if he was public enemy number one. She was thoroughly embarrassed by her behavior.

Seriously…while she'd been sound asleep last night he'd cleaned up the kitchen from dinner, run the dishwasher, vacuumed, dusted and run a load of laundry. He'd come to bed after her and gotten up before her, making her a delicious breakfast which he'd served her in bed. And she'd thanked him for all that by taking his head off.

Not that she was trying to excuse her behavior, because there was no justification…but she was not only upset and frustrated by the limitations forced on her by her injuries, but she felt guilty because she should be taking care of him. After all, he was still recovering from his own injuries. The staples were still in the back of his head and his cracked ribs had to be incredibly painful.

But the fact he'd reacted so calmly to her raving lunacy and never uttered a harsh word or complaint of his own in reply, had only provoked her more.

He'd just gazed at her silently for several moments and then left the room, leaving her to finish dressing on her own. Which was exactly what she'd wanted…or thought she'd wanted…at the time. Except pulling on her clothing, something that usually took her about five minutes, had taken her nearly a half hour to complete because every move she made, hurt.

In truth, the moment she'd had her meltdown, she'd regretted taking it out on Gary. But like a sulky child, she hadn't seen fit to apologize immediately. And she definitely hadn't had the nerve to call him back and ask for his help again.

Now she couldn't ask for his help if she wanted to, because he wasn't home. A short time ago Zach had called in a panic. A pipe had burst in their basement and the water shut off valve was frozen. Cassie couldn't budge it. Zach was on his way home and a plumber had been called, but he'd asked Gary to help shut off the water to stop the flooding.

After the way she'd behaved, Kate couldn't blame Gary for leaving, for wanting to escape the house and her irrational wrath.

Drowning in guilt after he left, Kate had grabbed her crutches and made her way down the hall from their bedroom to the den. And seeing what he'd done for her here only made her feel worse about the terrible things she'd said to him. She definitely owed him an apology.

Giving herself a swift mental kick, Kate sat down in her recliner and propped her leg up on the pillows Gary had left for her. And after pouring herself a cup of tea, she reclined in her chair and picked up the book she was reading.

Kate was engrossed in the novel when the sound of shattering glass caused her to jump. Before she could even register what was happening, the French doors from the patio crashed open and chaos erupted in the room.

With a shrieking alarm siren, hysterical crying and yelling voices all annihilating the peace and quiet of her home, Kate's startled gaze swung around in time to watch in horror as a man shoved Brittany Franks and her children into the den. Brittany struggled to comfort her hysterical toddler while Tyler cringed in terror at the wild-eyed man holding a gun to the boy's head. Whether it was a flicker of memory from her ordeal or the photograph Gary had shown her, she recognized Adam Franks.

Kate stiffened, a noose of fear tightening around her neck. But she refused to cry, refused to give into the tears pressing against the back of her eyes begging for release. For two and a half days she'd been at the mercy of this madman and she wouldn't allow him to defeat her this time.

How dare he invade her home with a gun, threatening her and his ex-wife…and even worse, his small children.

Steeling her spine, Kate drew on a healthy dose of rage.

"What are you doing?" she challenged irately.

"Shut up, bitch!" he snapped, his gaze bouncing around nervously.

It took Kate only a moment to realize he was looking for Gary, expecting him to appear in response to all the noise.

"Shut off that damn alarm…now!" Adam hollered over the eardrum piercing siren.

Still fighting to resist the panic trying to rise inside her, Kate picked up her cell phone.

"I said turn off the alarm," Adam screamed. "And don't even think about alerting your security company."

"I am turning the alarm off," she replied defiantly, surprised by the steady calm in her voice. "An app on my phone deactivates it."

As tempted as she was to enter the Trouble Code, alerting the security company monitoring the alarm to dispatch police to the house, Kate wasn't willing to defy Adam, especially with his children present. She'd never forgive herself if she did something to cause them harm. And besides, the Trouble Code wasn't necessary because Gary would already be aware there was a problem at the house.

When the high-end custom alarm system had been installed in their new home, Gary had it programmed to call his cell phone whenever an alarm was activated. He'd done it, not out of any concern about the alarm company's monitoring ability, but because he wanted to know if there was a problem at their home.

As she punched in the code to silence the alarm, Kate prayed she hadn't hurt Gary so badly earlier that he'd ignore the alarm this time. It would serve her right, though, if he did.

Still she breathed a huge sigh of relief when her cell phone rang with the unique ring identifying Gary as the caller.

"Don't answer that," Adam ordered.

Kate froze. She had to answer the call. If she didn't, Gary would rush home and walk right into an ambush. She couldn't let that happen. Somehow she had to convince Adam it was in his best interest to let her answer.

She thought only a moment before she found her argument.

"That's my husband checking on the alarm and if I don't answer, he'll call the police."

The phone continued to jangle while Adam considered his options. "Alright answer it, but put it on speaker so I can hear. And watch what you say or my little stool-pigeon here is going to die."

Tyler turned panicked eyes at his father and began to cry again, realizing Adam was referring to him. Adding to the bedlam Brittany hollered a protest at her ex-husband, yelling over Nikki's continued screams.

Kate stared at the man for a moment, wondering how a father could so cruelly terrorize his children. But before she lost Gary to her voice mail, she connected the call and put it on speaker.

"Katie…are you okay?"

She had to strain to hear above the pandemonium. But the urgent question that flew through her speaker as soon as she connected the call evidenced Gary's heightened state of alert. Kate wasn't surprised either. After all, they'd both known Adam Franks was still on the loose and that he knew where they lived.

Kate drew in a breath to steady her voice. "Hi honey. I'm sorry I worried you. Jennifer and the girls dropped in to see us and when she rang the front doorbell, I forgot to turn off the alarm before hollering for her to come in."

In the moment of silence that ensued, Kate could almost hear Gary's mind processing what he'd know was a blatant lie.

Jennifer had been their daughter-in-law. But five years ago Zach's first wife and their three adorable daughters had been brutally murdered during his investigation of a South American drug cartel.

Even if Gary momentarily thought she'd lost her mind with the bizarre message and even if the hysterical crying in the room wasn't filtering through the phone to him, he would still know something was wrong. Because the alert on his phone would be signaling glass break and a breach of the den door, not their front door.

Before the silence aroused Adam's suspicion Gary's voice came back through the phone.

"That's great," he replied, sounding upbeat. "Ask them to wait for me. I'm on my way home and should be there in about a half hour."

As Kate had expected, Gary realized someone was listening and his answer had been designed to mislead the eavesdropper.

"Okay," Kate replied. "Love you; drive carefully."

Like Gary, her answer had been calculated. Zach and Cassie's home was only two blocks away. Kate would be willing to bet Gary had left his car in the garage and walked, not driven to their home.

If she knew her husband…and she did…he was already sprinting home, shortcutting his way through neighbors' yards.

When she disconnected the call, she glanced at Brittany. The poor woman looked terrified. Not that Kate blamed her; she was terrified too. But she knew something Brittany didn't. Help was on the way.

Adam waved the gun at her. "Get over here with them," he said motioning toward Brittany and Nikki, but still holding a whimpering Tyler in a death grip with the gun at his head.

Her heart pounding so hard she could feel it in her chest, Kate searched for a way to stay where she was. Yesterday, knowing her movements were limited, Gary had placed a gun in the side pocket of her recliner. At the time he'd told her about it, she'd thought the move was a touch of safety overkill. Now she was glad he'd done it. And as long as she remained in her chair, she had a chance of retrieving the weapon and potentially stopping Adam. But if he forced her over with the others, it would be out of reach and useless.

Banking on Adam not knowing the extent of her injuries and not being able to see the crutches that were tucked on the other side of her chair, Kate made no effort to move. "I can't stand or walk," she bluffed.

Feigning her helplessness, Kate used her arms to lift her body off the chair and slightly shift her position. Thankfully, she'd been so startled by their arrival, she'd had no time to move and with a lightweight blanket covering her legs and the cast, the ruse just might work. In reality the only reason she'd shifted was so she'd better be able to reach the gun. And if she was lucky she'd convince Adam she was no threat, giving her a slight edge in any confrontation.

Being married to a federal agent for more than thirty years, Kate was very familiar with weapons and a good shot. But she'd only ever fired a weapon at targets on a range and she wasn't at all certain she'd be able to shoot another living being. It went against everything she stood for as a doctor. After what Adam had done to her, though, she had trouble mustering any thoughts of mercy for him. And if he made any move to harm the children or anyone else, she'd do whatever was needed to stop him.

Adam considered her for several tense moments before nodding. "Okay. You can stay there, but don't try anything funny."

She returned the nod and dropped her gaze to Tyler who was so terrified he was trembling uncontrollably. Kate heaved a sigh.

"Look, you've got us all here captive and you're holding a gun. There's no reason to keep it aimed at your son like that. Let him go."

To her surprise, Adam released the boy and Tyler immediately dashed to his mother for protection.

"Momma's boy," Franks spat with disgust.

The taunt drew a verbal reprimand from Brittany and he retaliated by back handing her across the face. While his assault horrified Kate, her attention was diverted by a brief glimpse of movement streaking across a corner of the back yard. It had happened so quickly she hadn't gotten a good look, but every fiber of her being told her it was Gary.

Now all she needed to do was keep Adam occupied so he wouldn't know help had arrived.

"Why are you here?" she asked testily. "What do you want?"

"To kill your husband. I should have done it the first chance I got, but no one is going to stop me this time. And when I'm through with him, the rest of you are going to die."

Kate's heart dropped to her stomach but her thoughts weren't for herself. Her heart ached for the two children who were listening to their father talk about murdering them. For the moment there wasn't much she could do except try to keep Adam calm until Gary made whatever move he was planning.

# Chapter Twenty-One

With his weapon drawn, his heart in his throat and blood thundering in his ears, Gary stood on the patio trying to assess the situation inside the house.

Kidnapping Kate had been only one in a long string of crimes Adam Franks had committed recently…violent crimes. And Kate and the others inside the house were dealing with a man who was as unstable as nitroglycerine. They had no idea how dangerous Franks really was. Gary had only made the discovery two days ago, when he'd finally connected all the pieces of his investigation.

Adam Franks was *Refrigerator Man*, the missing Phantom known as *Tiny*.

Any shadow of doubt he may have had about the accuracy of his facts had been obliterated the moment Gary had stolen a peek into his den and he'd seen Franks and heard him speak. *Refrigerator Man's* voice, just like Trayvon Jackson's, was one Gary would never forget.

While he'd known Franks would surface sometime, he hadn't anticipated the bank robber showing up at his house today. If he had, Gary never would have left; even though Kate had made it clear she needed time alone. Still, a showdown with the man had been inevitable and Gary kicked himself mentally for not foreseeing something like this happening.

Brittany had confided to Gary that her ex-husband's bullying of their children and his abuse of her had led to their divorce. And a simple review of Franks' criminal record and FBI background report had painted a picture of a man with a penchant for violence.

Wife, employers, strangers…it made no difference to Franks. Anyone who annoyed him was repaid by physical violence. Gary knew that from firsthand experience. But what puzzled him was that for all those physically violent episodes, Franks had never served more than a couple weeks in county lock up.

But in spite of that anomaly, the files had also enlightened Gary with answers to many of the questions that had been rattling around in his brain. And he'd had plenty of time to review the information while he'd been sitting at Kate's bedside in the hospital.

The first detail Gary had found of interest was that Franks had been an offensive lineman on his high school and college football teams. Photos had shown him to be a massive man at six foot four, hovering well above three hundred pounds.

Something about the man's photos had teased Gary's memory. Playing a hunch, he'd reviewed security footage from the Hagerstown robbery again. He'd noticed immediately the physical similarity between *Refrigerator Man* and photos of Adam Franks. Carrying his hunch one step further, Gary had contacted Brittany to ask if her ex-husband had any nicknames. He hadn't been at all surprised when she'd revealed that Adam's pals called him *Tiny*. Gary had also confirmed another hunch when Tyler confirmed Adam had taken him to a bank during their weekend together and that when his father had returned to the car, his pants had been stained red.

Realizing Adam Franks and their missing Phantom, *Refrigerator Man* were the same person had piqued Gary's curiosity. He'd reviewed the security footage of the first Hagerstown robbery yet again, this time picking up on something he hadn't caught before. A motive.

As the robbery had begun and Gary had first spotted Brittany and her children in the lobby, he'd rushed to protect them when one of the masked gunmen swung his weapon toward them. Gary had dragged them to safety just as the bandit had unleashed gunfire directed at where they'd been standing.

Based on the security footage showing the mask the gunman wore, Gary knew the man firing the potentially deadly round at Brittany had been none other than *Refrigerator Man*, alias Adam "*Tiny*" Franks.

Security footage from previous robberies supported Gary's contention that none of the Phantoms had ever aimed or shot at any civilians during their other heists. Their deadly violence had always been directed at uniformed guards or law enforcement.

And that dichotomy had turned Gary's thoughts to Trayvon Jackson.

During the robbery, when Jackson had admonished *Refrigerator Man* for trying to kill Gary, Jackson had told the massive bandit to *"shut up and follow orders. Cowboy again and you're out."* And during Jackson's conversation with Gary at the hospital, in addition to identifying *Refrigerator Man* as *Tiny*, Jackson had claimed the Hagerstown robbery would have been *Tiny's* first and last with the Phantoms because the *"idiot wouldn't follow orders. He was shootin' at customers instead of focusin' on the money."*

All the puzzle pieces had begun to fall into place for Gary, once he'd connected Adam Franks to the infamous *Refrigerator Man*. And his mind had snagged on something Brittany had told the group of captives in the vault. She'd said her ex-husband had asked her to meet him at the bank that morning to set up savings accounts for the children.

During Gary's call to her, Brittany had confirmed Adam had originally requested the meeting for later that afternoon, but that he'd texted her that morning to change the time. Since she and the kids had been running errands near the bank, she'd agreed to meet him.

The entire scenario smacked of premeditation and Gary didn't believe in coincidences. Adam Franks had lured his wife to the bank that morning, intending to kill her and possibly even their children and make it appear to be a tragic result of the heist. Gary's intervention had ruined that plan because once Brittany and the children had been on the floor, any chance of making their deaths appear accidental had been eliminated.

A search of Franks' apartment had uncovered a registered letter from the Washington County court, informing Franks of an upcoming hearing to revoke his visitation rights. The mental picture that formed in Gary's mind, imagining Franks' reaction to the letter, wasn't a pretty one, especially given Franks' violent streak. But Gary believed that letter provided Franks a motive for wanting Brittany dead. And most likely when Gary had interrupted Franks' plans, preventing him from killing Brittany, Franks' need for revenge had grown to include him.

Gary still wasn't certain why Franks had transferred the desire for revenge against him into kidnapping Kate. But if Franks had been trying to hit him where it hurt the most; he'd succeeded. Never in his life had Gary been as scared as he'd been during the agonizing two and a half days Kate had been missing.

Franks had motive, means and opportunity. And the fact he was now standing inside Gary's home holding Kate, Brittany, Tyler and Nikki at gunpoint told Gary all he needed to know. Adam Franks was intent on getting rid of his family and anyone who'd gotten in his way of doing it during the robbery or who could testify against him. And the fact Franks had his family hostage at all, didn't bode well for the Hagerstown police officer who'd been assigned to guard Brittany and her children.

With a sinking feeling that Franks had killed the officer, Gary prayed Franks didn't begin shooting here before he could stop the lunatic. He risked a quick glance into the room and caught Kate's eye, silently motioning her to be ready for something to happen. Although she didn't react, he could tell by her expression she understood. Every muscle in his body tensed, preparing to spring into action as soon as Zach made his move.

The last thing he wanted to do was kill Adam Franks in front of his children; they'd been traumatized enough already. But if he was given no other alternative, Gary was prepared to do just that, because no way was he going to allow Franks to harm Kate…or Brittany and the children.

The chime of the doorbell reverberated through the house. Zach's diversion. Waiting impatiently, Gary listened carefully for his opening.

As expected Franks went on high alert. "Who is that?" he demanded, yanking Tyler against him as a shield again, causing the boy to yelp in fear.

Kate turned toward the door with feigned ignorance. "I don't know."

"Well go get rid of them," Franks countered.

Gary watched as Kate turned back to the gunman with a look of indignation. "How do you expect me to do that?" she countered. "Thanks to you, I can't walk."

At first her reply stunned Gary, but then he realized Kate had managed to convince Franks she was paralyzed, which explained why the gunman had allowed her to remain seated, away from the others.

He couldn't help the smile that curved his lips. Knowing Katie, she'd done it to stay close to the gun in the pocket of her chair.

But after all this time, her inner strength, her calm presence of mind under pressure still managed to surprise him at times. Like now. She was definitely one amazing woman.

After several moments of considering Kate's response, Franks released his hold on Tyler and grabbed Brittany in a chokehold. "Put her down," he demanded, indicating Nikki. "And go get rid of whoever is out there."

Reluctantly, Brittany set the terrified toddler down. As Franks pushed his ex-wife toward the front door, Kate motioned both children to her side.

"If you try anything I'll shoot you dead like I did the cop," he warned, glaring at Kate and the children menacingly.

Gary cursed silently. He'd been right. The officer was dead. And that made Franks even more dangerous. If he'd been willing to kill a police officer, he'd have no qualms about killing Kate or his ex-wife and children.

Hauling in a deep steadying breath, Gary watched and waited to ensure Franks was gone before silently slipping inside through the shattered den door.

Tyler's eyes widened the moment he saw Gary, and Nikki bounced on her legs excitedly. For a heart stopping moment, Gary feared they would give him away by calling his name. But then, to Gary's relief and amazement, Tyler clamped a hand over his sister's mouth and whispered something to her. When she immediately stopped bouncing and settled down, Gary could only assume Tyler had cautioned her to be quiet.

He gave the boy a nod of approval and then let his gaze rest on Kate, their eyes meeting for a heartbeat. He tried to convey everything in his heart to her in that one agonizingly short second, but there was no time to waste. Refocusing on his mission, Gary quickly swept both children up in his arms and deposited them inside the powder room that adjoined the den. He motioned them to stay and with a finger to his lips, signaled them to be silent. When they both nodded, he closed the door, securing them safely inside, out of danger.

He wished he had time to do the same with Kate, but moving her would take more time than he had. All he could do was point toward the pocket holding her weapon.

She nodded acknowledgement and as she reached down to retrieve it, Gary slid behind one of the colonial style doors separating the den from the rest of the house.

"There's no one there."

Brittany's declaration reached Gary's hiding spot and let him know Zach had managed to avoid detection. And although he didn't know exactly where Zach was, Gary knew his son would be poised to take action as soon as Gary made his move.

"Get back in there," Franks demanded, giving Brittany an ungentlemanly shove that caused her to stumble into the room. As she flailed her arms trying to regain her balance, her gaze collided with Gary's and she gasped aloud.

Fortunately, Franks seemed to think her reaction was in response to nearly falling. But he immediately noticed the children were missing and went ballistic.

"Where'd they go? What did you do with them?" he shouted at Kate, his gaze flying everywhere except behind him. It was the reaction Gary had counted on when he'd chosen his hiding spot. Franks would know the children couldn't have left the den through those doors without him seeing them.

Focused on his anger, Franks never saw Gary emerge from behind the door. One long step brought Gary behind the massive man.

"Twitch and you're dead," Gary said, with a voice full of menace he wasn't feigning. He pressed the muzzle of his weapon against the back of Franks' head. "Drop the gun," he added with deadly earnest.

Franks cursed aloud and shot a glance over his shoulder to see who was behind him. When he realized it was Gary, he let loose a string of vile curses that threatened to turn the air blue. And while he made no attempt to resist, he did not release the gun.

When Gary motioned Brittany to get behind him, Franks swung his gaze around to see what was happening, giving Zach a chance to slip into the room unnoticed.

"Always the gallant gentleman, saving a lady in distress," Franks taunted Gary. "I'm going to enjoy killing you."

"You're not going to kill anyone," Gary replied with icy calm.

Franks barked an arrogant chuckle. "And who's going to stop me?"

"I am!"

The male voice coming from behind him caused Franks to spin around and he gasped when he saw Zach with a gun pointed at him.

"And so am I!"

Startled again, Franks twisted further to his left and froze when he spotted Kate with her gun trained at his chest.

"I'm not going to tell you again. Drop the gun…NOW!" Gary repeated more forcefully.

With his escape routes cut off, Franks unleashed a string of violent curses and dropped his weapon.

During the bank robbery, Gary had been caught off guard by Franks' attack. And then he hadn't been able to retaliate without risking other innocent people being hurt or killed. But here and now, Gary wasn't concerned about the fact Franks significantly outweighed him.

Using decades of law enforcement training, he quickly buckled Franks' knees and dropped him to the floor before Franks knew what hit him. And as added incentive to comply, Gary planted his knee firmly in the middle of *Refrigerator Man's* back and pressed the gun to his head.

"Hands behind your back," he ordered.

Although Gary rarely carried handcuffs on him when he was off duty, he always had a flex cuff in his pocket for situations just like this. And with his free hand he reached into his pocket to get one.

When Franks resisted, Zach came over to help. While Gary ground his knee more firmly into the man's spine and yanked one of his arms back, Zach grabbed the other arm.

As soon as Gary secured Franks' hands he looked up at Zach. "Do you have another one?"

He wasn't taking any chances the man could get free. When Zach handed him a second flex cuff, Gary added it to the first for double strength.

Satisfied Franks was secure, Gary sat back on his heels and glanced at Kate. "Are you okay?"

When she nodded silently he turned to Brittany. "How about you? Did he hurt you or the children?"

She shook her head. "Some bruises, nothing serious," she said glaring down at her ex-husband who'd turned his head to stare back at her defiantly. "He just scared them to death, but that's nothing new."

Gary shook his head in disgust and stood up, turning to look at the powder room door. He wanted to check on the children, but didn't think they needed to see their father lying on the floor in handcuffs. And to be honest he wasn't sure what Franks might do. He figured the kids were safer where they were, for the time being.

He glanced down at Franks, who had his eyes closed and appeared to be sleeping. To get his attention, Gary nudged him none-too-gently with his foot. The bandit's eyes flew open, glaring up at him.

"Adam Franks, you're under arrest for kidnapping, bank robbery, first degree attempted murder of a federal agent, aggravated assault of a federal agent, attempted premeditated murder, assault, desecration of human remains, and reckless endangerment…just to name a few. And if the officer guarding Brittany and your children is in fact dead, we'll be adding first degree murder charges as well."

Franks' response to the litany of charges was to merely grunt, as if he was bored by the whole thing.

After reciting Miranda rights to Franks, Gary nudged him with his foot again. "Do you understand your rights?"

Franks turned a defiant glare on him. "You think I'm stupid?"

Gary stared down at him, icily. "No. I think you're a cold-blooded SOB who has no regard for human life and you deserve to spend the rest of your life in a cage. Now answer the question. Do you understand your rights?"

Silence hung between them for so long that when Franks finally opened his mouth, it actually surprised Gary.

"Yeah, but you stole my son, so I stole your wife. And, I want a lawyer."

The confession, spoken matter-of-factly, without a hint of emotion or remorse, was the last thing Gary expected. And he felt like he'd been kicked in the gut.

Kate had been kidnapped and nearly died all because in Franks' twisted narcissistic mind, Gary protecting and befriending Tyler during a terrifying robbery in which Franks was one of the robbers, amounted to Gary stealing his son's affection? Unbelievable.

Considering Brittany had told him that Tyler had talked about him to anyone who would listen, Gary could only suppose that with Franks' insatiable need to control, having his son idolize someone else was unacceptable. And to avenge that intolerable situation, Franks had hit Gary where it hurt the most. Preying on Kate.

The motive had been unbelievably simple and just as unbelievably demented.

Probably the smart thing to do would have been to let the comment ride without response. But Gary couldn't resist the urge to point out the obvious.

"Well, Franks…you failed. Kate is alive and well. And from everything you've put Tyler and your family through…I'd hazard a guess you've killed any chance of him ever respecting you. And lastly, because of your own criminal actions, you're headed to prison for the rest of your life and possibly death row. So, you've lost on all counts."

Franks glared at him with hatred burning in his eyes. A second later he unleashed another string of vulgar curses directed at Gary.

It was bad enough Kate and Brittany were being subjected to the disgusting language, but while the powder room offered some privacy from those in the den, it wasn't sound proof, which meant the kids could damn well hear their father's diatribe.

"Shut up," Gary ordered, turning Franks' head until his face was ground into the carpet, muffling his tirade. "You might not care that your children can hear you, but I do, and I won't tolerate you or anyone using that kind of language in front of them. Utter one more curse and you'll find yourself gagged."

To show he meant business, he glanced over at Zach, who was sitting on the arm of Kate's recliner with a comforting arm around her shoulder. "Zach, there's duct tape in the kitchen drawer by the phone. Go get it."

The sound of sirens that for over a minute had been growing progressively louder, suddenly died just outside and when Zach re-appeared, he was carrying the tape and leading four police officers into the den.

Gary flipped open his credentials, assuming Zach had already done the same. And after briefly explaining the situation, he yanked Franks to his feet and handed the mammoth prisoner over to the officers.

Taking a firm hold of Franks' arm and angling it in a manner that made it virtually impossible for him to do anything but comply, the officers led him from the house.

Zach stared after them for a moment, then turned to Gary. "I'll follow them to the station and start the process of getting him transported to a federal facility."

"Thanks."

With quiet restored, Gary hauled in a deep breath. He turned a worried glance at Kate, who in spite of having sounded calm when she'd been dealing with Franks, was visibly shaken.

"Are you sure you're okay?" he asked again.

Kate nodded. "I'm fine."

Gary gave her an understanding smile, but didn't contradict her. No way was she fine, though. Hell, he made his living dealing with situations like this and his heart rate was still elevated. But as much as Gary wanted to go to her, he had an obligation to Brittany and her children, too.

After making sure Brittany was steady on her feet, he headed over to the powder room to free the children.

Nikki bolted past him the moment he opened the door, her little legs churning as she flew across the carpet to her mother. But with a smile that consumed his face, Tyler held his arms up to Gary. When Gary picked him up, the boy gave him an enthusiastic hug.

"I knew you'd save us, Agent Gary," he cried happily.

Gary felt a lump rise in his throat and when he glanced at Kate, she gave him a teary smile. He swallowed hard and hugged Tyler back. "I'm sorry all this had to happen to you and your mom and sister. But you were a brave young man today, Tyler and I'm proud of you."

"Is daddy going to jail?"

Unsure how to reply, Gary opted for honesty. "Yes, son he is. Your father did some terrible things. And I'm afraid he's going to be in jail a very long time."

To his surprise Tyler nodded with satisfaction. "Good. Den he can't hurt us anymore."

Gary gave him another hug. "No son, he can't."

He turned to Brittany again. "Are you sure you're all okay?"

The young mother gave her children an assessing once over before answering. "We're all okay…just shaken up." She gave Gary a tentative smile. "Thank you for coming to our rescue."

Nodding, Gary set Tyler on his feet and when the boy scampered over to his mother, Gary turned to Kate and smiled.

Two long strides brought him to her chair as she lowered the foot rest. When she took his offered hands, he pulled her to her feet. Wrapping her in an embrace, he just held her for several long moments, trying to reconcile how close he'd come to losing her again.

When he'd chosen his line of work, Gary had known the dangers of law enforcement, but Katie had never signed up for those dangers.

"I'm so sorry sweetheart," he uttered for her ears only. "I should never have left you alone with Franks on the loose."

Kate pulled back slightly and framed his face with her hands. "You're not a mind reader; you had no way of knowing he'd show up here today. And if anyone should be apologizing, it's me. I'm so sorry for the way I behaved and what I said earlier. I don't know what got into me. Will you forgive me?"

"Always." He pulled her back into an embrace and lowering his mouth to hers, he kissed her tenderly.

A chorus of giggles drew them apart and they turned to find Tyler and Nikki watching them with apparent delight. Mortified, Brittany tried to quiet her children, but Tyler wasn't having it.

"Is dat one of Dr. Kate's magic kisses, Agent Gary?" he asked.

With his arms still around her, Gary could feel Kate laughing silently and he had to fight to keep from joining her.

The innocence of the question and the fact the boy had so quickly rebounded from what had surely been a terrifying experience, showed promise that everything was going to be all right. And it would be. Adam Franks and the rest of the Phantoms were no longer threats. His stalker was behind bars. And most importantly, they were all safe.

Gary noticed both his wife and Tyler gazing at him, Katie with an amused smile on her face, expectantly awaiting his answer. He glanced at the boy and then turned an adoring smile on his wife. Something that was easy to do.

"You bet it is, Tyler. And I need another one," he answered before dipping his head for another of Kate's magic kisses.

Made in the USA
Middletown, DE
09 June 2023